SILK STOCKING

SILK STOCKING

Daughters of Ireland

Jeanne Charters

OPEN ROAD

INTEGRATED MEDIA
NEW YORK

ISBN: 978-1-5040-8643-1

Published in 2023 by Open Road Integrated Media, Inc.
180 Maiden Lane
New York, NY 10038
www.openroadmedia.com

SILK STOCKING

CHAPTER ONE

BOSTON, JULY 1879

NELLIE

Music blares through the swinging door of O'Halloran's pub as Mam and I enter. I am immediately drawn out onto the floor by Molly O'Halloran singing:

> "Now there's some take delight in the carriages a rollin'
> And others take delight in the hurling and the bowling
> But I take delight in the juice of the barley
> And courting pretty fair maids in the morning bright and early
> Mush-a ring dumb-a do dumb-a da
> Whack fall the daddy-o, whack fall the daddy-o
> There's whiskey in the jar"

With the celebration in full swing, I join a wild dance with three of my classmates. I'm the only one who learned the *Celli* as a child, but the other girls try the reels and jigs; one with some grace and two clumsily. Nobody cares about skill. What matters is the sheer joy we feel as we stomp and whirl, singing our hearts out. After fifteen minutes, the music quiets to a waltz, and laughing, we hug and congratulate each other and part, panting.

It's official, I'm a Wellesley graduate. My degree is propped up and sitting on the bar, soon to be framed and hung in a place of honor on our living room wall. Mam will make short work of the framing. She is so proud to have a college graduate in our family.

I was chosen to speak at graduation because in Wellesley's first graduating class of seventeen women, I was the first hired in my chosen major. I'll teach General Science at Girls High come fall. It's the first time in their curriculum that science is offered.

After the two o'clock graduation ceremony, Mam and I walked straight here to O'Halloran's to celebrate. I've dressed carefully, wearing my new blue dress, draped in at the waist with cascades ruffling back to a small bustle. My hair is freshly washed and pulled up into curls with a matching blue ribbon. My face feels flushed with perspiration now, but I don't care. My heart soars with the joy of accomplishment and pride.

Uncle Kam is here, of course, and comes quickly to my side. "Nellie, your speech was wonderful," he says as he guides me to the table where Mam waits. "Your students will be lucky to have you."

"Thank you, Uncle Kam. I can't wait to start teaching."

"And you'll be a great teacher. I am so proud of you."

As I sit with him, basking in his affection, a male voice interrupts our sweet connection.

"Excuse me, Blackie." Sean O'Halloran pulls me up to standing and his arm encircles my waist. I stiffen. His hug is proprietary—much too proprietary. Uncle Kam, always the gentleman, turns away and pours Mam a glass of wine.

Sean tugs me to the other side of the room, his arm still around my waist. Angrily, I say, "Sean, that was rude. Kamua Okafor is my family's best friend. How dare you speak to him like that!"

"Sorry, Nellie, but he is colored. Ace-of-spades colored. Since Dad died, I own this place, and I don't think he belongs here." As I protest, he pulls me closer in and tips my chin up to look him in the eye. I smell the alcohol on his breath. "Don't worry. I won't kick him out and embarrass you."

His tone changes in a split second, "Well, Nellie, I guess you did it, didn't you? Congratulations. You've come a long way from that little girl who ran away and joined the circus."

I stare up into those blue eyes. Two can play this game of degradation. "How's your nose, Sean?"

He stiffens at the reminder, but recovers with a shrug. "All healed, sweetheart. No permanent damage. Girls tell me this slight crook gives me a roguish look." He turns his head to show off his profile. "They like it."

I've seen Sean rarely since the night on my front porch when I whacked him. As I look closer, I must admit that he does look wonderful. He's right. The nose I broke adds a dashing bit of dangerous allure to his otherwise perfect face.

"Then you're welcome." I peer up at him and tap him on his nose, then turn to leave.

He holds me firm and grins. "Nellie, Nellie, always a tease. So, what's next now that you've graduated?"

"I begin teaching Science at Girls High this fall."

His eyes widen in disbelief. "Science? Why in the world would any girl need to learn science?"

True to form, he tries to demean me, make me feel smaller. It used to work, but this time it makes me angry. "Sean, you sound like a Neanderthal. This is 1879. Women around the world are beginning to learn about science. Louis Pasteur and Robert Koch will change the way physicians treat diseases with their germ theory. Women making similar discoveries won't be far behind them. Why would you degrade science? Your own sister is a medical doctor."

He shrugs. "But normal women? Molly's always been a bit different, don't you think? And keep in mind, she's now over thirty. You don't see a line of suitors waiting at her door, do you? She's going to be an old maid and I'll probably have to take care of her in her dotage."

Molly, standing near enough to overhear, pushes her way between us, a sardonic grin on her face. "What dotage?"

"Yours, dear sister. Getting a bit long in the tooth."

"Sean, you're such a relic. You'd better change your tune. You want to be in politics someday, and by then women may have the right to vote."

"Over my dead body," he says between clenched teeth, sneering. "It's bad enough they let the uppity coons vote. But women? Never."

Molly and I exchange a look of contempt and shake our heads.

"Oh, come on, girls. Just kidding."

"No, you're not," Molly says. "If our parents could hear you, they'd be ashamed. Our mam was an abolitionist and suffragist."

"You don't know that, Molly," he replies, scowling at her.

"But *I* do." The voice belongs to my mam who has quietly joined us. "Sean, your mam was my dearest friend. I attended her at your birth. She believed in equality for all people. I wish you could have known her."

Suddenly, he changes, becomes softer. Mam often has that effect on men. "Ah, now, Mrs. Kelly, so do I. Yes, indeed, so do I."

I don't believe him for a minute.

CHAPTER TWO

As Mam and I walk home from the party, dusk begins to darken the streets of South Boston. Lined with sugar maples, leaves dance in the slight breeze overhead. Soon, those leaves will turn a bright red before they crisp and fall to the sidewalk to crunch under our feet. Fall has always been my favorite season, especially now that my career is about to begin.

Basking in a lovely evening, following a splendid celebration, Mam startles my reverie. "Do you still find Sean attractive, Nellie?"

The question catches me by surprise. Though, by now, nothing Mam asks should catch me unaware. She's sneaky and very astute. I decide to be truthful because she knows in a minute when I'm being evasive.

"Not particularly, Mam. He's handsome enough, but I don't like his attitudes on things."

"Like what?" She slows her pace slightly and leans closer to hear my words.

"Women, society, and most especially, Negroes. I think if it were up to Sean, they'd still be slaves. Did you see the way he treated Uncle Kam?"

"Yes, and I wanted to smack him one. Kamua Okafor is a person I respect more than anyone in the world. He was your da's closest friend. Best man at our wedding. His honor is above reproach and to see that young fool dismiss him as he did makes me furious."

I take her arm and squeeze it. "Don't let it trouble you, Mam. Molly says Sean's a relic of a bygone time."

She shakes her head. "I wish. But sadly, that bygone time still reigns in Boston. Most of the important men here feel exactly the same way. From the Lowells to the Lodges, I've heard them voice their opposition to the cause of the Negro and the women's suffrage movement. I don't know what they're so afraid of. I guess it's losing power."

"Perhaps, but I don't think all men feel that way. Look at Uncle Kam . . . and Derry." I just needed to say his name.

She presses closer, linking her arm through mine. "Oh, yes, that handsome young one from Ireland, who I understand is coming to visit us soon." She jabs me playfully in the ribs, then hugs me. "No, I doubt he's afraid of women or Negroes. He's too busy trying to boot the English out of Ireland."

I smile to myself. Derry would find a passionate partner for Ireland's home rule in Mam. Da felt the same way. I didn't live through the Great Famine, but Lord knows I've heard about it all my life from my parents. It's never seemed right to me for one country to control another and starve it half to death in the process.

The sound of Derry's name brings an unmistakable quiver to my lower belly. He's coming to Boston and, truth be told, I'm almost more excited about that than I was about graduation. It's been four years since we were together. Our time started when he serenaded me at the Brazen Head Pub on the night we arrived in Dublin for Neo and Angelique's wedding. Derry was to be a groomsman at that wedding and was Neo's good friend.

That night, he sang "The Rose of Tralee" without ever taking his eyes from mine and then walked me back to our rooming house in the rain. I couldn't believe Mam would allow such a thing, but she was as charmed by the young Irishman as I was. He kept his arm around my waist all the way back to the house as he protected us from the rain with his bumbershoot. I never felt safer in my life.

Days later, just before the wedding, the wire arrived telling us Da had been murdered in our backyard. Dazed and weeping, Mam and I packed to sail back to Boston the next morning. Derry arrived at the front door to offer solace and assistance to us. Finally, exhausted by her grief, Mam went up to our room while Derry and I stayed in the parlor drinking tea. I was crying so hard he took me in his arms to comfort me and, without warning, his kindness turned to something different. A feeling of urgency. He led me to a dark corner of the room and kissed me gently. It was my first kiss and its sweetness suddenly turned passionate before I knew what was happening.

At first, I felt embarrassed about my response to Derry—worried he might think me loose or easy—but that was not the case. He's written me every week since, and I think he feels the same as I do. I've faithfully responded to each of his letters. Those letters have become the highlight of my life, and I read them over and over and then tie them with a pink ribbon for safekeeping in the bottom of my underwear drawer. His letters are so expressive, and I feel I know him better now than nearly anyone in my life. Is this love? I have no idea, but I cannot come up with another word to describe my feelings for him.

Though several young men have shown interest in me since then, I have never responded to their invitations, telling them I was too busy studying at Wellesley. But that wasn't the real reason. The truth is none of them measure up to Derry.

Surely you can imagine my excitement at the fact that right now he's on a ship bringing him to Boston. Graduated from the Trinity Law School, he is a practicing barrister in Dublin. His journey is partly an exploration of America, as a young Constitutional Republic, because his hope is to turn Ireland into a similar system once "Home Rule" is finally accomplished there.

He's a Fenian, like Da had been, and that frightens me since the Irish grow more and more weary of British rule, and there may be a revolution there just as there was here. People die in revolutions. *Please, God, not Derry. I couldn't bear it.*

I must not think such thoughts lest they manifest in some way. No, I will focus on the fact that Derry has asked me to meet his ship when he arrives in a few weeks. When I think about seeing him again, my toes actually tingle.

"By the way," I say to Mam, "Uncle Kam says he'd like to come to the house tomorrow to tutor me some more on African folk remedies."

"That's fine, just fine. I'll pick up a bottle of that wine he likes."

Although I learned a lot about the sciences at Wellesley, I was ahead of the curve even before I attended there. I grew up with Mam reading sections of *Quain's Elements of Anatomy* to me, an old medical text book they used at Harvard. She read it cover to cover as a girl and says it helped her establish herself as a midwife. Uncle Kam replaced it for me a few years back with a more modern text called *Gray's Anatomy*, but Mam still prefers Quain's. By now, it's so dogeared and annotated from my reading, I can find any subject in seconds. All that study, coupled with Uncle Kam's herbal and tincture knowledge, has me well prepared to teach my girls this year. Kam's father was a medicine man in Africa who saved sick, indentured Irish people in the Louisiana sugar fields when regular doctors couldn't help them.

I'll be a good science teacher, and the thought of informing young minds excites me. Perhaps one of my students will discover the cure for the awful wasting disease that killed Uncle Kam's wife, Imani.

It was such a tragic time. Exquisite Imani wasted away to a wraith so quickly. Her housekeeper, Martha, was still alive back then and tried to force food on her, but Imani was too ill to eat. Uncle Kam spent every waking minute trying to find a tonic to help her, but nothing worked. The medical doctors found growths and removed her breasts, but it was clear that whatever demon caused those growths was invading other parts of her body. In the end, when she finally passed, there was gratitude that her struggle was over and her pain ended.

Uncle Kam has never fully recovered from her loss. He still grieves, though it's been nearly three years now. Mam tells him that sorrow never ends, but it does abate with time. That's what she learned when Da was killed.

Sadly, many men don't understand my passion for science. Certainly not Sean O'Halloran.

Perhaps Derry will.

CHAPTER THREE

The next afternoon, Uncle Kam and I are sitting on my front porch, studying his book on formulas and potions. He wrote it at age sixteen while working for Mr. Mendel who owned a local apothecary when the man hired him as a delivery boy. I've been told Mendel quickly recognized the inherent genius of the young African and fostered it. Together, they compared the serums Kamua remembered from Africa and the medicines Mr. Mendel had learned as a pharmacist.

I used to worry about what neighbors might think as they observe the two of us, our heads close together, discussing the wonders of modern medicine and science. He, an elderly black man, and I, a young white woman. At first, there was gossip about whether such a relationship was proper in very proper Boston. But now, my neighbors acknowledge him as a part of my family, joined by affection, if not by blood.

His short-cropped hair is now peppered with gray, but his dark eyes dance with youth and excitement. "Nellie, do you understand that, perhaps, many of the questions people now ponder about illness, humanity, even our universe, may be answered by a study of such things as vegetation and the skies? When I was a cabin slave on that hell ship, I taught myself to navigate the seas by studying the stars. Isn't it possible that the cures for human ailments might be right in front of us, in our universe, just waiting to be discovered? It's important that you keep your mind open to all possibilities. You'll make mistakes. Some theories may be wrong, but you can't know until they've been tested. You have a wonderful brain. Use it, girl, to train young scientists."

"Thank you, Uncle Kam. That's my vision for my life's work. You've opened my eyes to so many things unavailable in any textbook, such as herbs like acacia senecal for infection and typhoid."

"Yes, that's what my father used in the sugar fields to save the Irish. Doctors had never heard of it. Your people have been ravaged for years by tuberculosis, and many Africans believe it can be effectively treated with honey bush."

"Why do you think those discoveries haven't been tried here?"

He chuckles and pats my knee once, smiling. "Ego, superstition, prejudice. How can anything from Africa possibly be as efficacious as the discoveries of American scientists? That kind of thinking enabled me to amass a fortune. The bark of the yohimbe tree had been used for centuries in Africa to help men remain virile into old age. I simply imported it and created my tonic, *Kamua's African Love Potion*. A bit of ground tree bark, some quinine, and a splash of alcohol and honey. Couldn't have been simpler."

Mam had told me of the day he'd taken off in a wagon to sell the tonic across New England. She'd laughed as she recalled how she and Kathleen O'Halloran had forced him to change the drawing on his truck to something less salacious.

"And obviously it worked," I say, grinning into his eyes.

"Yes, indeed. Hammacher Schlemmer is still selling it for me, all across the country."

"Did you test it in this country?"

He pauses, seeming to deliberate whether to continue, then, having chosen his words wisely, says, "Actually, my first experiment was on your mam and da."

"Are you serious, Uncle Kam?" I am flabbergasted.

"Absolutely. I was tired of seeing those two fighting the love that clearly existed between them, so I asked them to be my guinea pigs."

"And what happened?"

The retelling excites him. "Nellie, I wish you could have seen it. One small glass for each of them and suddenly, they both turned beet red. You could feel their attraction vibrate the air. Even they, stubborn Irish that they were, couldn't deny what they felt. We'd never seen that reaction in Africa, because it was difficult to see dark skin blush and flush like that. Your mam was so embarrassed she ran from the room."

"So, Uncle Kam, are you saying that without your African Love Potion, I might not exist?"

With a twinkle in his eye, he answers, "Quite possibly, that's true. And wouldn't that be a tragedy for this town? Another positive result from my tonic is that now my African village has an industry that keeps them alive; growing, harvesting, and shipping that tree bark to me. I can't tell you how gratifying that is."

A sad thought occurs to me. "It must have been devastating to you that you couldn't save Aunt Imani."

His countenance changes instantly, replaced by a look of grief so deep I regret bringing up the dreaded subject.

"I'm sorry, Uncle Kam. I shouldn't have mentioned that."

He sits straighter, again composed. "No, Nellie, scientists must be prepared to discuss all their findings. Soon after Imani became symptomatic, I had two herbs shipped here. One was Nigella sativa; the other, Trigonella. I brewed them into strong teas for Imani and tried to force them down her throat. Sometimes, I was successful. Other times, she couldn't keep them down and immediately vomited."

Suddenly, his eyes fill with tears. I reach to touch his face in comfort. "This is too painful for you."

He composes himself in seconds and takes my hand. "No, Nellie. If we as scientists refuse to discuss matters that cause suffering, how can we ever progress? How can we learn what does and doesn't work? My great hope is that you or one of your students will continue the study of the horrible disease that took Imani. Someday someone will figure it out. I doubt it will be in my lifetime and perhaps, not even in yours, but the search must continue."

There is a clatter of horse's hooves as Mam pulls up to our house in her wagon. She jumps down, limber as a young lass, happy to find Uncle Kam still there. "I was afraid I'd miss you, Kam. This has been a very long day. It's past six o'clock. Are you hungry?"

"Well, your fine girl here served me a piece of apple pie earlier with a cup of tea. But yes, I am feeling a bit empty."

"Lovely. There's leftover pork roast. We can peel some potatoes for mashing, then heat it all up in that pork gravy from last night and have ourselves a fine meal."

As she hangs her shawl in the bedroom, she calls over her shoulder. "Kam, I got some of that red wine you like. While Nellie peels the potatoes, you and I will catch up over a glass on the porch."

This pleases him so. "Sounds perfect, Mabo."

She claps her hands and goes into the kitchen, returning with an uncorked bottle and two glasses. As I watch them settle next to each other on the swing, my heart warms. These two have known each other since they were children. Both of them were orphaned young and helped each other survive the horrors of the coffin ship and the rigors of existence in a strange new country. Though silver streaks both her red hair and his black beard, when they see each other now, it's as though they're children again, planning a brave new adventure and reverting to childhood nicknames.

"Shall I tell her?" he asks.

"I thought you were hungry."

"Yes, but more excited than hungry." He holds onto her sleeve. "Nellie, stay just a moment longer. Your mam and I have something to tell you."

I sit balanced on the porch rail. A branch of the maple tree in our front yard stirs in a sudden small breeze and ruffles my hair. *Just what secret does he want to share with me?* For one moment, I think perhaps he's going to say he loves her. Even as the thought registers, I dismiss it. Of course, he loves her and always has. Like a brother. Silly girl, thinking of Derry has turned the whole world romantic. These people are too old for starry-eyed foolishness. He's nearly fifty and she's not far behind him.

Somehow, though, I find the logic of my thinking saddens me. They are both so lonely. I still hear Mam weeping in her room when she thinks me asleep. In spite of all the problems, a relationship between them would be nice. I love seeing them together like this. Aged. Settled. Happy.

"Nellie, before you start the potatoes, I want to show you something," he says.

"All right. What is it?"

"It'll take us a few minutes. We'll take my carriage. The place we're going is on Chestnut Street."

CHAPTER FOUR

Mam and I climb into Uncle Kam's stately carriage as he unties his two black horses. I sit on the back seat, while Mam sits up front. When he brings the reins down on the horses' backs, they begin a gentle cantor over the cobblestones.

"I always feel so grand in this rig," Mam says. "Our old wagon gets me where I want to go, but it surely isn't luxurious."

He turns to her. "You know I've offered to buy you a more appropriate one, Mabo, but you always refuse me."

She giggles. "I know, Kam, but at heart, I'm an Irish farm girl and don't want anything lavish like this. Most of the girls at The Haven come there on foot. Don't want to seem like a four flusher."

"As if you could," he answers. "You're the most down-to-earth woman I know."

"And I want to stay that way."

Soon, we turn the corner onto Chestnut Street. This is a commercial street where they sell everything from ready-made women's dresses to spittoons and wood stoves.

"Where are we going?" I tap Mam on the shoulder.

"Patience, Nellie. You'll find out soon enough." I can tell from my brief touch she is quivering with excitement. She darts glances over at Uncle Kam, and he returns them, excitedly. The two of them seem as eager as children on Christmas morning.

I may as well sit back and enjoy the ride because they're clearly not going to tell me anything about where we're going until we get there.

Dusk begins to fall over the streets of Boston and the lamplighters stand in clusters smoking together before they begin their nightly ritual. They wave cordially, heads tipped in respect, as we pass by. One is a young man about my age and when he smiles, I notice many of his teeth are missing. I am once again grateful that Mam was such a stickler about tooth brushing. I thought her a nag at times, but looking at his gapping smirk, I thank my lucky stars for still having all my teeth. *How embarrassing it would be to stand before a class of students afraid to smile lest they see missing molars.*

Finally, we pull up to a building at 103 Chestnut Street with a large sign printed in swirly gothic letters, *Chauncey Thomas, Ltd.*

Uncle Kam helps Mam to the street, and I clamber out of the back, asking, "What is this?"

"Let's go inside and you'll see, Nellie," he says.

We enter the front door and I am captured by a wonderland of magnificent carriages. Some look fit to transport Cinderella to the ball with gilt and glass and velvet seats.

"Now don't think of getting that one," Uncle Kam says, frowning, as I finger the handle of an especially ornate conveyance. "It's headed to Great Britain for use by the Royal Family. Come out back with me."

I follow him out the back door of the shop, Mam holding my hand. There it stands. A beautiful two-seat, one-horse wagon with a purple canopy fringed in yellow. My mouth hangs open in wonder.

"A young lady deserves a proper gift for her college graduation. Nellie, this is yours. The horse is around the corner."

I begin to stutter in excitement, "B-but Uncle Kam, I-I can't afford this. I'm only beginning my first teaching job."

"I said 'gift.'"

I had wondered how I would get to class at Girls High every day, and by seven in the morning at that. Horse-drawn buses were quite unreliable, and the train didn't go near there. I couldn't ask Mam to take me every day because her first responsibility was to the mothers at the Haven. As I touch the fringe on the canopy, I begin to weep in absolute joy. Then I turn to him and, with no concern for propriety or social ostracism, throw my arms around his neck and bury my sobs into the soft wool of his jacket.

CHAPTER FIVE

The three of us leave the carriage shop and walk one block down Chestnut Street to a horseshoe emporium.

"Bill, is she ready?" Kam calls out.

A male voice answers, "Out back."

As Uncle Kam leads me to the alley behind the building, I can feel the excitement and joy radiate from his trembling hand. My mam grins and takes his other arm. He closes the door to the shop behind us and says with a flourish, "Ta da! She's yours."

In the alley stands a horse that, for a moment, I think is the same one I rode in the circus when I was younger. But this one is a mare; five hands tall and black as midnight with a coat as shiny as my own hair. When I touch her silken flank, she presses against my hand as though she knows that she and I are going to be lifelong friends.

"She's mine?" I whisper in unbelief.

"What's her name, Nellie?" he asks.

I needn't think for a second. "Rosie. After my best friend now living in Ireland with her little boy."

"Are you sure?" Mam asks, knowing the heartbreak I suffered when Rosie Marino betrayed me with Sean O'Halloran. What she doesn't know is that I've missed Rosie with all my heart since she went to Ireland to have her baby. I've wondered how she is and if we'll ever see each other again.

But I no longer believe in shying away from sadness. Rosie and I mended some fences on our journey together over the seas. Now I'm ready to forgive her totally if I ever get the chance. In the meantime, I'll honor Rosie with her black hair and sparkling eyes by naming this beautiful new friend in her honor. I look into her eyes. "Your name is Rosie. You and I are going to be great friends, and I'll take care of you always." The massive head dips and when she lifts it again, she stares into my eyes as though she understands that something sacred and true has passed between us.

I turn to Uncle Kam. "Can I take her home tonight, along with the wagon?"

"She's all yours, Nellie. Enjoy her."

I lead Rosie back to the carriage shop with Mam and Uncle Kam trailing behind us. We hook her up to my new wagon, and I hoist myself up into the driver's seat. Rosie takes to the reins as if she were born to them. She senses my competence with horses and responds like a noble partner. Her cantor back to our house is perfect and her proud head stays high the entire ride. When we arrive, I jump down and tie her to a post, then run into the house to retrieve a carrot for her. She chomps on it eagerly. I then lead her around to the backyard and into the little shed that has not been used since Da died. When I open the door to the shed, I find that Mam has placed straw all over the floor inside and that there is a tying post, too.

I wonder how long these two old friends have planned this surprise for me? I am touched beyond words by their conspiracy. I tie Rosie to the post inside the shed and run her new brush down her sleek flanks and neck. Again, she presses her body against me as though she recognizes me as her mistress and this as her home. I have never felt such happiness.

"Nellie, come on now. Let's get those potatoes cooking," Mam shouts from the porch.

I kiss Rosie once on the snout and run in the back door. Mam and Uncle Kam are again sitting in the front porch swing drinking their wine. I join them and sit down.

"Uncle Kam, I can't thank you enough for the horse and wagon. I love them."

"You deserve them, Nellie." He turns to my mam. "Mabo, don't you think this college graduate daughter of yours deserves a glass of wine, too? She's a big girl now."

"Oh, alright, bring out a glass, Nellie."

I rush to do so, peeling potatoes fleeing from my mind. She pours me a glass and the three of us relax in the deepening dusk as we sip our drinks.

"When is your young gentleman arriving from Ireland?" he asks.

"Fifteen days, if the seas cooperate, Uncle Kam."

"Are you looking forward to seeing him again?"

Wild thoughts fly. What should I say? Should I admit that sometimes I can't sleep at night in anticipation? Should I share my fear that perhaps the romantic excitement Derry and I felt in Ireland will be gone now? That ours was a romance born of the tragedy of my da's death? That perhaps he just felt sorry for me that night in the parlor when he kissed me?

"Yes, I do look forward to seeing him. But who knows how we'll feel seeing each other again? It's been four years after all, and we both might have changed a good deal. He may have a lady in Ireland now that he feels strongly about."

"If so, why would he be coming here?" he prods.

"He wants to understand our government better. I think he envisions something like our republic in Ireland someday and sees himself as part of that. That might be his sole purpose for this visit."

"Do you really believe that, Nellie?"

I find myself wanting to escape what feels like an interrogation, so I say, "I'm going to start the potatoes."

They are laughing as I bolt into the kitchen.

I set a pot full of water on the cook stove. Sticking my finger in it to test for salt, I light the fire. Then I start peeling potatoes in a frenzy of brown skins and rapid heartbeats. *Why did Uncle Kam's questions bother me so?* As my hands whirl the skins off the potatoes, I mull over what I'm really feeling. *If I'm honest, I have to admit that I'm terrified to see Derry again. If he doesn't still have strong feelings for me, I fear it might break my heart.*

But what if he does? What if the passion we felt in Ireland that night is still ablaze? I've been taught all my life by my church that kind of feelings are to be reserved for the marital bed. Certainly, I can't marry Derry—at least not yet. I am to start teaching this September. By then, he'll be back in Ireland. And if I did give in to passion, what would he think of me? That I'm a harlot, like some of the girls hanging all around him in Dublin? It was clear that he could have any of them he wanted, with no strings attached. But I'm not a no-strings kind of girl. I've followed church rules, protected myself—my purity, my virginity. I've never even kissed a man, other than Derry. Except for that one disastrous night I tried to tempt Sean O'Halloran on my front porch. I needed to see if what I felt with Derry was something I could experience with Sean.

What a joke! Sean was clumsy and harsh and so rude that I hit him one, breaking his nose.

As I put the peeled potatoes into the boiling water, I chuckle at the memory of Sean's shock to find his nose bleeding. Although proudly I stood my ground, I chastise myself mentally for such thinking. Hitting a man is not funny. Violence is never a solution to anything. But, oh Lord, he was so surprised. My shoulders shake in spite of myself.

Setting the table and starting the sliced pork to warm in its gravy, I think again of Derry. The way he protected me from getting wet in the rain with his bumbershoot. How I laughed at what he called his umbrella. The song he sang to me in the pub as though there was no one else there but the two of us. The way his eyes crinkled at the edges when he smiled at me. That ornery shock of brown hair that always hung over his forehead, no matter how many times he pushed it back.

I find the potato masher in the drawer and pour the water off the hot potatoes, then start pulverizing them and adding butter. A quick taste reveals a need for salt, so I add some, grateful for the respite from my memories.

"Dinner's almost ready," I call out to the front porch. The swing squeaks as Mam and Uncle Kam stand from it and come in the front door.

"Good," he says. "I was hungry before. Now, I'm famished."

As they settle at the table, Mam folds her hands in front of her face for a quiet grace. Uncle Kam looks at her with such devotion that I truly wish he was white. They could make each other so happy, but some things are impossible.

Nearly as impossible as what I feel for Derry. There's no denying it. When I first saw my new wagon and horse, my first thought was how excited I would be to pick him up at the ship in such a delectable ride.

CHAPTER SIX

JULY 30, 1879

TWO WEEKS LATER

His wire arrived yesterday. He'll be here tomorrow. I am so excited I can scarcely breathe. My heart is racing in my chest as I prepare for bed. Sleeping will be difficult this night. The rags I tied in my hair pull at my scalp, but I ignore their discomfort. My hair must look its best tomorrow. My chosen dress is already hanging outside my little closet, ironed and ready. It's my everyday dress, not the fancy one I wore for graduation. I must not appear to be anxious, though if I were any more eager, I think I'd vibrate right out of my skin.

Nellie, stop this. You're acting like a foolish child, and that is unbecoming to a young woman of twenty-two years; a college graduate ready to teach other young women important things about science. And yet . . . and yet, I must be honest in my deepest soul. I have missed Derry terribly. I've lived for his weekly letter and prayed to God he'd never stop writing me. The memory of that one night in the dark shadows of Mrs. Conley's boarding house when Derry's kiss dispelled the grief of Da's murder still brings a thrill to my whole body.

25

Lighting my bedside candle, I reach for my latest novel. It's the seventh section of *Middlemarch* written by George Eliot. The first six sections were fascinating, and Eliot says the eighth section will complete the story. Everyone assumes Eliot is an Englishman, but study proves that a wrong assumption. This writer is a British woman named Mary Ann Evans who chose a masculine pen name because she wasn't writing the frivolous stories of romance typical of today's female authors. Fascinating stuff. She also embarked on a scandalous affair with a married English philosopher named George Henry Lewes and considered them married until his death two years ago. His wife disagreed.

After a few pages, I close the book and ponder whether I could be so bold a woman as she was. Could I abandon my religion, my social standing, everything I've been taught critical to my reputation to become the kind of woman whispered about by stodgy matrons in Boston, like a scarlet-letter tramp? *Am I so desperate for the fleeting passion of that night in Dublin that I would forsake all else for its recurrence?*

Am I?

I roll to my left side and close my eyes.

Am I?

The morning sun streaming through lace curtains awakens me. It's seven o'clock. I should be at the dock by nine. I may wait all day for Derry's ship because docking times are totally unpredictable, but I do want to be the first face he sees upon disembarking in America. Thinking back to getting off that ship four years ago in Dublin Harbor, I recall the excitement and anticipation of exploring a new country.

Before washing and dressing, I throw on chore clothes and head out back to muck out Rosie's stall and give her fresh water. She gets a special treat today. Oats. Purchased at Quincy

Market yesterday, this is the first time she'll taste them. Usually, she just grazes in our back yard and keeps our grass down, but she deserves a special treat for being such a good girl. I pour the oats into her feed bucket and hang it over her neck. She dips her long snout down into the bucket and begins to eat hungrily. For a second, she stops chomping and looks at me over the edge of the bucket. Then, back she goes into it, loving this new indulgence.

While Rosie finishes her breakfast, I pump fresh water into the bucket and set it to heat on the stove. Mam's note says she received word of an imminent delivery and went to work. While the water warms, I cook up oats for my own breakfast and set up the tin pot for coffee.

Gingerly taking the bucket of hot water from the stove, I go into my room to wash and dress. I remove the rags from my hair and watch my hair tumble down in curls nearly to my waist. Examining myself in the mirror, I wonder if I've changed much in the four years since Derry and I last saw each other. I can't see changes, but then maybe no one can in their own reflections. Looking closer, my face looks thinner, less girlish and round. But perhaps that's just my imagination.

Suddenly, I catch the scent of burning oats and run to yank the pot from the fire. Running a wooden spoon around the bottom, I am filled with a sense of relief that nothing seems stuck too badly. I pour myself a cup of strong black coffee and add a touch of milk fresh from our cow in the back, then dish the oats into my favorite bowl—the one with daisies in the bottom—and pour the remaining water into the pot to soak any remaining crust off. Adding milk and sugar, I settle down at the table, sinking my spoon into the oatmeal, and take a satisfying bite.

Again, my reverie turns to Derry. Daire O'Byrne from Dublin, Ireland, now a fine young barrister and gentleman. *Does he still play his fiddle*? I doubt he'd ever stop that. It seemed almost part of him. Eyes glazed over, I remember the music that night; the dancing and the joy of the Brazen Head. And the Guinness. *Ah, yes, I must pick up some of that on my way to the dock.*

After scraping the bowl clean and swigging down the last of the coffee, I clear the dishes and wash everything up so that the house is tidy. We will have a guest tonight for dinner. A very important guest eating his very first meal in America.

The town clock strikes nine times as I pull up at the pier. The ride over was exhilarating. As I passed other girls on the street, they stared at me and Rosie with wonder and, perhaps, concealed jealousy. Not many of them have such a fine wagon and horse to parade around town. It's also a bit scandalous for an unaccompanied young woman to be driving herself through the streets of Boston. At first, neighbors raised their eyebrows when they saw me, but, fortunately, Mam doesn't believe in old-fashioned rules any more than I do. I tie Rosie to a post and hurry toward the ships.

There's no worry that someone will steal my rig or horse. Stealing a horse is considered such a crime that if you do it, you can plan on spending a long, long time in jail. When Da was alive and practicing law, horse thievery was much more common and many of his cases involved defending or prosecuting such cases. I'm happy things have changed. If anyone stole Rosie, I'd want to kill them.

Walking down the dock, I look out at all the sailing ships and remember when we all boarded the ship to Dublin four years ago. That was for Neo's wedding to Angelique, and it was such a happy, festive occasion. Dear Martha was my bunk mate on that voyage, and I learned so much from her. I was coming into my womanhood then and had many questions about what was happening to my body. She eased my fears and my conscience with her wise, calm words. I wish she was still alive now so I could talk to her about Derry. She died a year after Uncle Kam's wife. I think her sweet heart was broken at losing Aunt Imani. Martha was an old woman by then but always remembered helping Imani rear Neo. She was forever grateful that Uncle Kam bought her from the cotton plantation in Georgia. Losing her felt like losing a second mother.

During that trip, some criminal shot Da. To this day, we don't know who did it, but the memory still makes me shiver. I thought Mam would not recover from the horror of that. But although it took her years, she did. An awful time for both of us.

Strolling along Boston Harbor, all those memories assail me. A sailor's whistle jolts me from my reverie. I remember why I'm here and excitement replaces the pain. Derry will be here today.

I enter the little shack where the dockmaster keeps his maps and find a man sitting there holding a pipe. "Sir, any word yet on when you expect the SS *Hibernia*?"

He takes his pipe from his mouth and picks up a spy glass. Staring out over the vast sea, he taps his pipe against an ash tray. "No, ma'am. No word yet. Last I heard, they was expected around noon time. It's been an easy sail with few storms to slow them." His brogue is so thick I can scarcely understand him.

I thank him and turn to leave.

"Expecting someone special?" he calls after me.

"No, sir, just a friend."

"Well, my name's Seamus O'Doyle. And if you've a mind to it, I'd welcome your company for a bit while you wait." He gestures to the other chair in the tiny shack and lights his pipe.

I hesitate only a moment before deciding to sit down with him. *He's a nice man, and it probably gets lonely sitting alone here at the dock.*

"So, what's your name, Miss?"

"Nellie Kelly, sir."

"A fine Irish girl. I thought so, with that black hair and blue eyes. Just looking at you makes me miss the auld sod."

"I'm used to hearing that. I've heard it most of my life and didn't really understand until I went to Ireland and saw the women there. There was an immediate affinity with them, both physical and emotional. So many of them had my coloring, and those that didn't had red hair like my mam. It really felt like coming home."

"Mr. O'Doyle, where in Ireland did you come from?"

"A town called Tullamore in the center of the island. Not a pretty town like Killarney or Adare. It's a manufacturing town."

"My da used to love a whiskey called Tullamore Dew."

He grins broadly. "Ah, lass, that's what we 'manufactured' in my town. Whiskey. I worked in the distillery till I was nineteen and then hopped a boat over here. That was twenty-two years ago."

"Do you miss it?" Remembering the green hills, I imagined he must. I've wondered if Derry could move here away from the beauty of Ireland.

"Nah. Life was hard there. All we did was work and drink."

Just then I noticed the broken blood vessels on his large nose.

"Haven't had a drop of the devil's brew in fifteen years. My wife, an American lass like you, swore she'd leave me if I didn't lay off it. So, I quit."

I'd seen the effects of spirits on some Irish men, staggering home to their families after working on the railroads all day. It frightened me. Mam calls whiskey the Irish curse. "Ah, Nellie, you should see the things I used to see at O'Halloran's pub. Men drinking down their wages every Friday night, and their women coming into the pub and hauling them out. The women, crying their eyes out because their husband's wages had been wasted on getting juiced up with not a penny left for the babies at home." She'd shake her head. "Be careful, Nellie, if you ever marry an Irisher, that he isn't more in love with the almighty bottle than he is with you."

Derry had had a Guinness or two when he stopped playing in the pub, but I didn't think he was a victim of the Irish curse. *I'll watch closely once he gets here.*

"So, it must be a good friend you're meeting to bring a lass like you down here, right?"

"Yes, indeed, sir, a good friend from Dublin."

"Is it a male or female friend?"

"It's a young man, sir. Someone I met when I visited Ireland four years ago for a wedding."

Mr. O'Doyle removed the pipe clenched between his teeth and lifted one eyebrow. "A young man, is it? And tell me, is this young man more than a friend to you, Miss?"

I am flustered by this man's familiarity. How dare he ask me such a question! In a huff, I stammer, "He's my friend, sir. I haven't laid eyes on him in four years and only knew him for a few days. Of course, he's not more than a friend to me."

O'Doyle holds up his hand in protest. "Easy, Missy, no offense intended. I just figured a pretty girl like you might just be meeting a handsome young bloke. Irish men are the best looking in the world, unless the whiskey gets to them."

All of a sudden, an instrument on his desk starts to send out a signal. O'Doyle begins a tapping sound with his fingers. This continues for the next five minutes. When it's over, he removes his headphones and grins. "The SS *Hibernia* just passed Skull Island. She'll be docking in forty minutes."

CHAPTER SEVEN

I stand on the dock as the tugs pull out to the ship approaching the harbor. My nerves feel as though they're coming through my skin.

Why must the tugs move so slowly?

A voice startles me. It is Mr. O'Doyle. "It'll be another half hour till they get that ship here, Miss. If you need to use the facility, it's right over there." He points to a small outhouse with W imprinted on its door.

I thank him and decide to avail myself of this opportunity to freshen up. Inside, I am happy to see a water bucket and mirror. I splash some water on my face. It's cold but feels good on my inflamed skin. I look in the mirror closely and take the comb from my little purse. I start to rake the comb through my long hair and adjust the blue ribbon holding it off my face. Looking more closely, my face looks pale. Pinching my cheeks, I take the Vaseline from my purse and rub it on my quivering mouth. My lips are quite full and I like the way they shine now. Taking a deep breath to calm myself, I open the door and walk out into the sunshine.

By now, two tugs are close to the big ship and men scurry up the ropes to attach sturdy metal lines to its bow. When they are certain the lines are secure, they rappel back down the side of the ship to the tug boats. The steam engines accelerate and the tugs lurch forward.

I turn to Mr. O'Doyle who has joined me on the dock, asking, "What powers the tugs?"

"There's a seven-foot propeller under each of their hulls," he answers. "Those tugs are little miracle workers the way they're made."

The two of us stand side by side as the tugs approach the dock. Now I can see passengers at the rails. *Where's Derry?* I can't see him yet. Suddenly, the wind brings up a big wave and some people standing at the rail of the ship let out a loud whoop of fear or excitement.

I hear him before I see him; that deep baritone yelling, "Holy shite, that one nearly took me over the rails!"

That's when I spot him, waving wildly from the aft of the ship, a young boy staring up at him as his mother steadies herself on the pitching deck and tries to hold onto his hand.

"Nellie! Nellie, there you are, girl. Wave back if you see me."

I flail both arms like crazed windmills and scream at the top of my lungs. "Derry, I see you. Welcome to America, to Boston. I see you."

O'Doyle chuckles behind me.

Derry pulls off his woolen cap and begins waving it in the air, his brown hair whipping away from a face burnished and tan from the sun. When the wind dies down, the forelock tumbles down over his forehead, and the sight of it turns my knees to rubber. I didn't know how much I had missed that errant flop of hair till I saw it again.

O'Doyle guffaws loudly. "I see, Miss. You two are friends, just friends, right?"

"Right."

"I'd wager a month's wages that eager lad at the rail has other ideas."

Why do his words excite me?

After what seems an eternity—but is only twenty-eight minutes by the clock on the dock—he stands in front of me, a knapsack in his hand and his fiddle case slung over his shoulder. His eyes dance and his grin looks about to split his face in half.

"You look beautiful, Nellie. Even prettier than I remembered."

I feel a blush start at my chest that travels up to my face. "Is that your blarney talking, or do you really mean that, Mr. O'Byrne?"

"On my mam's life, I swear it, Miss Kelly. The four years have only made you lovelier, though I'd have sworn that to be impossible when I last saw you. Your eyes are bluer and your skin looks like rose-colored velvet. I'd forgotten how midnight-black your hair is. I won't go into the other attributes I notice about you right now lest I scare you off."

My blush grows deeper and I lower my eyes. Then there's a poke in my side and O'Doyle says, "Are you not going to introduce me to this fine young countryman of mine? I want to warn him about American girls, even if their last name is Kelly."

I stammer an introduction. "This is Mr. O'Doyle, the harbormaster. He's been keeping me company this morning, waiting for your ship."

Derry shakes his hand and the two of them begin exchanging information. Where they're both from in the old country, relatives they might know, where they went to school.

Finally, O'Doyle says, "And how goes the fight against the filthy Brits?"

With that, Derry begins pumping his hand in earnest. "Heating up, sir. The young people are more stirred up than ever. Were you involved in it before you left?"

O'Doyle's chest visibly inflates. "Was I? Does the word Fenian mean anything to you, boy?"

"Yes, sir, I am a member of that fine group myself, though I try to keep it quiet in Dublin," Derry answers.

"Once I got too old to continue my fight as a Fenian in Tullamore, I came to America where I'm part of a club here, the AOH, that sends money back to the cause. That's why some of us came here, to help finance the fight back in the old country."

Derry's face deepens with respect. "The Hibernians. Yes, I know of your organization very well, Mr. O'Doyle. It's been critical to our efforts In Dublin. Ireland's too poor to finance the rebellion that's needed. Our Irish-American brothers are an invaluable resource to us."

O'Doyle warms to the conversation. "And have you heard of the Molly McGuires, lad?"

"Of course, I have. Who hasn't? They're the toughest crowd of Irish men here in America, right?"

"Indeed. My brother was part of that group in Pennsylvania, trying to keep the money-grubbing mine owners from killing the Irish laborers in the coal mines there."

"Was?"

O'Doyle's face contorts in pain. "Was! They hanged him last year for his involvement with the Mollies. Bastards."

"Mr. O'Doyle, I am so very sorry to learn about your brother." I touch his arm.

"Thanks, Missy. But this is not a day for grieving. This is a day for celebrating this young lad's arrival, now isn't it? Go on with it."

He squeezes my shoulder and shakes Derry's hand and we turn to leave. "I'll see you again, Mr. O'Doyle," Derry says. "I'll come see you here."

"I'll do better than that. I'm going to talk to the Missus about having you two come to our place for dinner. She's not a great cook, but she keeps a clean house and makes a mean apple pie if I do say so myself."

They exchange addresses and promises.

"We'll look forward to that," Derry answers, waving goodbye.

Chapter Eight

When we get to my wagon, he whistles. "Well now, isn't this a fine rig for a young girl to be driving. I'm gobsmacked."

"Uncle Kam gave it to me, along with Rosie, the horse, for my graduation from college. Isn't it marvelous?"

"Indeed. Uncle Kam. The colored gentleman who was with you in Dublin for Neo's wedding? Neo's father, isn't he?"

"Yes, and like a second father to me. He was on the coffin ship when Mam came here from Ireland. The two of them saved each other's lives, I'm told." I climb up to the driver's seat, then notice a slight hesitation from him.

"Would you like to drive it?" I asked, holding out the reins.

"Thought you'd never ask." He pats Rosie on the flank and tells her she's a pretty filly while I climb over to the passenger side. Then he leaps to the driver's side and takes up the reins, clicking his cheeks, saying, "Let's go, Rosie."

She arches her neck and neighs, then turns and looks at Derry with some alarm in her eyes.

"It's all right, Rosie," I console. "She hasn't been driven by anyone but me," I explain. "Guess she's a bit leery of this stranger telling her what to do."

"A typical female, I wager." His Irish brogue is running thick. "Don't worry, Rosie. I won't bring down the reins too hard on you. Don't want to aggravate you or Miss Nellie."

As we pull away from the harbor, Derry says, "Nellie, I want you to tell me everything about this city. I understand it's called 'The Cradle of Liberty,' though Philadelphia quarrels that's their name. I plan to visit there as well while I'm here."

In spite of myself, I feel disappointed. I'd hoped he'd spend his entire visit in Boston. "I can tell you a lot about Boston, but I've not been to Philadelphia."

"We'll have to remedy that. Maybe you can come with me."

What did he just say? Is he serious? My first thought is that Mam would never permit such a thing. My second is that maybe I can convince her. After all, I'm twenty-two years old now, a fully grown American woman. She and Uncle Kam would have a fit—but maybe.

He slaps his fiddle case. "I brought this along because I figure I can pay my way on this trip playing in some pubs. Are there pubs in Boston?"

"Lots of them. Mostly in South Boston, where I live. That's where the Irish all settled. Before I take you to your lodging house, would you like to look around Boston?"

"Love to."

"All right. Turn right at this corner." We ride along for several blocks and I say, "Stop here, Derry. I want you to see the Old South Meeting House."

He pulls the wagon to the curb. "This church is where the Sons of Liberty left a meeting and dumped hundreds of chests of tea into the Boston Harbor. It was called The Boston Tea Party."

"Ah yes, I've read about that. To protest taxation without representation, right?"

"Right."

"Just like in Ireland. Damn Brits think they own the world, don't they? But America showed them. See, Nellie, this is why I must visit America. I want to understand the process of your independence so I can use it for my country."

For a moment, my breath stops. "I thought perhaps you were here because you wanted to see me again."

He turns to me and takes my hand in his. "That's the personal reason, but there is a greater cause as well. Ireland's independence. Please understand that."

His eyes look deep and grave and his passion for his mission causes me to feel silly. "Yes, Derry, I do understand. I grew up hearing my parents express the same need. I just didn't grasp it before."

"Good," he says. "Because somehow I think you'll be part of my quest."

His words puzzle me. *How? How can I be part of Ireland's independence?* "Someday, you must explain your meaning to me."

He lightens the mood. "I will, as soon as I figure it out myself. Where to next?"

"Go left here and then right on Bromfield Street. We're going to the Granary Burial Ground."

He does as I say and pulls up at the old cemetery. "Now what?"

"We'll get out and walk it."

He ties Rosie to a hitching post and we stroll into the cemetery. "Don't step on any graves, Derry."

"No, I wouldn't. We have the same custom in Ireland."

"I understand Mother Goose is buried here," I tell him.

"Who's that?"

"A famous writer of nursery rhymes."

I stop at a grave. "This is where Paul Revere is buried."

"Yes, I've heard of him. 'The Midnight Ride of Paul Revere.'"

"That was the beginning of our Revolutionary War, when the British invaded Boston." We stand looking at the grave and then I guide him to another. "Three of the signers of the Declaration of Independence are buried here, too, but I'm not sure of the location of their graves."

"I'll come back here another time and find them, Nellie. Maybe if I say a prayer over them, they'll inspire me on how to free my country from the limey bastards."

We go back to the wagon and I give him directions to our next stop. We are both in quiet contemplation as we go on.

"A farthing for your thoughts, Nellie."

I forcefully shake myself free of them. "Well, the first thing you must learn is that we don't use farthings or pounds here. It's dollars and cents."

"Will you teach me, Nellie?"

"I'd love to."

"Someday, I hope Ireland will have monuments to freedom against the bloody Brits. I intend to make that my life's work."

My stomach constricts in fear. "Do you mean to go to war, Derry?"

"I hope not. I believe our revolution must be done politically. That's why I got my degree in Law. I want to be a part of England's Parliament and work from the inside. But if I must fight or even die for the cause of my country, I'll do it."

A great silence followed us as we climb back into the carriage and continue our tour of Boston.

"What is that?" he asks, pointing to a majestic building.

"The Massachusetts State House. The dome on top was finished by Paul Revere himself. He was a silversmith by trade."

As we meander along, I glance at him. His eyes are narrowed in deep thought. Both of us have much to consider.

A bit further down the street, I ask, "See that church over there with the spire?"

"Yes, yes, 'tis lovely."

"That's the Park Street Church. One of the oldest churches in Boston. Many years ago, it was instrumental in beginning the Abolitionist movement here in Boston."

"Abolitionist?"

"The people against slavery. You know, this country had slaves until the War Between the States. Da fought in that war. He said that slavery was our national tragedy."

"Of course. I knew about your slavery. I hadn't heard of that term, though. Abolitionist, eh?" He touches my hand. "I wish I had known your father."

I don't answer, but my thought is, *He'd have liked you.*

CHAPTER NINE

Pulling up to the house, I smell baking bread and mutton stew. *Good.* Derry and I had skipped lunch in favor of an ice cream on our ride around town. Now we are both ravenous. He'd insisted on buying a bottle of wine when I got the Guinness at Quincy Market, and I didn't argue. I knew Mam would appreciate such a gesture.

"Mam?" I call as we walk into the house.

"In the kitchen, love. Make yourselves at home. I'll be right there."

I take the beer and wine from Derry's hands and go to the kitchen.

"Well?" she whispers, her eyes dancing.

"Well, what?"

"Do you still like the lad?"

The rosy color of my face tells her all she needs to know. "I knew it. I knew you were sweet on him. Well, isn't that lovely, though?"

She washes her hands as I open the wine and pour the beer and we go into the living room.

"Mr. O'Byrne!" she exclaims, rushing to shake his hand. "And how was your journey?"

"'Twas good, Mrs. Kelly, but a bit long. Your fine daughter here has been showing me all around Boston this afternoon. Grand city, grand!"

Is it my imagination or are both of them speaking with a heavier brogue than earlier today? This pleases me so.

"Your house smells like heaven, Mrs. Kelly. Is that stew cooking?"

"Indeed, it is. I hope you like stew."

"Ha! Now have you ever known an Irishman who didn't?"

"Not really. My late husband never lost his taste for it. We'll eat after we finish our drinks. It's ready."

The three of us sit in the parlor, chatting easily and sipping our drinks. Mam asks him many questions about Ireland and how the quest for independence is going there.

"It'll come," he answers. "But I can't say when. The British are a wily crowd, you know."

"Well, it can't come soon enough for me." She takes a final swallow of her wine and then slams the glass down. "Those blackguards crushed my family and all our neighbors during the famine, burning down our pitiful huts and starving us out. And it had gone on for six hundred years before that, ever since that evil King Henry invaded us. 'Tis wrong for one huge country to destroy its small neighbor. Wrong." She picks up her glass and rises to her feet. "Nellie, I think it's time we feed this lad. He must be hungry."

He smiles. "Mrs. Kelly, that is an understatement. My mouth hasn't stopped watering since I entered this house."

She seats him at the kitchen table and puts the stew into a serving bowl, saying, "Nellie, slice the bread, please."

I slice the warm loaf, take the butter from the icebox, and put them on the table. When we bow our heads, she says, "Mr. O'Byrne, will you say the Grace?"

I grin. *She likes him.* She would never ask a man she didn't like to pray at our table. No man has said grace here since Da died. *Yes, she definitely likes him.*

Derry eats like a man starved, asking for seconds. Mam rises and goes back to the stove, opens the door, and removes a warm, fragrant apple pie.

"You baked?" I ask, surprised.

She hasn't made a pie since Da died. Says it makes her think about those she has lost; in particular, dear Kathleen O'Halloran, who taught her to bake when she first came to America, and Da, who loved her pies almost as much as he loved her. *But today, she baked.*

Cutting the pie, she says nonchalantly, "Of course, I baked. It isn't often we have company here from the old country. What else would I do?"

I'd forgotten what a baker she was. Though never a great cook, her pies were fantastic—apple, berry, peach—whatever she could pick from a tree or a bush used to arrive at our table wrapped in the most tender crust I've ever tasted.

As Derry finishes his second piece, he pulls back from the table. "Best pie I've ever tasted. Nellie, can you bake like this? If you can, I'll just have to marry you now, won't I?"

He caught me off guard and I blush. "Afraid not, sir. I've been too busy going to school to learn much baking. And Mam has never wanted me tied to a kitchen like some girls. Isn't that right, Mam?" I stare at her with a bit of defiance in my eyes.

She hesitates only a moment. "Yes, that's true, love. But maybe it's time I teach you a trick or two. Couldn't hurt now, could it? After all, you are a college graduate."

CHAPTER TEN

Derry and I spend the next two weeks exploring Boston. I take him to the Boston Public Library where he pores over history books while I prepare study plans for the fall. As I research every book they have on science, my heart quickens. I so look forward to meeting my class and teaching my girls.

I look up over my book and catch Derry staring at me quizzically, teasing his lips.

"What?"

"I'm just thinking how lucky I am. I've always wanted to know a girl who was as passionate about her future work as I am. Until I met you, I'd despaired of ever finding one."

His words warm me all over. Since he arrived, we've pretty much avoided moments of intimacy. He kissed me once, saying good night on our porch, but it seems he's more intent on knowing me intellectually rather than physically. That's all right with me. I think we both understand that the attraction between us is not going away, and I love getting to know him in other ways, like watching his excitement as he discovers some new morsel of information about America's independence from Great Britain.

"Just think, Nellie, if crazy King George had only allowed someone from the American British Colonies to serve in

Parliament, this town might still be flying the British flag. But he wouldn't. And once the boys convened the First Continental Congress, the die was cast. America wasn't going to put up with England's tyranny any longer. Good on you boy'os, good on you."

His last words are raised in excitement, and the librarian comes to our table, "Sir, you must speak softly, please."

He turns red and smiles up at her with puppy dog eyes. "I'm so sorry, Miss. I guess I got carried away here."

She grins back at him, clearly taken with this handsome young man. "Don't worry about it. Some of the people here might complain, you know?"

"Of course," he says. "I'll do better."

Can any woman resist this charming Irishman?

That evening, Uncle Kam comes to the house to see Derry. They had met on our trip to Ireland for Neo's wedding. Derry was a fellow classmate at Trinity with Angelique's brother, Jean.

"Tell me about my son." Uncle Kam opens the conversation. "I understood his reason for moving to Ireland. He and Angelique would never have been accepted here. We write often, but I haven't gotten back to Ireland for a visit. He was home only once for his mother's funeral. Is he happy?"

"He's great, sir. He and Angelique have a magic act and are getting bookings all around the island. They were at the Theatre Royal last month, and I got to see their performance. It was incredible."

I remember that was their plan when they married. I'm so happy that my old friend is doing what he always wanted to do: being a magician, and apparently doing well with it.

"Tell us about their act," Uncle Kam says, leaning forward. "I'd hoped he'd become a physician, but that didn't appeal to

Neo. I was worried he'd never make a living as a magician, but knew he must follow his dream just as I followed mine."

Respectfully, he says, "I'd say he's making a very good living, sir. They have a grand house on the outskirts of the city, and he and Angelique are made for each other. They're very happy. As to their act, Neo comes on stage first and does all kinds of magic acts, like borrowing a ring from someone in the audience and then having it turn up in the tiniest gift-wrapped box behind the curtain. I've asked him how the devil he does it, but his answer is always the same."

"A magician never reveals his tricks," I say, trying to sound like Neo.

"Exactly."

"I heard that line all through my childhood. You should have seen him when we ran away together to the circus. He was supposed to be a mind reader and, in truth, was very good at that, too."

"What did you do in the circus, Nellie?"

I look over at Mam and see her frowning. This is still a tender subject between us. She'll not ever forget the worry I caused her and Da back then. "Actually, I was a bareback rider. Until I fell off the horse and got a concussion."

Derry's gaze is rapt. "Nellie Kelly, I wish I'd known you then. We could've done some major mischief together."

"Hush now," Mam says. "She did quite enough mischief on her own. Nearly turned my hair silver with worry."

"How does Angelique fit into the act?" Uncle Kam asks.

"After Neo has dazzled the audience with tricks, the theater darkens except for one spotlight which moves to the top of the stage. Angelique is positioned there on a swing. She's dressed all in pure white and really looks like an angel. The whole crowd gasps when they see her. She is quite beautiful, you know."

We all nod our heads in agreement.

"Then, the swing is lowered to the stage where Neo takes her hand and helps her off. He takes her in his arms, and the orchestra begins an old Irish waltz. The two of them dance to the center of the stage, never taking their eyes from each other's. Part of the magic, I think, is the differences between them. He's so dark and handsome and she's so fair and lovely."

Closing my eyes, I can almost see them together on the stage. They would be breathtaking.

"Magically, an elaborate trunk rolls to center stage. Its top opens by itself and the audience by now is craning their necks to see how that happens, but no one can tell. They stop dancing and Neo leads her to the trunk where he gently lifts her and places her in it. Silently, without any assistance from him, the lid closes on her."

The three of us sit there enraptured by the story and breathless at the images in our imaginations of what is happening on that stage in far-away Dublin.

"What happens then?" I ask, eyes wide.

"The lights change colors on the stage, going from blue to lavender to pink and every shade in between. Neo stands stark still gazing down at the trunk which almost looks to levitate. Then a saw comes down to the stage from high in the ceiling. They must use an invisible wire, but it seems to be moving as if on its own accord. Neo takes it and cries, 'No!'"

"A voice booms down from the top of the theater roof. 'You must. It is destiny. It's the only way to save her.'

"Neo takes the saw in his hands, and his eyes glisten with tears. He told me later it's glycerin, but you'd swear he's crying. He starts to saw the trunk in half as the audience screams in fear. Sometimes, he seems to be stuck, as though he's hitting bones. Moans come from the trunk, high and agonized. When

I looked around the audience at that point, many women were in tears. He continues to saw until the trunk is severed in two pieces. He whirls the pieces around to the audience showing they are both empty. Then, he collapses on the stage, supposedly in grief. It's as if he's saying, 'What did I do?'

"Then, as he's writhing in agony on the floor of the stage, Angelique appears from the wings. She's dressed all in silver now and shines like a bright star. She comes to Neo and touches his shoulder. He looks up, stands, and they embrace, kiss, and bow to the audience."

Mam, totally enraptured by the story, says to Uncle Kam, "Well, we must see this. When can we go back to Ireland?"

CHAPTER ELEVEN

Later, after Uncle Kam had gone home, Derry and I are sitting together on the porch swing. The neighborhood is pretty much deserted now with no neighbors strolling by. Earlier, Sam Welch and his wife had asked us if we'd join them walking to Quincy Market for a root beer, but we were too full of pie.

The evening is cooling and I love the familiar squeak of the swing's chains. I stretch my hands toward the ceiling and ask Derry a question. "Was that true, the story you told about Neo's act or are you spouting blarney for effect?"

He raises his right hand. "Swear on my mam's life. Every word of it was true."

"It must have been . . ." I search for the right word, "magical."

"Surely was. Even though I know it's an act, they hooked me with it." He turns to me on the swing and takes my hand. "Those two really love each other, don't they? Neo and his wife?"

Nodding, I close my eyes and think back to when Neo first saw Angelique at the circus and how I worried about their color difference. "Yes, from the first moment they saw each other. It's strange how the things that worried me then are probably what makes their act successful. I mean, his being Negro and she so very white."

"It's understandable why that would have troubled you. I mean Negroes were still enslaved back then, weren't they?"

"Supposedly they were emancipated, but America hadn't accepted that yet. Even here in Boston. In truth, we still haven't."

He becomes very still, stopping the swing. "How could Americans think it's proper for a person to own another person?"

His question raises my defensive hackles, and I stiffen beside him. "Not all Americans," I answer angrily, "just some. Mostly in the South where they needed free labor to pick cotton and tobacco. Really, Derry, don't assume we all believe in slavery."

"No, of course not. I know you'd nay have a part of that, but it is confounding, don't ya think?"

I nod, embarrassed about what Da called our national disgrace.

Right then Mam opens the front door and steps out. "I'm going to bed, children."

We look at each other and grin. *Children?*

She rubs her back and yawns. "I need to be at Kathleen's Haven quite early tomorrow for a meeting with Kam. We're running low on funds again, and, as always, he's going to bail us out. I truly don't know what we'd do without his help. But he loved Kathleen as much as I did, and he wants her honored forever."

As she steps back inside, she stops as if remembering something. "Derry, did you know Kathleen taught Kam and me to read and write when we first came to America?"

"No, I didn't. How wonderful!"

"Now here we were, both illiterate in a new country that wanted naught to do with either of us. Lots of people hated Negroes then, even more than they do today. And the Irish? No one would hire the Irish. Signs of NINA—No Irish Need Apply—posted in every storefront."

"Why did they hate the Irish!?" he exclaims; back straight, eyes wide. "How could anyone hate the Irish? We're a fine bunch of folks."

Mam chuckles in agreement. "I suppose it was fear. Many of them were afraid we'd take their jobs from them. And really, there were so many of us invading these shores at that time it just made them crazy with nerves. I trudged these streets in Boston till my feet were raw to the bone looking for any kind of work, but no one would give me a chance . . . until Kathleen."

She clearly remembers something that annoys her deeply and scowls in anger, lips pinched. "Kam was employed before I was as a matter of fact. At the apothecary. The owner realized that a handsome black boy with a fancy top hat would be a hit delivering medicines to the fops on Beacon Hill. Abolition was popular among some of the upper crust back then. Made them feel charitable. But a red-haired skinny waif of a girl like me? No one wanted that, except Kathleen. Kam and I both feel we owe her our lives."

"Why do you think that the apothecary owner wasn't threatened at the thought of having a Negro in his employ?" Derry asks, transfixed. "After all, America was still bringing in slaves then, weren't they?"

"Indeed. But the owner was a very wise gentleman. And, being Jewish, he'd been through his own share of prejudice in Boston. And because he was smart, he recognized quickly that Kam had a brilliant mind and would do him proud. It was the smartest investment Mr. Mendel ever made. Once Kam hit it rich with his tonic, he kept that apothecary solvent for years. Still does, truth be told."

"Interesting," Derry murmurs.

"Yes, I have many stories I'll share with you about those early days here, but not tonight. I have a book waiting beside my bed. Behave yourselves." She goes in and closes the door, trusting them completely.

The two of us become pensive as the sky darkens into night. The chatter of the birds quiets, leaving only the faint buzz of insects. The new night air drifts over the porch.

"Are you chilled, Nellie? Shall I get your shawl?"

"No, I rather like the coolness; it being so warm during the day."

He moves closer on the swing. I feel the heat of his body and the hardness of his shoulder through the sleeve of my dress. It feels good.

"Do you believe in love at first sight, Nellie? I mean like what happened with Neo and Angelique?"

I ponder only a moment. "How can I not believe in it? I saw it happen to them with my own eyes. And it terrified me."

He lifts his hand and puts it across the back of the swing. His hand brushes my shoulder and, without warning, I tremble. He tips my face up to look in his eyes. "What is it, Nellie?"

"Just the memory of that fear about Neo, I suppose."

"Are you sure that's it?".

His eyes stare into mine. "Are you sure you're not afraid because the same thing happened with you and me when first we saw each other?"

His words raise goosebumps on my arms and I cannot respond to them. In confusion, I pull my eyes from his and drift back to four years ago at The Brazen Head and Derry on the stool in the center of the pub, singing "The Rose of Tralee" with his eyes never leaving mine through all the verses; how Derry held me in the Conleys' parlor and what happened between us. I was ashamed and embarrassed the next morning, but there he was at the dock to say farewell to me and Mam, sweet and solicitous to both of us. A real gentleman. A real friend.

And now, here he is in Boston so close beside me.

"Do you love me, Derry?" *Did I really say that? What a bold question.* My face burns in embarrassment. *What must he think of me? How could I be so forward?*

"I believe I do, Miss Kelly," he whispers, then kisses me ever so deeply, igniting a fire.

He loves me and I can't deny that his love is returned. I can't think straight; his every touch, his lips, the heat of his body and the urgent warmth between my legs. *With every bit of myself, I love him—Don't stop . . .—But soon, he'll leave for Philadelphia, and then soon after that, go back to Ireland—Never stop!—So what good is loving him? Our worlds are thousands of miles apart.* I cling to him.

Then my mind flits to when I thought I loved Sean O'Halloran. That feels like a different lifetime. Sean's done well for himself and is now a successful attorney right here in Boston. I wrap my arms about his neck, kissing him in return; the ozone in the air prickling the hairs on my arms. He still tries to get me to see him. You'd think that breaking his nose would've stopped that, but no. People say they think he'll be mayor one day— *Don't think that way!*—I wish I still loved Sean—*No!*—It would be so much easier if that were the case—*No!*—And surely Sean is every bit as handsome as Derry, perhaps even handsomer— *No!*—And he lives here. It would be so simple if I loved Sean— *Stop thinking of Sean!*

But I don't have any feelings for Sean. I love this Irishman with the floppy curl that won't stop falling on his forehead—*Yes!*— This man with a mission to get his homeland freed—*Yes!*—This man who will leave me soon and whom I may never see again— *No!*—I wish I could stop loving him, but I can't help myself.

"Penny for your thoughts, girl." He had pulled away and sought answers in my eyes.

Tears well and spill over. I brush them away angrily. "What good is loving each other, Derry? You live in Ireland, and I live in America. You have your life planned there, and mine is solidly here. It's impossible."

He puts his hands on my shoulders and turns me to face him. His grip is almost painful in its strength. "Don't say that. Nothing is impossible. Look at what Neo and Angelique did."

"Yes, but Angelique was an orphaned French girl with no prospects after she left the trapeze and the circus. I am about to be what I've dreamed of forever. I'm going to teach girls. I'm going to make their lives better through education. That is important to me."

By now, I'm sobbing uncontrollably. Things look so dismal. And I can't bear the thought that we have no future together.

"Nellie," he says, taking his handkerchief from his pocket and rubbing it against my streaming eyes. "I haven't figured everything out yet, but I will. I promise I will."

"How?"

"I don't know but you have my word that I'm thinking about solutions."

His words don't mollify my feelings one bit. It doesn't help that I have my monthly and my emotions are running amok tonight. That always happens to me during such a time.

He sits back on the swing. "Is there any way you'd consider coming back to Ireland with me when I leave?"

I jolt forward in shock. "What? I begin teaching at Girls High in mere weeks."

"Yes, love, I know that. And I'm on track to becoming a partner at Hollyfield and O'Brien in Dublin someday. But we must find a way, mustn't we?"

My temper flares. "So, you expect me to forego my dreams so that you can have yours? Is that right, Derry?"

"Now, don't get your Irish up, Nellie. I'm just trying to sort things out here. I need to tell you something important and difficult."

His tone is disturbing, serious, and dark. *So what is this important matter?* I compose myself and remain silent.

"I need for you to be calm," he says.

"Very well. What is it?"

He clears his throat, then asks me, "Have you ever heard of Jeremiah O'Donovan?"

I shake my head. "Who is he?"

"He's one of the reasons I'm here; to see him in New York City."

"But I thought you were going to Philadelphia."

"That's what I want people to think. In truth, I'm going to New York next week. I'd like you to come with me. When my business there is finished, I'll sail home."

My heart stops for a moment. "Your business there? Who is this Jeremiah?"

"An Irishman exiled by Great Britain to America. They didn't like his activities in Dublin with the Fenians."

Da was a Fenian . . . so is Derry. His words terrify me. "What kind of activities?"

"They're planning a rebellion against Great Britain. It's called The Dynamite Campaign. It's very well thought out, and their target is London. People could be hurt."

I stammer my words. "T-that sounds awfully v-violent, Derry."

"I suppose it is. But face it, we've tried everything else."

"But it's criminal. How can you be involved in such a thing? You could go to jail." My head begins to pound. I don't know if it's confusion or fear, but I want nothing to do with it. At a sudden slash of lightning, I nearly jump out of my skin. Then, immediately thereafter, the thunder and the torrential rain; harsh, pounding rain that sounds like bullets on the roof, making me shiver in either cold or terror.

Derry stands up and begins to pace back and forth on the porch. "I'm not going to actually plant the explosives. I'm just helping the Fenians financially."

"How can you help them financially? You're just out of law school and haven't even started making money yet. That's crazy talk."

He stops pacing and looks down at me. "It's not my money. I'm just a mule, a transporter. There are a large number of Irish natives here in America. Many of them banished from Ireland by the Brits for what they consider illegal behavior. Some of these Irish are becoming quite wealthy. They're committed to raising money for the cause of Irish freedom. I've met with several of them here in Boston—one your Mr. O'Doyle, the harbormaster—and will take their money back to the cause in Dublin. Jeremiah O'Donovan has raised a fortune in New York, and I'm to pick that up for transport as well."

Suddenly, Mam comes back out to the porch holding a cup of tea. She's wearing her wrapper over her nightgown and has rags in her hair. "Did I overhear you say Jeremiah O'Donovan?"

I close my eyes. "Derry, you need to know she hears like a fox."

Derry chuckles. "I did, Mrs. Kelly. Do you know him?"

"I don't, but my husband surely did. Daniel spoke of him often. Always with a hush of reverence in his tone. Daniel subscribed to his newspaper, even here in Boston. Didn't he end up in an English jail?"

"Four of them. The bastards jailed him for treason without a trial."

"Where is he now?"

"In America, Mrs. Kelly. He and four other prisoners were released in 1870 with the proviso they can never return to Ireland. He lives in New York with his wife, Molly Irwin."

"Ah, yes, Molly Irwin, the poet."

"That's right. Jeremiah believes the Irish must go a bit mad in order to get the British to see reason about emancipation. I'm thinking he might be right. He's plotting something called the Dynamite Campaign."

She shakes her head, staring him down. "Dynamite, is it? It breaks my heart to hear such things, but after all these years, I think that's all the English understand. God knows we've tried everything else."

"Mam!" I exclaim. "How can you say such a thing? Are you advocating violence?"

She leans against the porch railing and stares into my eyes. "Nellie, sweet child of my heart, you know how I feel about violence, especially after what someone did to your da. But it seems that's all men understand. It's kill or be killed." With that, she turns back to Derry. "What part do you play in all this, young man?"

"I can't say, ma'am. But let me assure you I won't be setting off any dynamite."

"Well, that's good, I guess. When you get to New York, tell the O'Donovans I said hello. And tell Molly Irwin I love her poems." She looks us one then the other in the eye saying monotonally, "Good night again," then goes back inside.

As I sit there in shock replaying their conversation, he comes to me and takes my hand and pulls me to my feet. "I'd better head to my boarding house now, Nellie."

I grasp his hand, not wanting him to leave. "But it's pouring, Derry."

He picks up his fiddle case. "Miss Kelly, my place is just three blocks from here, as you know."

"But you'll catch your death."

"Nellie, my love, remember, I'm from Ireland. This is but a wee trickle of a rain. Makes me feel at home."

He pulls me close to him and presses his lips firmly against mine, leaving me wanting more. Then with a grin, he dashes off down the street, whistling all the while.

CHAPTER TWELVE

First thing the following morning, I dress and prepare myself for battle—with my mam. Stomping resolutely into the kitchen, I am disappointed she isn't there. Oh yes, she told us she had to be at Kathleen's Haven early this morning for a meeting with Uncle Kam. I'd forgotten.

I wasted a good night's sleep practicing my arguments for going to New York with Derry, and now there's no one to present them to. But I want to write them down lest I forget any of them. I grab paper and pencil from my school bag and start scribbling:

1) I want to meet this Jeremiah O'Donovan and see what he's planning.
2) I need to see how New York has changed since I was there as a child with the circus.
3) A short vacation is definitely in order before I start teaching. I've worked so hard.
4) When I come back, I can tell her how the resistance is coming along, maybe give her news on Ireland's quest for independence.
5) She needn't worry about my virtue. I'll find a boarding house exclusively for young ladies.
6) I'm almost twenty-two years old, a college graduate, a grown

woman, and I don't really need her permission to take a trip. But because I love and respect her, I'm giving her the opportunity to grant me her blessing.

All of a sudden, I wonder if I need to go to confession. All my life, nuns and Father Ruzzo have said that impure thoughts are sinful, and I cannot deny that my thoughts about Derry have been impure for the past four years. Then I remember Martha, beloved Martha, who told me on the ship to Ireland that my passionate thoughts and dreams are simply God's way of preparing me for marriage when the right man comes along. Darling Martha, her dark eyes shining as she remembered her one true love, the son of her master, the father of her only child. Theirs had been a true love affair, and she never experienced true passion again with another.

My head is spinning as I try to determine if Martha is right or is my church?

I daren't tell Mam the real reason I want to go to New York; that I love Derry and need to be with him every possible minute before he sails back to Ireland. That he loves me, too. That I think someday he'll be my husband.

A sharp rap at our front door startles me from my reverie. *Who can that be? Perhaps it's Derry.* I race to open the door, then stop, shocked. There he stands, tall, blonde, handsome, grinning that grin that once melted my heart . . . and then broke it.

Except for that night at my party, I have only seen him in passing. His picture is often prominently featured in the *Globe's* society pages. He's quite the young man around Boston now and one of this town's most sought-after bachelors.

"Sean, why are you here?"

"To see you, of course." He steps into the house before I can think of a response.

I stammer awkwardly, "A-all right. Well, sit down."

"No, I want to take you somewhere. Grab your parasol. We can walk. It's a lovely day with no rain in sight. Let's go."

Dumbfounded at seeing him, I grab my shawl and parasol from the rack and pull the key from my drawstring bag. Silently, I follow him out to the porch and lock the front door behind me. He's right. It's gloriously sunny with a slight cooling breeze tempering the air. I breathe in deeply, then ask, "Where are we going?"

"You'll see." He takes my arm and leads me North on Dorchester Street.

As we walk on this balmy summer day, others pass by, smiling. Most of the men tip their hat to him. "Hello, Mr. O'Halloran. Good luck in the race," one distinguished older gentleman says, patting Sean on the back.

Wondering what race he means, I stroll with Sean all the way to Beacon Hill where he stops in front of a grand house. It stands three stories high, with a porch scrolled around the entire bottom floor. Elaborate bric-a-brac trims cornices and windows on every floor. The front door is painted a vibrant green.

"Oh my, what a grand place," I say.

Sean turns me to face him. "I just bought it."

My mouth opens, but shock silences my words.

"Come. I want to show it to you." He opens the ornate iron gate, takes my hand and leads me up the twenty steps to the picketed porch, which curves gracefully around the front and both sides of the home. Seven wooden rocking chairs adorn the space, making it look welcoming and homey. Each of their seats has a thick cushion covered in damask floral. The delicate wood is curved unlike any chairs I've ever seen.

"Have a seat," he says.

I sink onto the chair nearest the front door and start to rock. "Ahh."

"Comfy?" He grins.

"Beyond comfy. In heaven. This chair feels as though it was made for my body. It fits me perfectly."

He chuckles and says, "That's the magic of Michael Thonet. He was a German furniture maker famous for his bent wood chairs. Everyone who sits in one of Thonet's chairs swears it was designed for their body. I felt the same the first time I tried one out on my graduation trip to Europe."

I continue to gently rock the chair in the shade of the porch; a blessing after the long walk. Sean sits in one closest to me. It's companionable for the two of us to sit on this marvelous porch rocking away like two old folks.

People passing by smile and wave. One couple walks up the steps, and the man—portly, balding and middle aged—shakes Sean's hand vigorously. "Good luck, Sean," he says, while the woman looks on, stars shining in her eyes. I gaze over at him and realize again how very handsome he is. In my infatuation with Derry, I'd forgotten. But this woman can't take her eyes off him.

Sean introduces me and they stay and chat a few moments before descending back down to the street to wave their goodbyes.

"Why does everyone congratulate you, Sean? First, that man on the street, and now this couple."

He stands and pulls me to my feet. I leave the chair reluctantly. He faces me, puts both his hands on my shoulders and stares down into my eyes. This makes me uncomfortable and I try to squirm away, but he holds me fast.

"You haven't heard?"

I shake my head.

"I'm going to be nominated to run for the Boston Board of Aldermen. I thought you knew."

I am beyond shocked at his words. He's so young, scarcely three years out of law school. *An alderman? An alderman should be an old man with mutton chops, not a handsome blonde fellow still in his twenties.*

"It's my first step to eventually becoming mayor. It's going to take some time. The ward bosses want Hugh O'Brien to be first. He was born in Ireland and they need to appease the new immigrants. They figure he'll get four two-year terms. By then, I'll be in my thirties. If I play my cards right—and I will—I'll win in a landslide."

I stand there with my mouth hanging open. And then it dawns on me. "Is that why you bought this house?"

"One of the reasons. It looks good for an up-and-coming young attorney to have a nice home. Living here, I can get into the right clubs and mingle with Boston's kingmakers."

"Can you afford it?"

"With the help of some friends in high places, yes." He takes my hand. "Come, I want to show you inside."

He walks me to the front door and inserts a key in the lock. The door swings open to reveal a large foyer with a gleaming marble floor.

"Oh!" I exclaim. "So lovely."

At the back of the foyer, two graceful staircases curve up to meet in a hall on the second floor. To the right of the foyer is a large parlor with a highly polished wooden floor. To the foyer's left is a dining room with a crystal chandelier in its center.

"The maid's kitchen is directly through that door at the back of the dining room," he says, pointing.

Holding onto my hand, he leads me toward one of the staircases. As we get closer, I see it is covered in a thick maroon carpet. My ascension to the second floor feels as though I'm walking on a cloud. He leads me to three large bedrooms, each more elegant than the last.

Finally, he opens a door to a tiny room connected to the largest bedroom. "The nursery," he says. "The third floor is the ballroom. When I'm Mayor, I intend to fete my constituents there."

I am speechless as we descend back down the staircase. He takes me again to the porch and sits down on a rocking chair, gesturing me to sit next to him in another. "Nellie, I've brought you here today for a reason."

"What is it?" Dumbfounded, I cannot see the forest for the trees.

He crosses his legs and leans forward. "To accomplish my goal, I need a partner. Someone of good Irish-Catholic stock. It would help if she were beautiful . . . and cultured. Able to hold her own in a conversation with anyone. Does that sound like anyone you know?"

"Not really, Sean. I've been so busy completing my education I've neglected making friends with many girls." I don't tell him that it's difficult for me to trust other young women after he got my best friend, Rosie, pregnant a few years ago. "Now that I'm ready to start teaching, my spare time is really tied up in that."

He leans toward me and puts his hands on the arms of my rocker. He's very close now, and I feel trapped. I try to rock, but he holds my chair firm. "Nellie, don't play stupid with me. You're a smart girl. You know what I'm talking about."

I scan my brain, trying to understand his meaning. Frustration and a bit of angst creeped into my voice as I say, "No, Sean. I really don't. I'm not playing a game. I just don't understand what you want from me."

"What I want, girl, *is* you. What I'm describing *is* you. Irish. Catholic. Educated. And yes, beautiful. You are all those things, and you know it." He takes in a deep breath. "Our children will be gorgeous."

For a moment, I sit with my mouth agape. That's how shocked I am. Years ago. Sean had hinted I was the kind of woman to help him fulfill his political dreams, but I told him then that I didn't want to marry him; didn't even know if I would ever marry, nor if I even wanted to have children. Now that Derry's in my life, some of those feelings have changed. *Now if Derry asked me to marry him, I would do it. And welcome his children. But Sean?*

I put my hand gently on his. "I'm very flattered, Sean, and this house is magnificent. I would love to live in such a place. But really, nothing has changed between you and me since the last time we discussed this. I asked you then if you loved me, and you had no answer. I told you I didn't love you and I still don't. I can't be your wife or your partner or whatever it is you want of me without love."

"Don't be a romantic fool, Nellie. People grow to love each other. So would we." He kneels before me and kisses me. I feel nothing and just want the kiss to end.

How can I explain this to him? Lord, help me. His mam died at his birth, so he never observed the love that can exist between a husband and wife. *I don't think he'll understand, but I feel a need to try to make him comprehend what I'm talking about.*

"Sean, I want what my parents had. When Mam walked into a room, Da's face glowed at the sight of her. That's what I want. We don't have that, and I fear it wouldn't change."

At that, he stands up, clearly angry. For a moment, I feel a panic that makes no sense to me. *Tell him. Tell him now. Tell him that you're in love with Derry.* But some perversity in my nature stops me. Instead, I say, "Let me think about this, Sean."

CHAPTER THIRTEEN

"Mam, I want to go to New York with Derry." The three of us are standing in our living room. Derry is behind me, so I feel his presence and support in this difficult moment.

The twilight coming through our lace curtains is dwindling. A shadow passes over her face. "No, Nellie. It wouldn't be right."

I rattle off all the reasons I'd listed on my paper, and she still shakes her head. After I have completed my list, I realize she won't budge. It's time to play my trump card.

"I feared you'd not approve. But frankly, I'm a grown woman and can make my own decisions. Mam, I love Derry." I figure *that* she'll understand.

She sits upon the sofa, finds a handkerchief in her pocket and dabs at her eyes. Her look is one of pure defeat; one I saw on her face only once before, when Da died. I want to run and take her in my arms and agree not to go with Derry. But he touches my shoulder gently without a word. His hand reminds me. Stay firm.

"Mam." I sit beside her and put my arm around her shoulder. "I really need to do this. I'll only be gone for a weekend and then be back to start school. Please understand."

"I'll take good care of her, Mrs. Kelly. We already have a reservation for Nellie at a young lady's boarding house in Greenwich Village. That's where Jeremiah lives, and I'll be nearby."

Her shoulder softens under my hand, losing its tension. She wipes her eyes one last time and stands up. "Well, I can't stop you, I guess. I'll just have to trust in God and in you, young man." Her eyes bore holes in his.

"Thank you, Mrs. Kelly. Your trust is well placed. I promise you," he says.

Yes, Derry is a man of his word. I know that. But what about me? Can she trust me? *Can I trust myself?* My stomach knots. *I just don't know.*

The next day, Mam attaches Rosie to the rig and takes us to the train. As she kisses me goodbye, fear shadows her eyes, but I am so excited that I ignore it. I'm getting away for a few days with the man I love. That's all that matters.

After Derry has stowed our small bags in a compartment overhead, we settle in our seats on the train. He puts his arm around me so naturally. *This feels so much like a honeymoon*, I think, swooning and exhaling into his embrace.

"Why can't we take the train all the way to New York?" he asks.

I tip my head up to catch his gaze and explain, "Because New York City is an island. Just like Ireland. The only way to get there is by steamboat, which we'll catch in Fall River."

"Your country is quite complicated, isn't it?" His eyes twinkle in delight.

"I suppose so." I snuggle back in. "It's just so big that it takes a long time to get from one state to another, which makes no never mind how long it takes us to get there. I'm with you and that's all that matters. Everything is wonderful. I'm determined not to think about you leaving me and sailing home."

Even saying the words causes my heart to hurt. Ireland is so far away. Once he goes, when will I ever see him again? I must dismiss such thinking. Don't spoil the time you have with him worrying about him being gone, Nellie. If it's the end of your story with Derry, make this time together memorable.

Because of a sleepless night and the comfort of his arm around me, I doze off with my head on his shoulder. The coziness of his nearness and the sound of the wheels on the rails is almost hypnotic and soon I am in a deep slumber. I dream of green hills rolling to the sea and see Derry running toward me, arms outstretched. There's a small white cottage nearby and when he reaches me, he lifts me up and carries me inside. A fire blazes in the hearth, and he places me down gently on a soft couch in front of it. He kisses me deeply and presses himself against me until I'm lying down. His eyes ask the question that has been asked without words for all of eternity. I know the answer. But just as he begins caressing my breasts, I am suddenly startled by a loud voice.

"Next stop, Fall River, Massachusetts! Prepare to disembark!" The conductor comes down the aisle, jostling passengers with his bulk as he passes them, continuing to yell, "Fall River, next stop!"

I spring to sitting, wondering whether I said anything or made any sound in my sleep that I should be embarrassed about.

Derry peers down at me and says, "Glad you got a bit of sleep, love. Me, too."

Were his dreams as beautiful as mine? "Did you dream, Derry?"

"Nah. Once I'm gone, I'm gone. I seldom dream."

I stretch my arms up. "Too bad. My dream was delicious."

He looks at me quizzically but doesn't ask the question. "Best get our stuff down now and get ready to catch that steamboat."

He looks at his watch. "We sail at half past the hour. Are you hungry?"

My stomach rumbles, causing both of us to look at my belly.

"Does that answer your question?"

"Indeed, it does. Shall we get something to eat before we sail?"

I think about his question and finally answer, "They serve beautiful meals in the dining room on the ship. I'd love to eat there. It's very fancy. The last time I was on *The Bristol* I didn't get to take any meals."

"Why is that?"

"Well, I was with Neo, remember? And Negroes are not welcome in the dining room."

He shakes his head. "I shan't comment, sweetheart. Starting an argument with you is the last thing I want to do."

"Smart man. You'd lose."

In less than ten minutes, we have climbed down the metal steps to the platform. Derry stretches his back and takes my arm. "So, tell me about this town, love."

"Sadly, we won't have much time to see it, but I looked around it last time I was here. It's quite industrial. Lots of factories. Textiles mostly. Not really pretty at all as I recall and covered in soot."

"Then, I guess I'm not missing much. Sounds like Limerick." He turns and scans the ships. "*The Bristol*, is it?"

"Yes, it's right over there," I answer, pointing.

He takes my hand and pulls me along toward the ship. When we arrive, Derry exclaims, "What a grand girl she is!"

I poke him in his side. "Why in the world do you call it a girl?"

"Are you daft, Nellie? Of course, she's a girl. Anything that beautiful has to be a girl. Like you, for instance." He lifts my hand

and kisses it and, in spite of myself, I blush. No one has ever kissed my hand before. A shiver of pleasure runs up my arm.

He takes our tickets from his inner coat pocket and holds them up in the air shouting in glee, "Let's go! I can't wait to get on this magnificent ship with my magnificent girl!"

We climb the gangplank and he hands our tickets over to the porter on the deck. "All right, Miss, you're in sleeping bunk number twenty-three in the ladies' car. The gentleman is in twenty-seven, next section over."

We head single file downstairs to the sleeping quarters of the ship. I find number twenty-three and Derry heads on to the next car.

"Be right back," he says.

I toss my bag onto my bunk, retrieving a few dollars for dinner.

Derry returns and knocks once on the outer wall. I step forward through the curtain to his outstretched hand in excited anticipation.

"Let's explore," he says, grinning from ear to ear.

"Yes! I want to show you the canaries."

"Canaries?"

"Yes, the owner, Mr. Fisk, has more than two-hundred of them in gorgeous gold cages hanging all over this ship. He's named every one of them. When they start singing, you'd swear it was a heavenly chorus. But loud, very loud."

We find the first cage up on the aft deck. The yellow bird jumps from its perch and grabs the wire of the cage as it stares at us. "Look!" Derry exclaims. "His name is Charlie." He strokes under the bird's beak softly and says, "Hello, Charlie."

The bird coos and lifts its head, better exposing its neck to Derry. Derry looks at me with wonder in his eyes. "I think he likes me."

"Of course, he likes you. Why wouldn't he? You're caressing him so nicely."

"Would you like that, Nellie? My caress?" His eyes stare into mine, deep and dark and filled with something like lust. "Would you?"

My face flames. Yes, I want to say. Yes, I would like for you to caress me, too—everywhere. But I dare not. He might think me a harlot if I speak what I honestly feel.

So, instead of continuing this dangerous conversation, I drag my gaze from his beautiful eyes and grab his hand, leading him up the stairs to another deck.

"I can see why they call this a floating palace," Derry murmurs. "Never seen anything like it."

"Yes, and Mr. Fisk owns another ship, *The Providence*, equally as luxurious. He has canaries on that one, too."

Just then, a small man in a navy uniform covered in gold braid jumps up on a podium, welcomes us aboard, and shouts, "Set sail!"

"That's Mr. Fisk, the owner," I whisper. "He fancies himself an admiral."

The side wheel starts to turn and soon we are in the middle of Mount Hope Bay headed for the Narragansett Bay and onward to the Atlantic Ocean. Derry and I stand at the rail of the ship reveling in the salt air and sunlight.

"Look," I say, pointing to a distant horizon. "Once we round that curve, we'll see Rhode Island, the state next to Massachusetts."

"'Tis interesting that your country is divided by states. In Ireland, it's counties."

"Yes, I know. Mam says she found that confusing when she first arrived here. She and Uncle Kam also had trouble adjusting to the monetary system. They were used to pounds and pence, and suddenly it was dollars and cents in America. A man from Poland explained all this to them when they were on the transport boat to Boston Harbor from the awful ship they had just disembarked."

"'Twas a coffin ship, I'm certain," he says.

"Yes, and they both feel fortunate to have survived their journey on it. They watched a close friend, a young girl, jump to the sharks to escape more molestation from the crew. Mam was only thirteen years old, and Uncle Kam sixteen. He saved her after she was brutally raped by the crew. He was the crew's African slave boy. She says he was similarly abused, but I've never understood how."

Derry shudders and when he turns to me, his eyes are shining. "When I hear stories about those escaping the famine and slavery, I take pride in my Irish blood and coming from people strong enough to survive those times. I figure we're a pretty stalwart stock, Nellie."

I nod and stare out at the water, thinking, *I'll need to be of stalwart stock when he leaves me.*

Chapter Fourteen

At six o'clock, Derry goes to his berth to change for dinner, and I do likewise. I'd only brought one extra shirtwaist and a second pair of bloomers so as not to be heavy with luggage once we get to New York. Derry had sent his trunk ahead of him, and it had by now probably arrived at New York Harbor to be placed on the ship he'd booked to sail to Ireland.

Monday morning, but I shan't think about that. We have two glorious days together in the city before that. Right now, I must focus on making sure he'll miss me enough to return.

I pull the blue shirtwaist over my head—the one people tell me flatters my eyes—apply Vaseline on my lips, tidy up my hair with a ribbon, and pinch my cheeks, then step out through the curtain to wait for Derry. Within moments, he joins me from the men's sleeping quarters. He wears a fresh white shirt and has put pomade in his hair to control that wayward lock that always falls over his forehead.

"You look very pretty, Nellie. That color really complements your eyes."

"Oh really? Thank you." *He did notice.* My heart skips a beat.

"Let's get ourselves a good meal, shall we?" He takes my elbow and guides me toward the steps leading up to the deck.

At the entrance to the dining room, he takes my hand in his. I am struck with how different Derry's hands feel from Sean's. Rougher. Square rather than tapered. Sturdy. I squeeze his fingers in response. We're alone on this grand ship heading to a great city of nearly one-million people. Although Derry will stay at the apartment of a friend who relocated from Dublin two years earlier and I'll be at Miss Gibson's House for Young Ladies, we'll be alone in that city, nearly invisible to the world outside.

Mam had contacted one of the sisters at St. Augustine's and had her wire a nun she knew in New York to make sure they had a "No Gentlemen" policy at Miss Gibson's before she would stop nagging me about this trip. It is so good to be away from her for a bit. I love her dearly, but she worries too much about me. I'm twenty-two years old, a grown woman after all. It's time I become independent of her.

The maître d' greets us at the entrance to the elegant dining room and escorts us to a table for two. His black hair is tinged with grey, and I notice how slender his back is in the black tuxedo as we follow him into the room. He looks the very essence of gentility. Smiling, he leaves two menus on the white-topped table, and we both peruse them. I unfold my napkin and squeeze its softness in my hand.

"What strikes your fancy, Nellie?"

"I don't know. It all sounds delicious." To tell the truth, I didn't recognize some of the entrees, and the appetizers are mostly written in French.

A young waiter appears at our table. He, too, is dressed all in black, but not in a tuxedo. He looks very posh, and his blue eyes have a flirty sparkle to them.

"Hello, lady and gentleman," he says. "What looks good?"

Derry grins up at him. "What's your recommendation?"

"Well, my personal favorite is the filet of sole broiled in browned butter."

"What's that? I don't know it," Derry answers.

"It's fish. Fresh caught this morning in the Ipswich River and tender as your young lady's heart."

Derry chuckles. "Well, then, I must have it. In Dublin, we eat mostly salmon."

The waiter's eyes flash in recognition, and when he speaks, I notice for the first time the hint of a brogue. "Dublin, is it?" He looks around and whispers, "I hail from Armagh."

Derry leans back in his chair. "An Orangeman, eh?"

"Nay, mate. I want freedom from the Brits as much as anyone in the South. That's why I left, to get away from the Tans."

Derry extends his right hand. "Then I'd like to shake your hand, friend."

The two of them shake, their eyes fixed on each other. "I'm Kevin," the waiter says.

"Derry."

"Gentlemen," I say. "I'm glad you two are kindred souls, but I'm hungry," I giggle lest they think I am serious.

"Sorry, love. I got carried away." He turns to Kevin. "I'll take the sole. What's it come with?"

"Rice and peas."

"No potatoes?"

"I can substitute potatoes."

"Good. I'll take mine scalloped. Nellie?"

"I'll take the sole as well, but I'd like my potatoes mashed, Kevin."

"Good choices, mates," he says. "Would you like cocktails first?"
"Nellie?"

"I'd love a glass of red wine."

"Madeira?" Kevin asks.

"Sure." I had no idea about types of wine.

"And I'll take a Guinness."

Kevin salutes us and leaves the table.

As I scan the people seated nearby, Derry reaches into his pocket and removes a small parcel wrapped in tissue paper. "I brought this over from Ireland for you, love. It belonged to my mam." He extends the tiny gift to me.

I'm startled at the surprise and take it from his hand. "What is it?"

"Open it, Nellie."

Inside the tissue paper is a ring. It's fine gold and has an emerald heart at its center held by two golden hands. At the top of the heart is a gold crown. "It's beautiful," I whisper.

"'Tis the *Claddagh*." His eyes are dark and very serious.

"What does it signify?" My eyes lock onto his.

"Many things. Friendship, loyalty, love. How you wear it defines what it means to you."

I look at him quizzically.

"If you wear it on your right hand with the heart pointing outward, that means you're looking for love. If you point the heart inward, that means you've found love."

"And if I wear it on the left hand?"

"Well, if the heart points outward, that means you're engaged to be married. You turn the heart inward on your wedding day."

I hesitate, pondering my response to his words. Then, I remember the thirteen-year-old girl who ran away to join a circus. That girl followed her heart, not her head. She was bold and headstrong. *What happened to me? Why did I grow cautious? What would that thirteen-year-old have done in this moment?*

Knowing exactly what she'd have done, I put the ring on my left ring finger with the heart pointed outward. "I can't wait to turn it in."

He lifts my left hand to his lips and kisses the ring. I exhale in relief.

"Well now, this looks like something to celebrate." It's Kevin back with our drinks. He places the wine before me and the beer in front of Derry.

"Yes, 'tis." Derry grins up at him proudly. He lifts his glass and I click my wineglass against it. "To us! God help us!"

At that moment, a plan forms in my mind.

We sit staring at each other like simple fools, not saying a word. Words are not necessary now. Our pledge to each other is clear, not to be broken. His eyes hold the promise of forever, but then I remember, *He's going to leave me in two days.* The thought brings sadness but also resolution. I must make sure he returns to me. I'll do anything to make that happen. *Please, God, bring him back soon.*

Suddenly, Kevin materializes back at the table, two trays balanced over his head. "Well, well, I feel I'm interrupting something. But remember my friends, neither man, nor woman, can live by love alone. You need sustenance."

He places the trays on a stand beside our table and brings my plate over to me. "For the beautiful young lady," he says, then puts the other dish before Derry, "and the fine gent." He removes the silver domes covering the dishes. "*Slainte.*"

The scent of the food drifts up to me, reminding me how very hungry I am. "This looks marvelous!"

Kevin places a full bottle of wine on the table. "Compliments of *The Bristol.*"

Delighted, we stammer thank you as he uncorks the bottle. He offers me the cork to smell and I shrug my shoulders at the gesture. "Well, that's a first for me."

"But not a last, I wager." With a grin and a swagger, Kevin leaves us alone.

Derry picks up the bottle and refills my glass, then pours some in the wineglass Kevin left for him. "To us, Miss Kelly."

I lift my glass, nod and take a sip. "Yes. Let's eat."

The meal is so delicious we don't say another word for a good twenty minutes. At the end of the meal, my plate is clean enough to fool the dishwasher. I push myself back from the table and rub my stomach, moaning, "I am so full."

"Indeed. I love a girl with a healthy appetite." His grin has the devil in it.

A busboy in a white shirt and black pants appears and asks permission to clear our dishes. We nod acceptance.

Just then, Kevin returns. "Coffee? Dessert?"

"Oh Lord, Kevin. I don't think I can eat another bite," I answer. "But just tell me about the desserts anyway. And I would love coffee."

"Our desserts are incredible. We have crème brûlée, Baked Alaska, and every flavor of ice cream. But my personal favorites are the apple pie and chocolate cake *ala mode*."

Derry orders first. "Well, since Nellie's mam makes the finest apple pie in the world, I'll take the cake *ala mode*. Nellie?"

Rubbing my tummy again, I say, "I really shouldn't."

"But I bet you will," Derry says, a rascally grin crinkling the corners of his eyes.

"Kevin, I've never heard of Baked Alaska. What is it?"

"Truth be told, I've not had it. But the swells tell me it's even better on *The Bristol* than you'll find at Antione's in New Orleans. It's kind of a cake and ice cream wrapped up in meringue."

"Well," I giggle, "if it's better than at Antione's, I guess I'll have it." As if I've ever even heard of the place.

As Kevin leaves the table, Derry bursts into a full guffaw. "Good, gotta fatten you up some, girl. Put some meat on those bones."

"Do you think I'm skinny?"

"Nah, just joshing with you. As my dear old da used to say, 'The closer the bone, the sweeter the meat.' My mam was slender all of her life."

Suddenly, I'm struck with a wave of insecurity. "What if I get fat?"

He takes my hand, turning me into jelly. "Then, I'll love ya fat, girl. I swear I will."

I take this time to look around at the other diners in the room. They're mostly couples with a few all-male tables sprinkled in. *Businessmen*, I think. *I wonder if anyone here is as happy this night as I am. No, they can't be.*

When Derry's cake and ice cream arrive, Kevin makes a big show of placing the Baked Alaska in front of me. "Let me know what you think, will you? Maybe I need to try it," he says.

I take a bite and say, "Yes, you definitely should. It's heavenly."

Derry makes short order of his delectable sweet, and I'm not far behind him. Draining our coffee cups, we push away from the table.

Kevin magically appears beside us, proud to see our content countenances. "Satisfied?"

"More than satisfied," Derry answers. "I'm happy as a pig in shite."

I snigger and scold him for his gross comment, but inside, I love it. It reminds me of Da. No matter how successful, how rich, how accomplished they may become, most Irish men never lose their sense of vulgarity. I know Mam, though she rolled her eyes at Da's language, wouldn't have changed it for the world. Neither would I.

Derry stands and pulls out my chair. I rise to my feet, full but blissful. He takes my arm and turns to Kevin. "You've been sterling, mate. Thanks for a grand night, and for the wine."

They shake hands and I touch Kevin's cheek in gratitude. *Lovely lout.*

As we head out to the deck, a cool breeze ruffles my hair. It lifts off my shoulders and streams out behind me. Free of hairpins and convention, I turn to Derry who wraps his arms around my waist and I put mine around his neck, as we stand by the rail.

"I don't think I could ever be happier than I am at this moment."

Looking down into my eyes, he says, "Nellie, my girl, I promise you'll have many moments of joy through all of our years together. I'll make sure of that." Then, he kisses me.

I press myself against him and open my lips to him.

He pulls away. "Easy, love. I promised your mam I'd be a perfect gentleman."

"But I didn't promise to be a lady."

His eyes hold a question asked in silence.

CHAPTER FIFTEEN

His arm circles my waist as we stroll the deck under the stars of a full-moon night. Other couples pass us. Their glances are warm and sometimes envious. I silently wish them the kind of passion I feel for the man beside me. This man who has stolen my heart and, to a large extent, my reason. *I must have him.* The plan I thought of earlier begins to develop more clearly in my head.

"Penny for your thoughts, Nellie."

"They might surprise you, Derry. Even shock you."

"I see. The sea air is turning you randy, is it?"

A shiver runs up my spine as I answer, "Maybe."

"Are you getting tired, love? It's been a long day, y'know."

"Yes, but I hate to say good night."

"Tomorrow, we'll be in New York City. We'll have two whole days together. Get your rest this night, Nellie."

He takes me back to my berth and kisses me good night as I part the curtain. I watch him walk to the adjoining section; the gentlemen's sleeping area.

I remove my outer clothes, folding them carefully so as not to wrinkle them for tomorrow, then my pantaloons, leaving on only my petticoat; soft and white with a lace trim over the bodice and is pretty enough to pass as a wedding-night nightie. To save space, I brought no nightgown.

Lying back against the pillow, I close my eyes, willing myself to waken in four hours. It's something I've been able to do since childhood. If I set my mind to wake up, I do it. In minutes, I am into a sound sleep.

At exactly three o'clock, my eyes pop open. I spring to sitting and wrap my shawl around me, fluff my hair, and open the curtain. The world is asleep; the only sound is the paddlewheel and the waves outside my porthole. No one stirs in their berth. I creep silently on bare feet toward the door between the ladies' and gentlemen's sleeping quarters. I hear the sounds of snores and grunts from some of the berths. I stop beside number twenty-seven. Taking a deep breath, I open the curtain.

Pale moonlight drifts over him from the tiny porthole. He sleeps . . . until I crawl into the narrow berth beside him.

He jerks in shock and gasps. "Nellie," he whispers, "I promised."

But then I slip the straps of the petticoat down to reveal my breasts.

"She'll never know," I whisper back.

Groaning, he pulls me to him. What happens that night once the initial pain subsides is so exquisite it cannot be described. Derry is worried about me and makes sure to disengage before each emission. We make love three times before I creep back to my berth at five-thirty, all while the ship still slumbers.

Slowly I pull the curtain to and reach down to adjust Derry's handkerchief between my legs. *Thank you, God, for all that bareback riding years ago. I know that was why I did not bleed a great deal.* I then lie back against my pillow a deeply satisfied woman. There is no regret, no guilt. Only joy. As Martha told me when we shared a room on our trip to Ireland, all the dreaming raptures

I experienced as a young girl were happening to prepare me for this man; the man I will someday marry.

Holding my *Claddagh* ring up to the porthole in the dawning sunlight, I pray that every young woman will someday experience this bliss of love consummated. No god I could ever worship would condemn it.

Chapter Sixteen

After two hours of sleep and cleaning myself up as best I can in the cramped bathroom, I dress and meet Derry to go to breakfast.

He touches my cheek. "Ah, love, I fear I've hurt you. Your chin is red from my whiskers."

"It'll fade. Until then, I will wear it as a proud badge of a woman in love with a handsome Irishman." He needn't know how sore other parts of me are this beautiful day.

"I'd call it a brute with a rough beard. Not handsome, but in love."

He's in love . . . with me. His words warm my soul. I reach and pick up his violin case. "This is so light, Derry."

He grabs it from my hand. "Yah, I sent the fiddle back to Ireland with my luggage."

Without its case? How strange. I wipe the question from my mind. *No matter to me.*

After a quick cup of coffee and piece of warm bread, we gather up our belongings and walk down the gangplank. In spite of wobbly sea legs, I'm floating on air with happiness.

On the dock, a burly man in his fifties stops us. "Are you Daire from Dublin?"

Derry wraps his left arm around my shoulders and extends his right hand. "You must be Jeremiah Donovan," he says. "I saw your picture once. I'm Daire O'Byrne, and this is Nellie Kelly from Boston. Call me Derry if you wish."

The man pumps Derry's arm up and down in welcome and looks at me with intense gray eyes that feel as though they might leave a hole in me. He has a full white beard and snow-white hair. His head is topped by a large-brimmed black hat tilted at a tantalizing angle. He carries a suitcase and wears a dark suit, a crisp white shirt, and a blue cravat. Quite an imposing figure.

When he speaks, his voice is deep and resonant, "'Tis Jeremiah O'Donovan Rossa, after Rosscarbery, my hometown in Cork. Good to meet ya, Derry. And your pretty friend here," he glances around him as though to make sure no one is within listening distance, "does she know why you're here?"

"Yes, indeed she does. You can speak freely in front of Nellie."

"Mr. O'Donovan Rossa," I say quietly, "I was born in America, but my parents came over on coffin ships and have prayed for Ireland's independence every day of their lives."

He nods his approval. "Are they living still?"

"My mam is. Da was murdered four years ago."

He shakes his head. "Murdered? Why?"

"We still don't know the answer to that, sir. We think he was shot by members of an Italian gang because he questioned the legality of their business dealings. He was a lawyer, you see."

The piercing eyes soften. "I'm sorry for your loss, girl. I used to think such violence was reserved for Ireland, but living in New York, I've learned different."

I lower my eyes and hope he doesn't see my tears beginning to form. Thinking about what happened to Da still hurts. Or am I tired from so little sleep last night? Or perhaps I can't escape the realization that Derry will leave me soon. I'm not sure what brought the tears, but I feel better when Derry wraps his arm around my waist and squeezes. He reads my feelings like no one else.

With that, this tall and robust man takes my arm and steers me off the pier and onto a street lined with carriages. We walk to the fourth one in the line and he says, "Here's mine. We're to meet Molly at O'Lunney's pub for lunch. She's anxious to meet you, Daire. And will be a fine friend for the young lady."

Wait'll Mam hears I had lunch in New York with Molly Irwin! She's loved her poetry for years. An old uncle sent Da copies of the Irish newspaper that featured her work. She didn't use her real name, but everyone knew who did the writing.

Jeremiah brings down the reins on the horse, rather roughly for my taste, and we're off. He gives a running commentary on things we pass along the way. "That's where we buy our meat," he says, pointing to a shop with slabs of beef and pork hanging out front. "And that's the theater me and Molly went to when we saw Rose Eytinge play Lady Macbeth. She was good at it, though I found Lady Macbeth quite daft. As did Molly.

"After the play, Rose Eytinge talked to the audience about the time she met President Lincoln. How tall, thin, and morose looking he was. 'Twas a shame what they did to that man, and all because he freed the slaves. And what a grand night! It was right after me and Molly settled here. Yes, indeed it was."

New York is a big, muscular place, and the people on the streets walk fast, much faster than in Boston. The buildings are taller, too. Some look to be ten stories high. Those buildings must have elevators. Nobody would want to walk up that many staircases every day. Carriages of every sort cram the streets, some so grand they take my breath away. The stores have big glass windows and some display the most beautiful dresses I've ever seen. And hats! Huge hats with feathers and veils. My guess is they could cost as much as ten dollars each. *Who can afford to buy such things?*

Jeremiah pulls on the reins and we head down a side street and park in front of a building. "Here's O'Lunney's," he says, jumping to the sidewalk and extending his hand up to help me down. He ties the horse to a post and the three of us walk in the front door.

In spite of the bright sun outside, the inside of this pub is dark. And smoky. Men line the bar with glasses of beer or whiskey in front of them. Though it's scarcely past noon, some of them seem inebriated. I catch one man's eye, and he looks me up and down in a way that makes me uncomfortable. Derry wraps his arm around my waist again in a most proprietary way and walks between me and the bar.

In the back of the room, which is brighter because of oil lamps, there are four wooden tables. Three are empty, but at one of them sits a tiny woman dressed all in black. Though her hair has a streaks of grey, her face is young and pretty, especially after she smiles. And smile she does as Jeremiah leans down and kisses her.

"Molly, my love, meet Derry and Nellie."

She stands and embraces me, though she only comes as high as my shoulder. "Grand," she says. "I didn't know there'd be a girl. Are you two married?"

"Not yet," Derry answers, "but someday."

"Well, you'd better make it someday soon, young man. A colleen this beautiful won't wait around forever, you know." She turns to me. "Are you from Ireland, too, Nellie?"

As I sit down, I answer, "No ma'am. I'm from Boston. But both my parents were born in Ireland."

"Ach," she says. "I'm not a ma'am. Call me Molly. I'm Molly Irwin O'Donovan Rossa." She grins, eyes shining. "Now isn't that a mouthful, though? Just call me Molly."

I feel as though I've known this tiny dynamo all my life. And in a way, I have. I remember Mam reading me her poems when I was a child.

"Are you still writing, Molly?"

"Only for myself and himself," she says, pointing to her husband. "When I wrote for the Irish people, I had to use the pseudonym, Cliodhna, or I'd have been jailed like him." Another finger toward her husband. "'Twas a Fenian newspaper, you know, and the authorities wouldn't have cared that I was pregnant. They'd have thrown me in one of their prisons like the others. Brits have no souls."

"When I was sent to the third prison, I made her move to New York with the children," Jeremiah says. "The conditions in those prisons were deplorable—all rat infested—and I was half starved; hungry enough that those little rodents were beginning to look appetizing. My Molly wouldn't have survived there. I lived in fear when she and the children were in Ireland that they might figure out she was writing rebel poetry under that fake name. Those limey coppas would have surely slammed her in one of their hellholes. Friends got her settled in Brooklyn, and I joined her as soon as I got released."

"I thought you were in Greenwich Village," Derry says.

"Nah, that's what we tell people. It's safer that way," Jeremiah answers. "Now let's have some lunch, shall we?"

A waitress brings us large platters of corned beef sandwiches and pitchers of beer. Derry pours four glasses and we begin to eat the delicious sandwiches. They drip so with juice and fat, I have to snatch up my napkin and politely wipe off my chin several times.

When we've finished, Jeremiah leans back in his chair, drains his glass, and says, "So, lad, have you a place to store it?"

Derry opens his fiddle case. Empty.

Ah.

Jeremiah picks up the suitcase from beside him on the floor and opens it. It is filled with bills of every denomination. I gasp. I've never seen so much money. The two men scoop up the bills and transfer them to the violin case.

Derry says, "How much is there?"

"More than sixty thousand dollars, lad," Jeremiah answers. "There's lots of men in New York from Ireland who want to see their homeland freed. And they're becoming better and better fixed. Lawyers and politicians mostly. These boys have connections—gents they strong arm when necessary for a good cause. All it takes is a Guinness or two and a chorus of 'God Save Ireland' and the swells open their wallets like they came over with the rest of us." He slaps his thigh. "I swear, some of them Greeks and Italians are sporting shamrocks like they were born in Clonakilty for Christ's sake, especially on St. Pat's Day."

Molly chimes in, "Not just men, love. The ladies of the churches know how to coax a nickel from the biggest tightwads around. They're good, they are, with their widows' weeds and holy water. When I go in a house and see the picture of the burning heart of Jesus, I know I've got a goldmine sitting in front of me."

I grin. "You two are quite the pair. I doubt anyone could refuse you anything."

Molly tilts her head and says, "All for the honor and glory of God, love . . . and for Ireland."

After lunch, the four of us stroll the streets of Manhattan together, the two men up front while Molly and I follow, window shopping the stores. Derry carries the violin case, and I worry lest he drop it.

"Would you like to meet me tomorrow for a bit of shopping, Nellie?" Molly asks.

I look at Derry. The shake of his head is barely discernible, but I see it. "I would love to normally, Molly, but you see Derry sails back to Ireland in a day and a half, and I want to spend every waking moment until then with him." I blush at the thought.

"Love, I do understand. Next time, though."

I sincerely hope there will be a next time. Molly is charming and fun. She and Mam would like each other. Someday perhaps they'll meet.

At five o'clock, our feet aching, we stop at a place called Ben V. Moise. "This is the finest tea house in the city," Jeremiah says. "Of course, you can always have coffee or beer, but I do recommend their English tea service. It's about the only decent thing that ever came out of that godforsaken country."

We sit at a table in the back and order. Derry carefully puts the violin case on his lap. The tea and small cakes arrive twenty minutes later with a bowl of clotted cream at the side. The tiny tea cake melts in my mouth and the tea with the sweetened cream is unlike any I've ever tasted.

"Delicious," I say.

"Yes," Jeremiah answers. "Can't have you going back to Boston never tasting Moise's tea. It's one of the finest flavors in New York."

An hour later, after hugs and promises to write, we part with the O'Donovan-Rossas. I feel we've made fast friends and vow to stay in touch with Molly.

After strolling for two blocks, Derry stops and whispers. "I need to be alone with you, sweetheart." He takes my hand. "Come sit here with me on this bench." I do as he asks. He puts the violin case between us.

He takes some bills from his pocket. "Jeremiah gave me one hundred dollars for my service. He said to treat you to a great dinner on him. But with all this money, we can go to a hotel, too. We passed a Hotel Albert earlier. He says it just opened."

The reality of his suggestion dawns on me. While the thought excites me, I am frightened. What would Mam think? And my church? His suggestion is scandalous. Will he think me a trollop if I agree? Because we took a chance last night, will God punish me with a baby? That could destroy my life and all my plans. I could never teach, expecting. Even married women can't teach, let alone pregnant women.

I rub my temples and try to think. "Derry, I can't. I'm too scared. What if I become pregnant?" Even saying the word embarrasses me. I would be considered a bad example for the girls. Me, Nellie Kelly, who hadn't even kissed a boy until Derry. "Aren't we tempting fate and God by continuing this?"

When I look at him, his face is so forlorn that I reach up and touch his cheek.

"I understand, love, and if you don't want this, I'll take you to your rooming house right now and go to my friend's place."

"But can't we just spend this evening together?" I am devastated at the thought of leaving him.

"Yes, Nellie, we can. But I want you so much I fear I might try to make you change your mind, and I mustn't do that. You're right. Let's be smart about this."

"You want to leave me now?" My voice trembles, ready to break.

"I never want to leave you. I want to marry you." He takes a deep breath. "Come with me to Ireland."

The shock of his words takes my breath. "But I start teaching in two weeks. It's what I've worked for all these years. Don't make me choose, please."

He puts his arms around me, lifting the violin case so it presses into my back. Neither of us care that passersby stare at us.

"I understand," he whispers into my ear. "I want you to have your dream, too. Plus, this mission I'm on is dangerous. You could get hurt. I'm sorry, love. We'll write like before and plan a proper marriage when it's a better time."

I lean back and start to cry.

"Nay, love. Don't cry." He dabs at my eyes with his handkerchief. "We'll work it out."

His words and the plaintiveness of their tone tears at my heart. I can't leave him. Not this man I want so desperately. I make a decision and take a deep breath. "I want to go to a hotel with you. I want to be with you until you get on that boat. And I will."

"What if. . . ?" His forehead creases.

I cover his lips with my fingers. "Isn't there a way? Isn't there protection?"

He kisses my fingers. "Yes. I must ask someone where to get them."

We sit together quietly on that bench for nearly an hour, both of us deep in thought. Then, we hear an enchanting giggle. It's a young woman with very dark hair, cut much shorter than others passing by. It curls prettily around her face, and she wears a jaunty beret. Holding her arm is a tall, elegant young man with a waxed moustache. He taps a silver-tipped cane merrily as he walks. When they get closer, he murmurs something in her ear, which elicits another giggle. He speaks in a foreign language, French, I think. Stopping at the corner, the man tips the pretty girl's face up slightly and kisses her on the mouth. She caresses his face, and a diamond ring flashes on her left hand.

"I speak a little French," Derry says. "I'm going to ask him."

He approaches the couple and stops them. "*Excusez moi*," he says politely. The rest of his words I am unable to understand. It takes just a moment before the couple turns and smiles at me in a most friendly manner. My grin back at them feels foolish on my face, and I flush in embarrassment.

The man shakes Derry's hand, then turns and points in the direction from which they came. He murmurs in French, then they turn to leave. The girl calls to me over her shoulder, "*Bonne chance*," and throws me a kiss. "*Vive l'amour*."

When he returns, I ask, "What did you tell them?"

"That we're newlyweds like them and need to buy protection. They're here on their honeymoon. He says there's an apothecary two blocks down that keeps them under the counter."

Now I am truly embarrassed, but also excited. "You mean those things made of rubber?"

"Yes."

That's when the guilt hits me. From childhood, my church had said that control of birth is sinful. Mam had many arguments with Father Ruzzo about that after Kathleen died having Sean. She also says that they are less than foolproof.

He turns me to face him. "We took chances last night, but we need something safer."

I take a deep breath and vow to act like the mature young woman I am. I stand. "Let's go."

Derry takes my hand and leads me in the direction the man pointed. Soon, we arrive at a small store with all kinds of herbal bottles in its window. A sign says Metropolitan Apothecary.

"You stay outside, sweetheart. I'll be but a minute."

I sit on the bench in front of the store, stare at my fingers, and avoid the glances of passersby. *Why am I so self-conscious?* Of course, I know why. Because my lover is buying something to prevent pregnancy. That means I'm definitely going to be having sex again with him. I blush, remembering last night. The memory excites me, even as I hear the priest in his wooden confession box telling me I've committed a mortal sin and giving me an embarrassingly long penance.

So what, I tell myself. *As Martha said, God understands. If my church doesn't, so be it.*

I hear the strains of a familiar tune. *My grandfather's clock was too wide for the shelf, so it stood ninety years on the floor.* The sound is scratchy and only plays the first two lines, but it is unmistakably the song I'd heard at Wellesley right before I graduated. The music teacher had printed up the lyrics for all us girls, and we sang it as a round at graduation. The audience had loved it.

But where is it coming from now? Drawn to the music, I walk two stores down the street where I find in the open window a strange machine playing it. The machine is a shiny metal with a cylinder covered with what looks to be tinfoil. A store clerk turns a handle, which rotates a cylinder, and the music plays from that. A crowd is assembling.

I run back to the bench. I can't wait to tell Derry about this. He comes out of the apothecary with a bag in his hand. I'm so excited about my discovery, I forget my embarrassment about what's inside the bag.

I grab his hand. "Derry, I must show you the most miraculous thing. Come with me."

I take him to the store and pull him inside. At that moment, the clerk starts turning the cylinder again. An unfamiliar song plays. It sounds like a hymn. A large crowd has now gathered, many of them asking for an explanation.

When the song is finished, the young clerk says, "Ladies and gentlemen, this is the first phonograph in the city of New York. It was invented last year by Thomas Edison, a young man from America's Midwest. This machine records sound. Then, by turning the crank, you hear it back. It's a miracle, and will someday be available to you right here in New York."

People pepper the clerk with questions about this miraculous machine as Derry takes me out the door.

"That little machine will someday change our world, Nellie. I love Ireland but marvel at the discoveries happening in America."

"That's true, Derry. At home, a man named Bell invented a machine that lets people talk to each other when they are in different places."

He shakes his head in wonder and leads me into a nearby alley where he kisses me.

"Now, my love, let's find that hotel."

CHAPTER SEVENTEEN

That evening and the next day, we leave our room only for meals. The violin case rests on the little table next to the bed. Sometimes, in the middle of the night when I awaken and see it, my stomach tightens in fear. Then, I roll over and look at the face of my lover—my wonderful Derry—trying to memorize his features for the long time apart.

Before he stirs, though, I am questioning my decision to stay in Boston. *Perhaps I should go off to Ireland with him when he sails. We could be married there and not ever have to part.* But even as I dream of how it could be, I know I won't do that. Instead, I'll report to Girls High next month. The tugs of obligation and desire are too strong to deny. I'll be the youngest teacher ever hired there, and one of only four female instructors at the school. And I'll not teach Home Economics or Music like the others. I'll teach General Science, a subject new to the school. When I was hired, I was told I'm part of a grand experiment of great importance to the school.

After my hiring interview with the president of the school's Board of Directors, Miss Spencer, the principal, had invited me into her office. In spite of the eight years that have passed since she accepted me as a student, I still felt intimidated to be sitting in front of her desk.

"Congratulations, Nellie. I'm very proud of you." The British accent was as strong as it was that first day.

"Thank you, Miss Spencer."

"Call me Marjorie, won't you?" She went on, "I welcomed you to this school because I believe that women have opportunities now far above what was available when I was a girl. But to take advantage of them, a girl has to have pluck. Be willing to take risks. Not be afraid. In you, I saw a daring girl. Expelled from St. Augustine's. Because of a boy's lies, you ran off to the circus." She chuckled softly. "How many young girls have such nerve?"

"I'm grateful to you, Miss . . . uhh . . . Marjorie, truly grateful."

"Your performance at Wellesley did much for the reputation of Girls High and, frankly, for my own reputation."

This shocked me. "Really?"

"Yes, Nellie." She stood and took a letter from her pocket-book. "Read this."

The letter was on high-quality ecru paper with Cambridge University gold stamped at its top. As I read it, I realized that Miss Spencer had been offered a position there as Dean of Girls.

"Girls can go to Cambridge?" I was so impressed.

"Only recently. That's why I am so honored to be offered this position. I think your performance at Wellesley may have contributed to their estimation of me."

"Oh, my!" I breathed. "Are you going back to England, Miss Spencer? I mean Marjorie."

"I'm quite torn, Nellie. Cambridge is home to me, and I am so honored to be offered such a contract. But Boston is dear to me, too, and this school in particular. I have felt like a pioneer of sorts in starting here. I just don't know."

"Whatever you choose will be the right decision." My words sounded trite in my ear, but it was the most appropriate response I could think of.

She smiled then and gave me a good luck hug.

Remembering, I roll over and look again at Derry, the man I love more than anything, except the opportunity to follow my dream. Perhaps I'm selfish, but I want to teach.

His eyes open. "Hello, my love," He takes me into his arms. "Any chance you've changed your mind about coming to Ireland?"

"That's what I've been pondering; about my teaching and all. And no, Derry, I can't give it up. As much as I'd like to. As much as I love you. Too many people are depending on me. I'm sorry."

He kisses me softly on the eyes. "Don't be, girl. It'd be like asking me to give up my dream of Irish independence. We mustn't lose ourselves in loving each other. We must first do our duties and then find our way back together. And we will. I promise that."

Sunday morning dawns much too quickly. When Derry wakes up and takes me in his arms, my eyes start to burn. *I mustn't cry. I will be brave.* Chuckling, I smack hm on his bare rump and say, "Get that arse in gear, Mister."

He climbs from our bed and goes into the bathroom. Then the tears come, but I stop them as quickly as I can. He mustn't remember me red eyed and sad. He's given me the most wonderful two days of my life, and it's important that that is the memory he carries with him over the seas.

We bathe together in the hotel's deep bathtub and make love one last time. Then, silently we dress, pack, and leave the room. Before I close the door, I look back at the bed and remember the bliss I experienced there.

Downstairs, we walk out onto the street and look for the carriage Derry booked to take to his ship. When we arrive at the pier, the violin case tucked securely under Derry's arm, the vessel sits there like a great hulking giant with steam already stoking the propellers, which turn slowly. It's called SS *Hibernia*, the same ship he came on, a freighter which also carries one thousand passengers. It's not a grand ship like *The Bristol* but is seaworthy and will get him back safely to Dublin.

"I'll send you a wire from the ship and write every week, Nellie. Please write back to me as often as you can. I know you'll be busy with planning lessons and all, but I will need to hear from you."

He takes me in his arms. The violin case pressing against my back reminds me that Derry is on a perilous journey. "Please be careful, my love. Of course, I'll write all the time. Derry . . . Derry, I shall miss you so much." No matter how hard I try, the tears still well.

He holds me like he can't let go of me, then holds my left hand up and kisses the ring. "One year, Nellie. One year, and I'll be back to claim you as my bride. Wait for me."

That's when the dam breaks and rivers of tears course down my cheeks alongside deep, choking sobs. "I'll wait, love. Till the end of time if need be. I love you."

In a rush that tells me he, too, will soon weep, he grabs his duffel bag off the dock, hoists the violin case to his shoulder and runs up the gangplank.

I stand there waving as the giant ship huffs and chugs to movement. Tug boats pull it off from the pier, and Derry becomes smaller and smaller as he stands at the rail, one arm flailing wildly, the other clutching the violin case. I don't move until I can't make out which tiny figure is my love; the reason my heart beats. With great purpose and steadfastness, I pick up my satchel and walk back to the wagon Derry hired to bring us here and take me back to *The Bristol*.

How different I feel boarding the grand ship this time than

when we did in Fall River just a few days ago. As I close the curtain, I take my off my Claddagh ring, tears flowing without restraint, kiss it and then hide it in my bag. *No need for Mam to know just yet.*

The journey back home nearly does me in. The only thing that eases my pain is the fact that soon I'll get his wire and his letters will begin to come.

CHAPTER EIGHTEEN

I keep myself busy with lesson plans for teaching my girls and find I love it. When I tell my class we'll start our study of science with teachings from Africa, they roll their eyes. But when Uncle Kam visits as a lecturer, one and all, they are enraptured. They've all heard of him and his vast fortune and know he and his tonic come from Africa. He introduces himself as a primitive scientist.

Only recently has the word scientist been used in schools. Conservative teachers still refer to its practitioners as natural philosophers; especially if the scientist is female.

At first, I was annoyed by that, but Aunt Molly told me some men still refuse to call her a physician because of her gender. She says I should not let it bother me, and she's right. They look at women like me and Molly as interlopers on a discipline they consider proprietary, and male. Mam has told me tales of when she, as a midwife, was called before the Boston Council of Physicians. They were threatened because her outcomes with mothers surpassed their own. That's when she told them, "If any of you gentlemen are willing to attend to and deliver a woman's baby for a sack of corn, have at it."

I laughed at that, but must admit things haven't changed much.

After we finish two weeks of African folk cures, we address

the most recent scientific discoveries here in America. A man named Charles Darwin has written a book called *On the Origin of Species*, which posits the theory of evolution by natural selection. My girls giggle at this, especially when they examine the drawings of apes and gorillas down through the centuries.

I talked to my priest about the possibility that we evolved from apes, and he said it was a mortal sin for me to even think like that. But I do wonder.

We study germ theory, the new concept by Louis Pasteur that I tried to tell Sean about. Pasteur thinks tiny organisms called germs cause many illnesses common today, like black plague and cholera. Doctors here in Boston still believe in the miasma theory, which says that organisms are transmitted from rotting organic material to humans. I don't know which is correct. I hope I'll find out one day.

Scientific discoveries are exploding all across the world. In chemistry, a man named Dimitri Mendeleev created the first periodic table of elements and other scientists are touting something called electromagnetism as yet one more undiscovered field.

It's dizzying how fast things are changing in the world for some women. I told my class yesterday about a girl in her twenties who is a journalist for the *Pittsburgh Dispatch* newspaper. Her name is Nellie Bly. First, she wrote an article on abusive factory owners in a new modality called "investigative journalism." Before she was hired by the *Dispatch*, she wrote an expose called "The Girl Puzzle," which focused on how divorce laws are unfair to women. That caught the attention of the editor at the *Dispatch* who hired her. But the factory owners complained to the newspaper about her articles, and she moved to Mexico for a while, where she was nearly imprisoned for writing about corrupt politicians. What an exciting girl she must be. I'd love to know Nellie Bly. Of course, that's her pseudonym. Her real name is Cavanaugh and her grandfather emigrated to America from Ireland.

Here in Boston, everything moves at its usual pace—slowly. Men still believe that women have no place in society except as a wife and mother. They refuse to accept that things are changing.

As we enter late September, I begin to teach the girls about photosynthesis in preparation for Autumn. I am so enthralled in explaining why leaves change color that I hardly notice the maples turning red with still no word from Derry.

Where might he be? Why didn't he wire me from the ship? If he's still aboard, he should be arriving in Dublin soon. I resolve to wait one more week before I allow myself the panic beginning to churn inside me.

But after that week passes, I can no longer bury my fears. And for very good reason. My monthly blood, always so regular, has not come.

I must do two things quickly. First, see Molly O'Halloran. Molly is practical and smart and I trust her to keep my visit private. Though I call her Aunt Molly, she's less then ten years older than I am and feels like a friend. As a physician, she often works at Kathleen's Haven with Mam.

Next, I wire Neo and ask him to find Derry in Dublin.

I sit in the sterile white waiting room, nervous as a kitten. Molly comes through the door and takes my hand. "Nellie," she says, "so good to see you. Are you here to chat or for an examination?"

"Examination, my monthly is late," I murmur, embarrassed to my core.

I am struck again by Molly's resemblance to her brother Sean. A likeness not attractive in a woman. She's a bit stocky, and the square jaw that gives his face a look of strength tends to emasculate her. Her hair is light like Sean's, but looks drabber than his. Today, she wears a simple gray skirt and blue blouse. The ever-present stethoscope hangs around her neck. In spite of her plainness, her eyes are beautiful and exude complete kindness.

She leads me into an examining room and tells me to remove my clothing and put on a long green gown that ties in the back. It looks like the ugliest nightgown I've ever seen. Once I've hung up my clothes, I sit on an examining table and wait.

She's back seconds later and asks me to lie down.

First, she examines my abdomen and breasts, which is terribly embarrassing.

Removing her stethoscope from my chest for a moment, she says, "Everything seems normal, but I must ask a delicate question."

I feel a hot blush from the roots of my hair down my neck. "Go ahead."

"Have you been sexually intimate with a man?"

After a deep inhalation, I squeak, "Yes."

"Derry?"

"Yes."

"I see." She takes the stethoscope from around her neck and puts it on the examining tray.

"And he is back in Ireland?"

"Yes, he left five weeks ago."

She rubs her eyes and temples. "Dearest girl, from the looks of your breasts and their tenderness, you may be expecting."

My heart sinks. Though I'd suspected this, to have the possibility confirmed is devastating. "Are you sure?"

"Not absolutely, but if your monthly blood doesn't come this week, I will be more certain as each day passes."

Every day that week, I run constantly to the bathroom checking to see if the moisture I feel is blood. It never is. Worry causes a lack of sleep and I find myself losing patience with my students over each wrong answer. I don't like being like this with them, and they react to the difference in me. Classes no longer excite them, and they make that obvious with every pout and complaint. One girl who was early every day and bright eyed becomes tardy and sullen. When I ask her why, she says she hates school now. I despise myself for doing this to her.

After a week, I go back to Molly's office. When she sees me in her waiting room, she raises her eyebrows inquisitively.

I shake my head.

"Come in, dear," she says.

When I am seated on her examining table, she takes my hand and says, "Perhaps you'd better tell Derry."

I burst into tears, and she takes me in her arms. "Hush, dear one. We'll figure this out. I'll help you any way I can."

"I haven't had a word from him," I sob. "He said he'd wire me from the ship and didn't do it." Putting my face in my hands, I continue, "I wired Neo to see if he's seen Derry. No word. But Aunt Molly, Derry was transporting cash from people in New York to the Fenians in Dublin. He may be in trouble."

"Oh, no."

Her whisper sends my heart diving further into terror. Molly never sounds afraid. She's always optimistic and cheerful. The worry in her voice alarms me into a convulsive trembling.

"Nellie, please calm yourself. This will be all right. I promise."

We agree that she will come to my house this evening, after her last appointment.

"We'll tell your mam together," Molly says.

Thank God for that. I'd never have the courage to tell her alone.

CHAPTER NINETEEN

Arriving at home, I find the house empty with a note on the table. "Nellie, dear, I'll be home by six. Please light the stove."

Trembling, I gather the wood from outside and put it in the stove. Then I sit down and begin to cry. *How can we tell Mam this?* She warned me many times that a pregnancy can ruin a girl's life, but I thought Derry and I were careful. *How could this have happened?* Even as I think the question, I chide myself. *Not careful enough. Not every time.*

Molly arrives at seven o'clock. Mam's face brightens. "Molly, love, come in and sit yourself down. I haven't seen you in ages. We're seldom at The Haven at the same time it seems. How goes your private practice?"

"Pretty good," Molly answers. "Busy."

"Wonderful! Nellie, be a dear and get a kettle going so we can all have a cup of tea, won't you?"

At the stove, I light the fire under the kettle. I hear them chattering cheerfully in the sitting room. When the kettle whistles, I dread going back to them, but I must. I carry the three cups on a tray with sugar, milk, and lemon. My heart is leaden.

I hope Mam doesn't cry. I just could not bear it.

"Well now, here it is," she says. "Thank you, dear." She takes a cup and extends it to Molly who adds a bit of sugar and milk and then sets the cup down.

"Mary, Nellie and I need to tell you something." Her voice sounds different. It is professional and somber. It catches Mam's attention instantly.

"Sounds dire. Did somebody die?"

She clears her throat nervously. "No, no, nothing like that."

"Well, for Pete's sake, tell me what's going on. Your faces look as tragic as a four-horse funeral."

Molly looks over at me. We hadn't decided who would tell her. I nod to her. I can't speak.

Molly stirs her tea. "Mary, I examined Nellie in my office last week."

Mam jerks and her teacup tips, spilling tea on the table. She starts to mop it up with a napkin; her hands trembling. "Why? Is she sick? There wasn't a lump or anything, is there?"

"No, nothing like that."

"Thank God! Remember when we found that lump in Annie Carter's breast? That was terrible, wasn't it? She was young, too. Same age as Nellie is now."

Molly covers Mam's hand with hers. "Mary, she might be expecting."

The silence in the room is total. I'm aware of the tick tock of the grandfather clock in the corner and the sound of crickets outside. I hadn't noticed them before.

Mam turns to me. "Is this possible, Nellie?" Her eyes beseech me to deny it.

I am unable to speak a word. I nod my head as the tears roll down my cheeks.

"Oh, no," she whispers, her voice a dirge.

We sit together in silence until some long minutes later, when Mam says, "Well, what do we do?"

We jump, startled at the change in her tone. She sounds strong, determined, and in charge.

Molly says, "Well, as I see it, we have options. Let's talk about them, and then Nellie can determine which suits her best."

The first option mentioned is to have Molly terminate my pregnancy, but not one of us considers that seriously. My church calls such a procedure murder, and Molly concurs. "I could do it," Molly says. "But I won't."

"She could go to Ireland, have the baby, and turn it over to the nuns," Mam says.

My heart sinks at that possibility and forcefully say, "No, this is mine and Derry's baby. I won't give it away."

Next, the discussion turns to Derry, and both women seem angry at him.

"Why hasn't he contacted you, Nellie?!" Mam shouts. Her implication, unspoken but clear, is that he had had his way with me and has now turned his back.

"He's disappeared. I wired Neo on Monday and asked if he's seen Derry. He wired back that he'd spent the week with Derry's mother and sister searching for him. The ship arrived in Dublin ten days ago, but Derry wasn't on it." With that, I burst into tears. "Neo fears the Brits traced him in New York to his meeting with Jeremiah. They know about Jeremiah's 'Dynamite' campaign and put two and two together. Neo says Derry might be dead; murdered by English sympathizers on that ship." My tears become sobs, convulsing and unstoppable.

"Nellie, you must calm yourself," Mam says, clutching my hands. "If not for your sake, for the wee one you carry."

Molly puts her arm around my shoulder. "She's right, dear.

You have every right to cry, but it won't help." She redirects her focus. "Mary, what's our next option?"

I compose myself. I don't want to hurt this innocent baby.

"I suppose she could stay in the house until the baby is born and then we could tell neighbors that the new baby is from some cousin in Ireland." As Mam speaks, her head shakes. "Ah, shite, I'm fooling myself. Nobody'd fall for that. Everybody met Derry. They'd figure it out. I can just see them counting the months on their fingers."

Molly starts to speak and stops herself twice. Finally, though, she says it, "Nellie, have there been any other men?"

I am both hurt and furious as I snarl, "How can you ask that? I've never so much as kissed another man . . . except for . . ."

"For whom?" Molly asks.

"It's nothing."

"For whom?" she presses on.

"Well, before Derry arrived, your brother, Sean, came here and asked me to take a walk with him. He took me to a grand new house he'd just purchased to impress the swells of Beacon Hill—and me, too, I suppose. He expects to be mayor someday, you know. He said he wants me to be his first lady."

Molly rolls her eyes. "Yes, that sounds like him all right."

My voice sounds like I am reciting a dirge. "When I told him I didn't love him, he grabbed me and kissed me. I guess he thought that would convince me. All I could think of was how different it was from Derry's kiss." The memory of Derry's caress assails me like a warm blanket ripped away on a freezing night. *Where is he?*

Again, the silence.

Molly breaks it. "Sean really wants to marry you, Nellie. He's spoken to me and my sister about it."

Mam shakes her head and wags her finger.

"What, Mary?" Molly asks.

"He's no good for Nellie. You know that."

Molly purses her lips. "I know you think that, Mary, but it could solve this problem. We're discussing options. Can you think of another?"

The two of them glare at each other, their eyes steely. Slowly, the realization of what they're arguing about hits me as an attack to my morality. *Are they really asking me to whore myself to a man I don't love for the sake of convenience? Do they really mean that?* I must be sure; voice trembling, "Are you suggesting what I think?"

The night pounds on. Arguments veer from loud to tearful. First, Mam storms to the porch and then stomps back into the living room, slamming the door shut. Molly remains the calmest of us. My head aches so terribly I fear I'll vomit. Only the knowledge that I mustn't hurt the little one I am surely carrying calms me.

"She doesn't love Sean," Mam chants as she paces the living room like a caged panther.

After her fourth repetition, Molly stands and takes her hand. "Mary, put on that hard-headed practical cap of yours and think."

Mam finally acquiesces and sits down; heart pounding, face beet red, visibly shaking. The two women stare at each other for a long time, two smart Irish-Catholic women, one as strong willed as the other. Mam has been Molly's rock since Molly's mother died birthing Sean. I know all the stories. Mam taught Molly as a child, dried her tears over lost loves, and once locked her screaming in her room when, as an unruly sixteen-year-old, Molly threatened to drop out of school. Then later, she introduced Molly to the wonders of science through her ancient medical books. She did the same for me. She, who had never gone to school herself, showed us both the way. And now Molly is the lone female doctor in Boston, and I am a teacher of science.

Finally, the doctor has the last word. "Mary, be smart. There are worse things than marrying the future mayor of Boston, living in a beautiful home, and bringing up your child in the lap of privilege. Think about it."

Mam's face reflects every conflict going on in her brain. My heart breaks as I see her surrender to Molly's logic. "I haven't been able to think of anything else," she says, her voice a whisper.

"Hold on just a minute!" I shout. "Have you two forgotten that I have a say in this. I will bring up my child alone!"

They look at each other forlornly and shake their heads. Then Mam turns away, wiping a lone tear scrolling down her cheek.

Molly asks, hands clasped in her lap yet open to any logical ideas, "How will you support the baby, Nellie?"

Mam. Surely, she'll help me. My eyes go blurry, full of tears, as our desperate gazes lock onto one another.

"Nellie, we're barely scraping by now, even with your teaching position. I can't support us alone. I've sunk every penny into Kathleen's Haven. I have no money."

Things had been hard since Da died, but I had thought my salary would carry us. Now I remember home repairs undone, meals seldom including meat. In my excitement about my new position, I'd ignored all the signs.

"What about Uncle Kam?!" I exclaim. "He'd help me. I know he would."

"No, I can't go to him with this. He's done so much for us through the years, but not this. No, not this." Her shoulders slump.

Why not this? He loves me like a father. I know that. Is she so ashamed of me that she can't seek help from our dearest friend? The thought hurts me to my core.

"I'll get another job," I say. Looking at their stony faces, I go on. "I can't teach as a single, pregnant woman, but surely there must be something I *can* do."

Neither of them acknowledges my statement.

"What?" Molly questions.

My head spins in search of an answer. "I could be a governess."

Mam shakes her head. "No one in this town would hire an unmarried mother to take care of her child."

She's right. "Maybe I could get a job in an office."

Molly takes my hand. "Can you use a typewriter, Nellie?"

"No, but I could learn."

"Do you know Pitman?"

The question confounds me, and I stammer, "What's Pitman?"

"It's a way of taking dictation from an executive. Men insist that any woman they employ as secretaries knows how to use it."

I need to think. If I can just figure out a way to take care of my baby alone, I can make this pain stop. I rush to the back-yard pump and splash my face with water. As I dry it, sad reality takes hold. I am not employable. Like Mam said, no one in Boston will hire an unmarried mother. Who will pay for my baby's food? Will he or she be hurt when neighbors look down their noses at the two of us—the whore of a mother and her bastard child? I dry my face and go back to the parlor. *I'm sorry, Derry. I'm so sorry.*

Mam takes one look at my face and knows. "I guess we're out of options," she says sadly.

All I can think of is Derry. My sweet, loving Derry. Although I hate him each time the post brings no word and fear he's abandoned me, my heart tells me different. If he could get word to me, he would. *Is he dead?* That thought brings bile up into my mouth each time it occurs, and it nags me often. I banish it each time, unable bear to think such a thing. No, he isn't dead. I know that somewhere he's alive. I know it in my soul. But where is he?

Molly jolts my reverie. "Sean must believe this child is his. His ego is much too large for another possibility."

And thus, the three of us begin the mechanics of a despicable ruse. And I, God forgive me, become the chief engineer.

CHAPTER TWENTY

The next morning, Mam takes her wagon to Marietta Langford's Lingerie store in the Faneuil Marketplace. Although she's embarrassed to walk in the shop, she purchases a ruffled red corselette and the most expensive silk stockings in the place.

When I unwrap the package and caress their softness, my heart hardens to stone.

We agree that Molly, when my time comes, will deliver the baby and tell her brother, "Sometimes, a big healthy baby can be born a month early." That will appeal to his vanity and abet bragging rights about his virility. She will also give me a small vial of blood to be used as proof of my virginity.

His political allies might wonder some, but they'll be afraid to ask questions.

In the afternoon, Mam will visit Father Ruzzo and will tell him the truth about my condition, with one exception, the name of the father. She'll say, "Father, my girl is so ashamed of herself. This scandal could ruin our family. We need to get them married quickly. There's no time to post the banns, but you baptized and confirmed both Nellie and Sean and gave them their first Holy Communion, so will you do it?"

After a bit of arguing, she'll become tearful, after which he'll agree and they'll set a date for a quiet wedding on a weekday afternoon when the church is empty.

He's done it for others.

He'll do it for us.

The rest is up to me.

The following day at four o'clock, I dress in the pretty blue dress with the bustle and the matching parasol. As I slip the silk stockings up my legs and fasten each one to the frilly corselette, my thoughts are of Derry. *I'm sorry, my love, wherever you are. I just don't know what else to do.*

Sean had told Molly he'd be at home all day working on a brief. *So, it must be today.* I tuck the vial of blood Molly delivered to me into the waist of my pantaloons. Then, I leave home and begin the trek that will seal my fate.

Though Autumn has begun to turn some leaves, it's a warm day. Under other circumstances, I would enjoy a stroll to Beacon Hill. But today, it feels as though both of my feet are encased in cement.

I ascend the steps to the beautiful porch with its rocking chairs and knock on the door. I force a smile onto my lips as it opens to a woman in a black maid's outfit. She has gray hair pulled into a severe bun at the back of her head. When she sees me, her mouth purses and her glasses slide down her long, hawkish nose. She shoves them back up to her eyes and says, "Yes?" Her voice is haughty.

"Is Mr. O'Halloran at home?" I ask.

"And who's asking?" Her voice is tinged with a slight brogue.

I pull myself to my full height and say, "You may tell him Miss Kelly is calling."

With obvious reluctance, she gestures to come inside. "Stay here," she orders, then turns away, scurrying down the hall.

The foyer wall is now covered with maroon velvet. It is so soft and luxurious that I'd like to run my hands over it. An elegant, tufted matching settee is placed to its side, but I don't think I should sit down since the maid didn't offer me that option.

In minutes, Sean appears, followed by the housekeeper. "Nellie," he says. "Good to see you. Mrs. O'Keefe announced you." He turns to the woman hovering nearby. "Marie, this is Nellie Kelly, one of my oldest and dearest friends."

She nods to me and takes a hasty leave.

"Come in." He guides me to his drawing room, furnished elegantly now. A painting on the main wall catches my eye. It's a watercolor of two men in a rowboat on a rough sea.

"This painting is magnificent, Sean," I say as I study it closely. "I can almost feel the waves."

"Yes, it's a Winslow Homer," he answers. "Do you know him?"

I shake my head.

"Actually, he was born in Boston but now lives somewhere in Europe."

He gestures for me to sit on a striped satin settee and says, "Mrs. O'Keefe is my new housekeeper. I hope she was cordial to you."

"Cordial, yes."

He chuckles, lowering himself into a brocaded chair opposite me, and crosses his legs. "I know she takes herself quite seriously and sometimes is brusque with strangers. But she does a good job." Then he leans slightly forward and whispers, "She's a shade protective of me. Has three daughters at home and, I think, hopes I'll take one of them off her hands." Abruptly he rises, goes to the door, looks out in the hall—left then right—then closes it. "That's not likely. They all have the Irish hook."

I know what he means. It seems most Irish women are either quite lovely or are cursed with a hook nose. It's a common joke on the south side of Boston.

Taking in his overall demeanor as he returns to his chair—decked in a fitted white linen shirt and tan trousers. Everything reeks expensive. A waistcoat matching the trousers has been carelessly tossed across his nearby desk, along with a patterned ascot. Under different circumstances, I would be thinking how strikingly handsome he is. But that was before Derry. Now, I must get on with the task that brought me here today.

"So, Nellie, how've you been?"

"Very well, thank you. I'm teaching now and enjoying it very much."

"So, I've heard. That's quite the topic of gossip at the Club. I mean, that a young woman like you is teaching science, of all things." His tone is cynical, demeaning.

I ignore his sarcasm, forcing the bile down with a hopefully undetectable swallow. "Yes, and my girls are splendid; smart and so willing to learn."

"I see," he says, displaying a cocky sneer. "Though I still don't understand why they want to study science. How would they ever use it? They'd be better off asking you for beauty tips so they can catch a successful husband."

With that, my spine straightens. I cannot allow myself anger this day.

He recrosses his legs, cocking an ankle on a knee and leaving them open at that suggestive angle I remember. "I also heard around town that you've been seen with a male visitor from Ireland."

Of course, he'd heard. For a second, I am taken aback by this unexpected comment but quickly recover my bearings. "Yes, that was Derry O'Byrne. He was one of Neo's groomsmen when he married Angelique in Dublin four years ago. He's a good friend."

He raises his left eyebrow. "Is that all he is?"

I silently pray the color of my skin does not give me away. "Absolutely that's all. He asked me to show him around Boston because he's trying to understand our democracy for when Ireland gets her independence from England."

"Fat chance, that," he replies. "With their pitchforks and ploughshares, there's no possibility of that for at least a hundred years." He places both feet on the floor and leans forward. "You know, Nellie, our Irish ancestors are not regarded as the smartest people on earth."

His remark riles me, though that is certainly the opinion of the powerful men in Boston. I choose to ignore it and flutter my lashes. "Then, why do people want you to be in politics?"

"Well, dear Nellie, I am the exception that proves the rule." He strides across the room and points to his Harvard diploma, gilt-framed on the wall. "Plus, I am considered to have a certain charm that appeals to the ladies. Not that they can vote, thank God, but my backers feel it's a good idea to have the support of the little women at home."

"Sean, why did you say, 'Thank God?'"

He sits back down. "Because that would be a whole different kettle of fish politically. Women are quite emotional, you know. Men will never trust them with anything as important as voting."

His words annoy me, but I grit my teeth and lean forward, using my arms to push my breasts up over the scooped neckline of my blue dress. They are larger now. Molly says pregnancy does that to a woman's body.

He glances at my chest, licks his lips, then stands and goes to a side table where he pours himself a glass of whiskey then lifts the decanter toward me. I shake my head. In an obviously domineering way, he takes a large swig of the brown liquid in his glass, then cocks his head to one side and says, "So, the last time I saw you, I told you I was interested in making you my wife."

I nod politely.

"But you weren't interested."

My stare is bold, and I know it. "Yes, but a girl can reconsider."

"What about the man from Ireland?"

"Derry? As I said, he's just my friend. He doesn't seem interested in girls."

"One of those, eh?"

Sorry, my love. I must betray you. "Possibly."

"Hmmm. Where'd he go to school?"

"Trinity College in Dublin."

Sean's nostrils flare. "Maybe it's something in the water."

I stutter my next words. "What does that mean?"

"Just that one of my partners did a year at Trinity and said the school was loaded with that kind. You know, gentlemen who prefer other gentlemen."

I blush, appropriately.

"He mentioned a writer named Oscar Wilde," he continues. "He tried to get my partner to, you know, participate."

Derry would be furious at this conversation; irritated that Sean would talk about such things with a lady. *And* that he speaks this way about Trinity. But although this conversation would incense him, Derry isn't here. *I don't know where he is. And I'm expecting his baby.* So, instead of acting offended at Sean's remarks, I say, "Hmmm, maybe it is the water," hating every syllable.

"So, you think your friend from Dublin is one of them, huh?"

"I don't know for sure. I just know he's shown no interest in me . . . or any other girl that I know of."

His blue eyes lock on my bosom again. "Then, he must be."

Embarrassed, I lean against the back of the settee to ease the pull on my bodice.

"So, tell me, Nellie, what brings you here? When I first showed you this house, you didn't seem particularly interested in it *or* in me."

"Sean, that's not true." I squeeze my upper arms to my body, increasing my cleavage and causing an uncontrollable whimper to escape him. "I was just taken aback by your comments. I love this house and think you've done a marvelous job decorating it. It's beautiful."

"Molly helped some, but most of my ideas I got from a British firm called Lapworth, a designer of minor castles in London."

"Well, it's magnificent." To emphasize my approval, I let my gaze wander over his face. His stare is unnerving, as if he is unclothing me.

"So, here you are calling on me alone. Tell me, are you more interested in my house or in me, Nellie?"

I swallow every bit of pride I've ever had. "Both."

He stands and walks to a corner of the room where he tugs at a purple velvet cord. Within seconds, the housekeeper walks through the door braced for orders.

"Mrs. O'Keefe," he says, "Miss Kelly will be joining me for dinner. Please tell cook."

With a sour mien, she turns to leave.

Sean sniggers. "Well, she didn't look very pleased, did she?"

"Not pleased at all. But thank you, I'd love to join you for dinner."

Like a cat about to pounce a mouse, he picks up the whiskey decanter and again offers me a glass. This time, I accept. Though I'm not partial to strong spirits, I must play this game through to the end. When he returns with a glass, I sip, trying not to make a face at its bitterness nor allow a shiver to betray my naiveté.

"Very good," I force out.

He is pleased, and it shows. "A girl should enjoy a glass sometimes, but never overindulge. In my world, that's a criminal offense for a woman."

As the drink burns its way down into my stomach, I pray the little one I carry doesn't get any of it. Then, I throw my head back and finish the glass, unable to hide the redness of my face.

He comes across the room to sit beside me on the settee. There was a time when having him so near would have thrilled me beyond reason. I loved him as a girl, even after he broke my heart with Rosie. But she was Italian and didn't fit into his political plans back then. So sad to remember. And now their son lives somewhere in Ireland with Rosie who works as a barmaid. She who was one of the brightest lights at Girls High.

I thought Sean was everything I wanted in a man—handsome, smart, clever, and ambitious. He was like a god who shone in the sun. Went to Harvard and Georgetown Law School, then secured himself a position with the best law firm in Boston. His wife will have everything—money, position, and prestige.

But she won't have love. And now that I've had that, can I live the rest of my life without it? As Sean wraps his arm around my shoulders, I almost recoil from his embrace. But then I stroke my stomach, knowing that inside it is Derry's baby. Scarcely a baby yet, but on its way to becoming one. A child who may have Derry's curly hair and gentle hands. Maybe his musical talent and passion for freedom. *This child deserves a good life; a life I cannot give it alone.*

When Sean tips my chin up to kiss me, I think of that and open my lips to him.

At first, his kiss is soft, almost tender, but quickly becomes demanding.

What is expected of me here? Can I give it?

Sean whispers in my ear, "After we finish dinner, I'd like to show you the master bedroom. I have a big brass bed with the softest mattress money can buy."

Our eyes lock. A tinge of fear tickles my insides and goosebumps cover my body.

What he expects is now quite clear. *But what if he's testing me? What if he thinks me trashy for succumbing to him easily?* I decide that I just don't care. There's no other way to carry out this dastardly plan we three women have concocted. Let him think as he will.

"I can't wait to see it," I say, fluttering my eyelashes at him, even as I grit my teeth.

CHAPTER TWENTY-ONE

That night is everything my time with Derry was not. Rough, awkward, degrading. Sean tries, I know he does, to arouse me but my body remains frozen, unable to respond.

At one point, he says, "I hope you're not frigid."

"I think it's just because this is my first time," I say, barely audible; resolving to be a better actress next time. When he dozes off, I tip the vial of blood Molly gave me between my legs and onto the sheets.

My adjusting the covers awakens him. As he reaches for me, he feels the wetness, bringing up his hand to sees the crimson fluid, and actually sheds a few tears of relief. I am frozen, not knowing how to react.

Through it all, through that long night, I feel . . . nothing, absolutely nothing. Not fear, not pain, not pleasure, nothing. If it hadn't been for Derry, I might think I am truly frigid. Scientists do believe that some women are, but Mam thinks it's often a term used by clumsy lovers.

Sometime, in the middle of the night, he again is aroused. I pretend pleasure, and Sean believes the hoax.

After his release, he pants, "I love you, Nellie."

Hearing the words, there is a long silence. This is a lie I do not want to tell. Not to him. Not to any man but Derry. Then, remembering the baby, I clamp my eyes shut and whisper, "I love you, too, Sean."

With the proper response received, his body relaxes and he rolls to pull me to him; his heat and rhythmic breathing to the back of my neck, his arm wrapped tightly about me, as if to hold me in place. I lie awake for hours staring at the wallpaper, weeping quietly. Finally, I force the tears away. *This is the bed I've made, and I must learn to lie in it, literally.*

The next morning, I rise before daybreak, dress hurriedly and open the bedroom door. Sean sits up, still half asleep. "Nellie, come back. You needn't leave."

"I don't want Mrs. O'Keefe to see me. She might gossip."

He rubs his eyes, saying, "Yes, she surely would. I'll stop by this evening after work." With that, he collapses back onto his pillow and begins to snore.

As I walk back in the dark, amidst the early morning sounds, a deep mix of shame and sadness overcomes me, and I begin to cry. Stop it, Nellie. This is the only solution for you and your baby. Be a realist, not a whiny fool.

Reaching my home, I open the door to find Mam sitting in the parlor, looking as though she has not slept at all.

"Well?"

"The deed is done. In three weeks, I'll tell Sean he's going to be a father. I've no doubt he'll want to get married quickly to avoid scandal."

"Sweetheart, I'm so sorry it has to be this way."

I turn on my heel to go to my room to clean up and change. "I must hurry or I'll be late for my class."

Throughout that day, I operate as an automaton, going through the motions of teaching and following my lesson plans to the letter. I don't believe anyone notices anything different about me until my student, Meryl Bradshaw, says, "Miss Kelly, are you alright?"

Startled, I snap. "What a question! I'm fit as a fiddle, girl. Don't be impudent."

Meryl shrinks down into the seat of her desk and looks ready to cry. While I'm sorry to have hurt her feelings, my heart is cold. She must learn toughness. I certainly have.

CHAPTER TWENTY-TWO

MARY

The hardest thing I've ever done in my long life is telling my Nellie that I cannot help her rear her baby. Because of money. *Hmph, that is a lie.* I cross myself. Though we're certainly not rich, I could have figured out a way were it not for the secret I must protect. There've been many lies over the past two months. That I had to be at The Haven all night delivering a baby. That I was attending a weekend medical conference in North Hampton when no such conference existed. Lies tear people apart, and I've feared this deception of mine might drive Nellie away from me.

How I've hated deceiving her and all my friends at Kathleen's Haven. But none of them would understand, I know it. Some sacred things must be kept silent lest they lose their value. This secret is one of them.

Though some would consider my secret unholy, I have now committed a sin far more serious. I have become an accomplice in turning my own daughter into a whore. A respectable whore, but none the less, a true whore. That's what I call a woman who marries a man she loathes for his money. And that's what my Nellie has to do. Surely, she does.

After that night she first seduced Sean, he came calling for her every evening, playing all nice and gentlemanly. He doesn't fool me, though. I've known what kind of man he is for years now. Sometimes, I wish I'd saved his mother's life instead of his. *And I've told the priest that sin in confession, haven't I?*

Nellie still rushes to the post office every day after work, praying for word from Derry. It never comes. I see her disappointment, and it hurts my heart. As the days pass, Nellie changes. She becomes more resolute in her movements, and her face changes from the sweet, trusting girl she's always been to something harder. She is still beautiful, but there's a set to her jaw that wasn't there before. I remember turning tough like this as a young girl on the coffin ship. I had hoped to spare her this alteration, but one must survive, and that's what Nellie is doing now.

Often, she goes home with Sean after dinner in a restaurant and does not come back till morning. I know what's happening. Of course, I know. I am part of the planning.

Three weeks after that first awful night at his house, I see her working herself into a practiced agitation before he arrives. I stay in my room but crack the door to see and hear.

He enters the living room and reaches to embrace her. She falls into his arms, weeping. "Oh Sean," she laments, "I am late." The tears become convulsive. "And I'm always so regular. Every twenty-nine days. I'm ten days late . . . Sean, I fear I'm pregnant."

At first, he recoils from her, shocked. "I thought you were protected. I thought you knew how to do that from your mother. She's told half the girls in this town how to keep from getting pregnant. Didn't she tell you?"

Nellie sobs into his shoulder. "She didn't think she needed to. She knew I was a virgin . . . until you." She looks up into his eyes, then appears to crumple in his arms. I marvel at her acting skill. Then, before my very eyes, his face changes. I see the wheels turning in his head as it dawns on him that her pregnancy will accomplish what he's wanted all along. Marriage to a beautiful, well-educated, Irish-Catholic girl.

"Hush, Nellie. Don't cry," he soothes. "I'll marry you." He gets down on one knee and takes her hand. "You're perfect for me. We must marry quickly, though."

Shocked, she wipes away her tears.

Then he ruins what could have been a tender moment. "So that no one realizes there's a shotgun involved."

Bastard. Truth be told, that fits in perfectly with our plans. And with my agreement with Father Ruzzo.

But Sean doesn't want a quick afternoon wedding in the rectory. Oh, no, he wants to make this the social event of Boston's Fall calendar. He'll invite the Lowells and the Cabots, after all. It's surely the first time those limey snobs will set foot in St. Augustine's Church.

"Many plans, but it must be accomplished quickly, of course."

Of course.

The date is set for two weeks away, Saturday, October 10. A High Nuptial Mass at St. Augustine's. Sean makes it clear that money is no object. He'll pay for everything. But there's so much to do before then.

First things first. Nellie needs a dress.

Next day, we hook up Nellie's pretty wagon and head to the Clementine Smythe Bridal Salon in Quincy Market. I've passed the place often but haven't ventured inside. It's said to be a terribly snooty spot, in keeping with its Beacon Hill clientele. Sean has insisted that Nellie's wedding dress be of the highest fashion—and white.

She is downcast as we enter the shop. Thinking of Derry, I figure. It's a beautiful store for sure, all white and fancy. In the center of the room is a step-up pedestal surrounded by full-length mirrors. On the main wall hangs a large painting of Queen Victoria in her white wedding gown. Before her, brides seldom wore white. I study it closely and I nudge Nellie to look at the picture.

"No one could say she was a beautiful bride, eh?"

"Hush, Mam!" she exclaims, hissing. "Lower your voice." She walks closer to the picture and looks. "I certainly can't quarrel with your assessment of her looks."

The two of us put our heads together and giggle like school girls until a tall, striking woman approaches us. "Miss Kelly, you're here for our two o'clock appointment. Such a pleasure to meet you. I'm Clementine Smythe. Mr. O'Halloran says to make sure I take very good care of you." She turns to me. "And is this your dear mother?"

Nellie seems startled at the woman's haughty effusion, so I take the conversation. "Yes, indeed, Miss Smythe." I stick out my hand. "Mary Kelly."

She shakes my hand and I get the distinct impression she would like to rush off and wash hers.

"I've pulled some dresses appropriate for the occasion. It's quite important to choose something today so that alterations can be made in time."

She leads us to dressing rooms in back of the shop, and we sit on uncomfortable little gilt chairs as she leaves to get the gowns. Nellie looks around at the mirrors and gilded walls and raises her eyebrows to me.

"Gaudy, yes," I respond, "but it's what the swells like."

Miss Smythe returns with a rack of white confections. "I believe these are close to your size, Miss Kelly, though your waist is so tiny we'll probably need to take them in."

Not for long.

Nellie steps out of her plain dress and Miss Smythe slips the first dress over her head. I gasp. It is so beautiful. Like the finest dresses in *Godey's Ladies Book*, the gown is gathered up under the waistline into a perfect pleated bustle. Inside the bustle are fake lilies of the valley. Its sleeves are long and tight to Nellie's arms, and the gently scooped neckline shows a modest amount of her swelling bosom. It is perfect.

"How much is it?" Nellie asks.

"Five-hundred dollars," Miss Smythe answers.

I gasp. With that kind of money, you could buy the grandest carriage in Boston. Or it could be the start of buying a house.

Miss Smythe arches her eyebrows. "Mr. O'Halloran said that money is not an object."

I get the distinct impression that she's looking down her aquiline nose at me, so I say, "Yes, I know he said that, but it does seem an exorbitant amount for one dress, pretty as it is."

Miss Smythe chuckles in a decidedly superior tone. "Mrs. Kelly, I guess you don't know what fine dresses cost now-a-days." As she says it, she scans down the plain cotton Sunday-best frock a neighbor lady made for me. I love this dress. Its green color sets off my red hair, and I get compliments on it every Sunday at Mass. But now I hear a distinct lilt in Miss Smythe's speech. I've always had a good ear for accents. The cultured Buckingham Palace enunciation fades into a slightly cockney inflection.

"You're probably right, Miss Smythe," I answer. "I haven't bought a new dress in a posh shop for quite a spell. But tell me, dear. Where do you come from?"

Taken aback, she answers in a huff, "London."

I nod. "The east end, I'd wager. I bet you miss the peal of the Bow Bells, don't you?"

Her face falls and she stammers, "N-no, I'm from the west side."

I lower my lashes and purse my lips at her. We both know better.

CHAPTER TWENTY-THREE

My sense of dread is as deep as the Atlantic this October 10 morning. The day my girl marries Sean O'Halloran. Though it's all gone as we planned that night with Molly, the reality of her marriage to him truly singes my soul. It's a mistake for sure, but none of us could figure another way for her to keep the baby. Nellie hoped against hope to hear from Derry, but word never came. So, today is the day.

Somehow, we pulled it all together in time. She bought the first dress she tried on with a matching veil, shoes, and gloves. We booked the best calligrapher in Boston and Sean paid top dollar to get the invitations done quickly and hand delivered. He was lucky to book the Somerset Club on short notice for the reception and has arranged lodging for all his posh friends from Harvard.

A white beribboned carriage will take me and Nellie to the church at eleven for the noon-day High Mass. Boston's best hairdresser will arrange Nellie's hair in the rectory to complement the veil. It's the first time she hasn't done her hair herself. Everything is in order with Father Ruzzo still thinking this baby is Sean's. In my most wicked thoughts, I figure that alone might justify an annulment someday. I confessed as much in a

New Hampshire church without mentioning names, and got absolution, though I did wonder if the priest was playing dumb with me.

Molly will be Nellie's Maid of Honor and has her dress ready to go. I wanted to wear my regular Sunday dress, but was shamed into a new one by Sean. The new one's pretty enough, but the corset it comes with is enough to stop my breathing. How can women wear such things every day? When I showed the outfit to Kam, he gasped and said, "Mary, you are as pretty now as when I first met you on that ship."

Very funny. Pretty as a half-starved, filthy thirteen-year-old with her red hair tucked into a sailor's cap to hide it from the crew. *Some pretty, I'd say.* But he means well, does Kam. And, best of all, I know he means what he says.

I tiptoe from my room and go to Nellie's. She lies there, her eyes fixed on the ceiling, looking steeled for whatever happens this day. "Morning, darlin'. Did you sleep?"

She rolls to her side and replies, "Not a lot, Mam."

I sit on the edge of her bed and stroke her long, black hair like I did when she was a little girl. Her blue eyes stare into mine with painful resolve. There are no tears, which hurts me more than if there were.

With steely resolve, she pulls back the covers and stands; bare feet on cold floor. "This is my last night of sleeping here."

"Don't say that, Nellie. This room will always be here for you, with the bed made and fresh. I promise."

She touches my cheek. "Thanks, Mam."

When I think of how much I wanted her to call me Mam a few years ago, my eyes nearly spill, but I won't let that happen. I must be strong for my girl. And for the wee bairn she carries. As Molly said, there are worse things than living in a mansion on Beacon Hill, probably married to a future Mayor of Boston. *But* what worse things? If you don't love the man who shares your bed, isn't that worse? I wouldn't have traded one day with my Daniel for any life of luxury and privilege. Nellie feels that way about Derry. I could see it in her every gaze. But Sean? Come now.

Stop it, Mary Boland. Get moving lest your sadness spoils even more of this day. You've gotten what you wanted, a da for your grandchild. I stuff my regrets and call out, "It's nine-thirty already. I'll go and make some breakfast for us. You get washed up and dressed. Needn't fuss with your hair since that'll be done in the rectory. Just wear an everyday dress. We'll take the finery in the carriage and you can dress there."

As I bustle about the kitchen, she passes me to get water out of the pump.

"I wager you'll not need to pump water in your new home, love. Most of the mansions have water that runs out of a faucet. Won't that be grand?"

"Yes, I suppose so," she answers.

"Does Sean have a proper bathtub?"

"Yes, it's big *and* deep. You just turn a spigot, and there's hot water."

"Imagine such a thing!" I exclaim. "Perhaps one day when he's at work, you'll let me come and take a bath?"

She puts the full bucket on the stove to warm and turns to me. "Mam, you can always come to Sean's place and visit or take a bath or do anything you want. I hope you know that."

"Well, see love, that's the thing. It's Sean's place. And I am not his favorite person. He's made that *abundantly* clear."

She shakes her head. "And you to him, don't you think?"

She's right, of course. "I suppose I have been distant to him at times." I hold up my right hand and face her. "I swear to you right now, on the memory of your da, that I will make a better effort with Sean. Just watch me."

Her water is warmed now, and she takes it to her room, along with a basin, a towel, and a wash cloth.

"Wash your hair, too, love, but leave it loose," I say after her.

Turning on her heel, she comes back into the kitchen and gives me a peck on the cheek.

As I scramble eggs and make coffee, I say a silent prayer. *Dear God, please let her learn to love him. Let him be a good husband to my girl, and for everyone's sake, make me nicer to him. Amen.*

After a time, she comes back to the kitchen and looks around. "I'll miss this kitchen. Sean has a woman who'll do all the cooking for us. Heaven knows I'm not much of a cook, but I think I'll miss trying to learn."

We sit down and begin to eat the toast and eggs. "Well, I sure wouldn't miss cooking. Though I'm not much of a cook either. I'm a good baker because Kathleen taught me, but she always cooked the real food. Nellie, I wish you could have known her. She was a corker."

"I can tell just looking at that painting of her in The Haven. She looks *nothing* like Sean."

"No, not a bit, I'll grant you that. I don't know where he gets his looks. Tommy wasn't much of a looker either. But how Sean's parents loved each other. Fought like cats and dogs, but the love was always there. I didn't think Tommy'd make it after she died. Without Sean to rear, I doubt he would have."

Nellie rises and takes her dishes to the sink. "Molly says he spoiled Sean rotten."

"I suppose he did, but you couldn't really blame him. His girls were grown and leaving him, and that little boy was his life. Couldn't do enough for him. Then he married that skinny widow just to give Sean a mother. Tommy didn't love her and made that quite apparent."

Nellie turns to me. "Maybe that runs in the family now—not loving, I mean."

Her words twist my heart. She knows that something's missing in Sean. Affection or empathy, something. *The boy doesn't have them. Never did.*

After washing up the few dishes, I go to my room to dress. Picking up the despised corset, I hook it up the front and then turn it so the hooks are down the back. Some women have maids to do their hooking and lacing. I can't imagine such a life. A strange woman always around looking at me naked and all. I'd feel like a total eejit.

After I'm hooked up, I pull on the petticoat and crinolette. The thing makes my behind stick out in the bustle that is considered so fashionable now-a-days. *Why do women wear these things? It must be to make other women jealous.*

I've not known a man who didn't like the normal curves of a woman. Perhaps I've been lucky in that way. But why in the world would a man want a woman he's taking to his bed to be uncomfortable and squashed by such confining garments? It'd be like unwrapping a plum pudding at Christmas time and finding it all wrinkled and lined from its package. But today, I'll wear this *fuathfar* corset like the lady in the shop says all the stylish ladies do to keep the peace with Sean O'Halloran. *God help me.*

When I look in the mirror, the image looks like someone I don't know. Pretty but alien. Quit your bleating, Mary Boland. It's only for a day and then you'll never have to hook up this contraption again in your lifetime. My constricted form would be enough to turn any red-blooded male into a flapdoodle, I wager.

But when Nellie sees me, she exclaims, "Mam, you look beautiful!"

That's what counts. She's the one I want to please this day. And her intended. Kam won't be coming to the wedding. Sean didn't want him, and Nellie didn't feel the matter worth a battle. 'Tis better he not be there. He and Sean can't stand each other, and Kamua Okafor is not one to bluff his feelings well. Nellie would have had him walk her down the center aisle were it up to her, but now she'll have a husband to consider in deciding such things. A husband much more indebted to the swells of Boston than to people like me or Kam. Today, she'll be escorted to the altar by Sean's senior partner.

When it's almost time to leave the house, Nellie touches my arm. "Mam, I need to give you something for safe keeping."

I raise an eyebrow.

She takes my right hand into hers and uncurls my fingers, then drops a beautiful *Claddagh* ring into my palm. "Do what you wish with this," she murmurs, anger coating every word. "Obviously, he didn't mean what I thought he did when he gave it to me."

"Ah, Nellie, he must have loved you to give you this."

She laughs bitterly. "Clearly not, Mam. I guess you're as big as sap as I was."

Her rancor is heartbreaking, but understandable. I turn and take the ring into my bedroom where I hide it in my bottom drawer where I keep all my mementoes from Daniel.

"The carriage is here!" she calls to me.

Wiping away my tears and squaring my shoulders, I grab the long bag holding her dress, veil, shoes and gloves and pick up the other satchel with her underpinnings in it. She'll need no clothes for a honeymoon. Sean says that'll come later . . . after he speaks at the Democratic Convention in Springfield next month.

As we climb into the grand carriage, Nellie takes one long

look back at our little house. *Do I see mist in those blue eyes? Or is it in mine?*

The driver brings down the whip on the two horses and off we go to St. Augustine's. It's a short ride, and before we enter the church, we stop at the cemetery and stand for a moment over Daniel's grave. Nellie places one white flower there with a Kelly-green ribbon tied round its stem. Neither of us says a word, but my heart is breaking that he isn't here this day.

"Time to go in," she says, her voice flat.

In the rectory, we find Marguerite, the hairdresser Sean hired, ready to do her work with Nellie's hair. I'd hoped it would be long and loose, but the woman pulls it up into a tight chignon and then loosens a few tendrils around Nellie's face. "It'll look better this way with her headpiece," she says.

When she's finished with the hair, she asks Nellie to sit down in front of a mirror. "I'd like to do a teeny bit of makeup to enhance your natural beauty."

"Makeup?" Nellie is shocked. "I don't want to look like a tart."

"You won't, dear. What I do is very subtle."

She takes a cream from her bag and smears it around Nellie's face and neck.

"That feels good," Nellie murmurs.

Then, the woman takes a huge powder puff and dips it into a tin of powder. She flicks the thing around in her hands and suddenly, there's a thick puff of white over everything.

Poor Father. He won't know what happened to his rectory with this sweet-smelling, snowy film all over his desk.

Next, Marguerite takes a small pot of pink rouge and applies a hint to Nellie's cheeks, then blends it up into her hairline. A final dust of powder completes her face, and I figure she's done. But no, she pulls a tiny vial of coal dust from her bag and a hairpin. She dips the hairpin into the coal dust and runs it around Nellie's long eyelashes.

"Now bite your lips right before you walk down the aisle. I'm not going to use lip rouge on you. Your own natural lips are perfect as they are. There, that's it, sweetheart. You look beautiful," Marguerite says, quite pleased with herself.

And she does. Indeed, she does.

As she steps into her wedding dress, Marguerite and I stop breathing for a second. She truly is the prettiest bride either of us has ever seen, and Marguerite's seen most of them in Boston. At first, the idea of makeup was repugnant to me, but I must admit, Nellie looks magnificent.

Though it seems like gilding the lily, this lily couldn't be prettier.

Marguerite attaches the veil and Nellie puts on the gloves. "Let's go," Nellie says, "and get this over with."

Marguerite's eyebrows shoot up into an arch, and my stomach takes a dip.

Now that'll be all over Boston tomorrow.

The new organ strikes up a rousing hymn and some young man I don't know comes to escort me to the second pew on the left, the place of honor for the bride's mother. Then, Shannon's husband walks her down the aisle, their five children in tow, and seats her on the right. She smiles and waves to me. Shannon is Sean's sister, the other little girl I took care of, along with Molly, when I arrived from Ireland. Her blonde hair has dimmed since those days and she looks older than her forty years. I do hope she's happy. There's been gossip that Kevin, her husband, has someone on the side, but I can't bring myself to believe that.

Molly comes down the aisle next and bows down to kiss me on the cheek before she goes to the altar. There is a hush in the church as the organist pauses . . . then begins to play "Panis Angelicus," the hymn Nellie chose for her processional.

As she appears, I hear audible gasps from the congregation. My tummy is attacked by butterflies. I bet none of these English snobs have seen a bride as stunning as my Nellie. I've seen their daughters' pictures on the "Society" page of *The Globe*, and most of them are pinch-nosed plain.

There is a photographer here today from the newspaper. Sean, of course, made sure of that.

And there he stands at the railing, next to a man who is, I imagine, a friend from Harvard. I will be the first to admit Sean is a fine-looking man, standing there dressed in his morning coat and striped trousers. He's so tall, so blonde, and so convincing as he gazes at the beautiful woman coming toward him. One would think the two of them are madly in love.

Father Ruzzo welcomes them and asks who gives this woman in marriage. I stand up and in the strongest voice I can muster say, "I do, along with her departed father, Daniel Kelly."

The priest had questioned a woman saying this, but who else but me could do it? Nellie wanted to ask Kam, but Sean objected vehemently. That's when Kam suggested that Daniel would have wanted me to give our daughter away. So although such a thing is not traditional in the church, that's what I chose to do. When I sit down after my little outburst, Nellie turns my way with an Irish determination in her eyes. That does it for me. I burst into tears.

Through the long Mass and all the hymns, I remind myself that this is for my child and for hers, too. She'll have a decent life as Sean's wife, if not one filled with passion. Maybe that isn't important to her. Ach, but the foolishness of that thought. I saw her with Derry. I felt the attraction between them. It was palpable. But maybe a woman is only supposed to experience real love once in her life. Even as I think that, my own life experience tells me differently. But look at me, I have it now for a second time.

Finally, the Mass ends, and it's time for the vows. The priest is positioned in the center of the altar facing Nellie and Sean who stand side by side at the rail. I see a slight trembling across her shoulders, which makes me want to rush to her side and embrace her, But, of course, I can't do that. Not in church at her wedding. Not in front of Boston's upper crust. It wouldn't be right.

Father Ruzzo asks, "Have you come here willingly to enter into the Sacrament of Matrimony this day?"

Both Sean and Nellie nod and say yes.

The priest then addresses the congregation. "Does anyone know any reason why this couple should not be joined in the Holy Sacrament of Matrimony?"

The church hushes as it always does at this time during a ceremony. Molly coughs, but does not speak. Nor do I, though God knows we'd like to. In a better world, this is the moment Derry would run down the aisle and grab Nellie into his arms. But this is not a better world, it's the world we've got.

"Dearly Beloved," Father begins. "You have come into the house of the Church so that, in the presence of the Church's minister and this community, your intention to enter into marriage may be strengthened by the Lord with a sacred seal."

He continues with the hallowed words about fidelity, duty, and the rearing of children, and then asks them to state their intentions.

"Sean O'Halloran and Ellen Kelly, have you come here to enter into marriage without coercion, freely and wholeheartedly?"

Both Sean and Nellie say, "I have."

He asks, "Are you prepared as you follow the path of marriage, to love and honor each other, for as long as you both shall live. And are you prepared to accept children lovingly from God and to bring them up in accordance with the law of God and His Church?"

"I am," they answer.

"Then join your right hands."

They do and face each other.

Father nods to Sean.

"I, Sean, take you Ellen, to be my wife. I promise to be faithful to you, to love and honor you in good times and in bad, in sickness and in health, as long as we both shall live."

Father now turns to Nellie. She repeats the vows from the priest, sounding mechanical. She stumbles a bit over the pledge to obey Sean and the congregation titters slightly. Her reputation as a working woman is known, and this is considered rebellious.

After repeating the vows once more, Father asks them to pledge their fidelity to each other until death. Both of them say, "I do."

The priest takes the ring from the Best Man, blesses it and says, "May the Lord bless this ring as the sign of your love and fidelity." He hands it to Sean who repeats the words and places the ring on Nellie's finger.

"Then by the power given to me by Almighty God and the State of Massachusetts, I pronounce Sean O'Halloran and Ellen Kelly man and wife. What God has joined together, let no one put asunder."

The organ strikes up a loud, celebratory hymn and the two of them turn and walk down the aisle together. Sean pats the backs of several men as he passes them. Nellie forces niceties. Molly looks as sad as I feel.

It's over.

Chapter Twenty-Four

Rice and streamers assail us outside the church. Bulbs flash, nearly blinding me, and a reporter from *The Boston Globe* grabs my arm and says, "Mrs. Kelly, how does it feel to be the mother of a girl who may someday become the First Lady of Boston?"

I stammer a suitable response and say a silent prayer for my girl's happiness. As if she reads my mind, Nellie comes to me and takes me into her arms. "Mam, don't be sad," she whispers. "I will learn to love Sean. I know I will. I loved him when I was a girl. I can love him again."

Then she's whisked away from me by friends clamoring for her presence. Sean stands with his arm around her waist, beaming like the happiest groom in the world.

Maybe he will be a good husband. Maybe she will learn to love him. Maybe.

We all climb into our carriages and head to the reception. The Somerset Club is at 42 Beacon Street, right in the heart of Beacon Hill, also called Snob Hill. I've never been inside, of course, so I'm curious about what it's like. Riding alone in my fancy carriage, I watch the neighborhoods change as we leave South Boston and head toward Beacon Hill. Houses become larger and grander with each passing corner. I sit back in the cushioned seat and decide to enjoy the ride. *Boston is a lovely town*, I muse to myself. *I could have done worse when I left Ireland.* Though even now, I miss the old country, especially the green hills and hedgerows. Both Boston and Ireland are on the Atlantic Ocean, but in Kinsale, the waves seemed so much closer. I saw them every day. Smelled the salt. Watched as the surf rose to the clouds and magically turned into rain. I must stop romanticizing my memories of Ireland. In truth, it almost killed me. But when I went back there for Neo's wedding, I felt wonderful, so much at home. Which, of course, I was.

And I wasn't the only one. Nellie and Kam loved it, too. The people, the countryside, Trinity College's beautiful campus, and our visit to the Gnarly Head Pub. That was where Nellie first saw Derry. I worried that night about her clear infatuation for that Irish charmer, and it turns out I had good cause. Where is he? Neo says no one's heard a word from him. He wasn't on the ship when it docked. Where in God's name can he be?

Stop thinking about Derry! Your daughter just married another man; one she swears she will learn to love. So, you must learn to love him, too.

In my musing, I don't realize we are on Beacon Street until the carriage pulls up in front of a large stone mansion at number forty-three. How majestic it is. John Singleton Copley once owned this parcel of land and called it his farm on Beacon Street. Sure doesn't look like any farm I've ever seen. Its stones are white and it covers half a block of the most exclusive street in Boston. How in the world did Sean O'Halloran end up a member of this club? If any of these swells could have seen his da serving up spirits in O'Halloran's pub and singing Irish songs, with his red face and bulging belly, they wouldn't believe this classy young lawyer grew up as part of that life. But he did, and so did I. And it was fun, it was. Probably a lot more fun than what we'll have in this tony club that would never let Tommy O'Halloran near its door if he were still alive.

When the carriage stops at the curb, the driver opens my door and extends his hand to help me down. I thank the man and walk up and into the Somerset Club.

In the foyer, I hear the strains of a waltz. A lady in black takes my cloak and a gentleman extends his arm to escort me into the grand ballroom. On the stage, a string quartet plays, and a few couples have already started to dance. It's strange to see men and women dancing together this way in a posh setting. Partner dancing has only recently come into fashion among the upper class. I did waltz with Daniel at the Irish Fellowship Hall on Saint Patrick's Day, but the Irish always danced together. These couples do look beautiful gliding around the floor. Like gentle colored swans floating across a lake. The men all wear black. But the colors of the women's dresses are magical! All shades of the rainbow in soft silk and tulle. *How I wish Daniel was here to see this.*

I am seated at the first table, a place of honor for the bridal party. As Nellie and Sean enter the ballroom, the quartet strikes up a tune. A woman at my table who introduces herself as Evelyn, the wife of an usher, says, "It's 'The Wedding March.'" Marguerite, Nellie's hairdresser, had told us that this is the music now played at the most elegant weddings in America, and that it was composed by a man named Wagner for the opera, *Lohengrin*. It is a pretty tune, and quite ceremonial, but I fancy more the tunes played on the Celtic harp and bodhran I've heard at other weddings.

To each her own, Mary Kelly, I tell myself. *To each her own.*

Waiters come to the tables serving champagne and tiny crackers covered over with something black.

"What is this?" I ask Evelyn.

"Caviar," she replies. "The eggs of sturgeon."

I take a nibble and find it much too fishy and salty for my taste, but I tell Evelyn, "It's delicious." Finding it hard to chew and swallow, I do anyway, even though I would have preferred to spit it into a napkin.

Her approval is seen in the way her posture adjusts. "Wait'll you taste the *kutti pi*. The Somerset is famous for its *kutti pi*."

"*Kutti pi*? What is that, pray tell?"

"It's actually a braised unborn goat. It's wonderful, bones and all."

I try not to choke. *What is wrong with these people? Why do they feast on unborn fish and goats? It's barbaric.* Politely, I put a hand over my plate when the waiter comes with the *kutti pi*.

The afternoon goes on with me drinking champagne and eating next to nothing. I watch Sean as he circulates around the tables, shaking hands with all the men. Nellie looks more tired by the hour, and I worry about her. I hope he'll take her home soon so she can rest.

By five o'clock, I am feeling woozy and hungry. I stand and bend over Nellie's shoulder to tell her I love her and would like to excuse myself.

She looks up, her blue eyes wide and says, "Are you all right, Mam?"

"I'm fine, love. Right as rain. Just a bit tired."

She walks with me to the front door of the club, then asks the doorman to fetch my carriage. "I'll visit this week, Mam. I promise."

"Do, love. And bring Sean, won't you?"

The carriage takes me to my house. I go inside, then through to the alley in back and climb into my own little wagon. I bring the reins down on Maeve. She takes off at a leisurely trot back toward Beacon Hill but goes to the back side of it.

I guide her to the rear of the house, as always, tie her up, and make sure there's water and hay in the troughs. There is, so I go around to the front door and knock.

When he opens the door, he takes one look at me and knows it's been a trying day. He guides me into the house and feeds me toast and eggs, then accompanies me upstairs where he slowly removes the dress and corset, unwrapping me like a treasured present. When he sees the lines in my body from the stays in the corset, he kisses them, saying, "My dear, poor love."

We lie together then, and he asks me about the wedding, the club, and how I feel about the whole thing.

"They fed me fish eggs and goat fetus. How do you think I feel?"

This seems to amuse him greatly as he pulls me to him where I stay until morning.

CHAPTER TWENTY-FIVE

For the next month, I go about my business as always. There is a great burst of births at Kathleen's Haven. We blame it on the full moon rising. Some doctors in town say that's old-fashioned superstition, but those who've birthed babies as long as I have known better. You can't separate the magic of birth from all the other wonders of our universe. There's a pull from the skies, the seas, even the other animals on earth that regulates our rhythms as humans. As a midwife, I see it every day. Father Ruzzo calls it God, and he may be right, for after all, who created all the universe but God.

When I see finally get to see Nellie, I notice dark shadows around her eyes. I ask if she's sleeping all right, and she says, "Yes, Mam. Don't be a worrywart." But I do worry. Although her belly is expanding normally, she looks thinner in the face and neck.

But time passes and fall turns into winter. When New Year's Eve comes round, Nellie insists to Sean that they come with me and Molly to the Irish Fellowship Party rather than the Somerset Club. At first, he refuses, but when Molly points out that it's important for him to maintain his ties to the Irish community in Boston—that they now represent a large portion of the electorate—he agrees.

The Fellowship Hall is quite festive when we enter at nine on New Year's Eve. Christmas trees still adorn the perimeter of the floor, and mistletoe hangs from the ceiling all around the ballroom. The women are dressed in their Sunday best. Molly wears green taffeta and I am in my fine dress from the wedding. I left the corset in the drawer so the dress is a bit tight around the waist, but it's certainly more comfortable than with that blasted thing strangling my ribs.

We join our friends, Marty and Ruth Anne Walsh, who lived in the old neighborhood before he was elected alderman. They've already begun celebrating and their faces are flushed and ruddy.

"Mary, Molly, so good to see you! Haven't seen you in a coon's age!" Ruth Anne exclaims as she hugs us both tight. I feel the tight corset constricting her middle and marvel again that women still wear them. I'd like to see a man forced into one of those contraptions.

Marty chimes in with, "Can you believe it's almost 1879? By the saints, where does the time go? Where's that pretty daughter of yours and her fine husband?"

His merriment is intoxicating as I answer, "They'll be along any minute now. Save two seats for them, won't you?"

"Indeed, we will. It's not every day we get to mingle with the lad we're banking on to be mayor of Boston someday," Marty replies. "Wouldn't old Tommy be thrilled with his bairn?"

Molly beams as the band strikes up "Carry Me Back to Old Virginia." The song is popular now in Boston though it's all about the South and was composed by a black minstrel man.

"Dance with me, won't you, Marty?" Molly says. I sense she wants to escape the conversation about Sean. "You don't mind, do you, Ruth Anne?"

"Holy Jesus on the cross, no, I don't mind. Glad to get rid of the bloke for a bit."

She chuckles as he leaves the table and pats him on his posterior.

Claiming her turf? My eyebrow arches.

The two of them go out onto the floor and Ruth Anne turns to me. "So, Mary, how is Nellie? Must be getting pretty big now, I wager."

"Yes, she is, and relieved to be over the morning sickness, that's for sure."

"Well, she surely landed the catch with that handsome Sean, didn't she? Marty says he's the rising star in the Democratic party."

"Yes, I suppose so. But in a way, he's the one who got the catch."

"Nellie is a prize, that's for certain." She pauses for a moment. "She did get pregnant quickly, now didn't she?"

Is she scavenging for gossip? Aye. I've always liked Ruth Anne, but a forced marriage would be a tasty morsel to spread around town and the St. Augustine's Women's Guild. "Yes, a honeymoon baby. Like many young Catholic women."

"So, when is her baby due?"

"Sometime in July, I'd wager." Keep it vague, Mary.

"Hmmm," Ruth Anne says.

I see her fingers moving as she counts the months since the wedding. I feel a pang of disappointment in this woman I considered a friend. To hell with her. Between Molly and me, we'll convince the yacky windbags in town that Nellie's baby is merely early. As if all of them were virgins when they walked down the aisle. Ha! I know better. I did their premarital checkups. Hypocrites.

Suddenly the noisy crowd quiets. Heads turn toward the entrance to the ballroom. When I look, there are Nellie and Sean. Such a dazzling couple. She wears a Christmas-red dress and hardly looks pregnant at all even though she's nearly six months along. I wager there's a corset under the dress, a practice I vehemently advise my expectant mothers against. But Nellie is being attended by Dr. Benjamin Forsythe, a well-known obstetrical specialist and the President of the Somerset Club. Sean insisted on him being her physician.

I do not agree with Dr. Forsythe's advice to mothers-to-be. He tries to keep weight gain under fifteen pounds and tells his patients that if they eat sour foods, the baby will have a sour disposition. I craved dill pickles during my pregnancy with Nellie, and no child could have been sweeter than her.

I rise from my chair and go to greet them. Nellie's hug is tight and warm, but Sean's feels mechanical and forced. So much of what the man does is for show. "Come to our table. We've saved chairs for you. Molly and the Walshes are there." Marty Walsh is chairman of the Boston aldermen, and that clearly pleases Sean.

As we join the others, Marty stands and shakes hands with Sean. "Good to see you, lad." Ruth Anne stares up at Sean with stars in her eyes.

"Nellie, dear, you look so pretty. I understand congratulations are in order," Ruth Anne says after kissing Nellie on the cheek.

Marty hits Sean on the back. "And congratulations to you, too, you lucky bloke. You didn't waste any time, now did you? Come on, Sean. I'll buy you a drink to celebrate."

As the two men head to the bar, Ruth Anne descends on Nellie like a scavenging crow. "How is married life, Nellie? That snooty housekeeper, Mrs. O'Keefe, is something, isn't she? I met her once when Sean invited us to a political gathering at his new place. She nearly scared me to death with her airs."

"She's all right," Nellie answers, "now that she doesn't hate me any longer for marrying Sean. She so hoped to catch him for one of her daughters."

As if he'd marry a housekeeper's daughter.

Nellie cradles her bare arms, shivering. Excusing herself, she goes to a nearby fireplace and rubs her hands in front of it. When she returns, she says, "Hasn't this been a beast of a year weatherwise? All those hurricanes this summer, and now a deep freeze."

"Shall I get your shawl?" I ask.

"No, Mam. I'll be warmed up soon."

She looks around the hall. "Where is Sean, I wonder? Surely it can't take this long to get a drink."

Ruth Anne attempts to brush off her concern. "Get used to it, dearie. Both of us are married to politicians. And, oh, how they love to mingle. They're probably in the bar hitting up some drunk for a campaign contribution."

"Yes, I suppose so," Nellie answers and the four of us women settle in for a long evening . . . alone.

Molly stands up. "Well, I want a beer. I'll get a pitcher."

"Whiskey for me, please," Nellie calls after her.

Don't say it, Mary. You have no proof that alcohol harms a baby. Many women drink all through their pregnancy. You'll just be thought a nag.

The three of us watch the dancers on the floor as they whirl and prance. And we gossip, of course.

"That Maisie Grady should not be wearing such a tight dress. Not flattering at all," Ruth Anne whispers.

Nellie and I turn to see Maisie and, God forgive us, we nod in agreement. Poor Maisie. She can't help it. Her mother was stout, too.

All in all, it's a pleasant evening. The men drop by occasionally, and even once ask their wives for a dance. Nellie has a second whiskey, and looks as though her eyes are about to close as we get nearer to midnight.

At half past eleven, she says, "I'm going to find Sean. We should be together at midnight."

Molly stands up, too. "I'll go with you."

I wonder if she suspects something I don't know?

Marty comes back to the table, glass in hand, leans down and kisses Ruth Anne, then whispers to us at the table. "I think Sean's a favorite to be mayor someday," he says, almost giddy. "All the money boys say so."

Ruth Anne grabs my shoulder. "Mary, isn't that exciting? To have a mayor in the family. And he's so young. Who knows? Someday, he might be governor."

I smile but don't reply. I'm not sure that would be such a great thing. But that's not for me to say. I cannot interfere in their lives, even mentally. I'm on thin ice with Sean, as is. Keep your own counsel, Mary. Stay out of their affairs.

Molly returns to the table, nervously pulling up her gloves and adjusting the combs in her hair. One look tells me she's upset about something. The others don't notice. They're putting on their New Year's hats and preparing to unravel streamers.

Marty takes Ruth Anne to the floor. "Come on, Missus. This'll be our last dance for 1878. Then we'll kiss in the New Year."

"What's wrong, Molly?" I lean in, asking.

She seems so distressed she can hardly speak. "Uhhhh."

For a second, I think possibly something happened to Nellie. "Molly, tell me."

She takes a deep breath. "I don't know if I should."

"Of course, you should. And quickly."

"Well, Nellie and I were looking all over for Sean and couldn't find him anywhere."

"And?" My heart pounds in my chest.

"Nellie said, 'Maybe he's in the cloak room getting something from his coat pocket.'"

Molly's eyes are almost bleeding pain.

"Tell me, Molly. What happened?"

"He was there all right, hiding in the pack of coats. And not alone."

Oh, no! Please, God, no! Finally, I can control my voice and ask. "Who was with him?"

"Mary, I don't want to say, but you know that floozie, Bernadette Ryan?"

"Yes, I know her from church." *Pretty girl though a bit flashy. Never takes communion.*

"She was with Sean." Molly's eyes fill with tears.

I wait breathlessly.

"And they were kissing."

The band begins to play "Auld Lang Syne" and couples go to the center of the dance floor, counting down the seconds. "Twenty-five, twenty-four, twenty-three, twenty-two . . ."

"Where's Nellie now?" I ask, sounding calmer than I feel.

"I don't know, Mary. She ran outside."

I dash through the hall to the front door. As I open it, I am slapped in the face with a cold burst of snow. I desperately look up and down Beekman Street, then run down the stairs and call out, "Nellie?"

No answer. My heart starts to beat like a bodhran in my chest. Frantic, I call her name again. And then I see her. She's two blocks down Beekman Street, staggering on her high heels, her head down. Oh, Father, please don't let her lose the baby.

I run with all my being. Reaching her, I grab her by the shoulders and turn her around to my arms. "Nellie, love, you'll catch your death. What happened? Why are you outside?"

Her eyes swim, dazed and distant. "I just wanted to get some air, Mam."

Turning away, she walks back to the Hall, goes up the stairs, and never speaks of what she saw.

CHAPTER TWENTY-SIX

That night, I weep in his arms and tell him about Sean's behavior. He is quiet for a good long time, but finally breaks his silence. "There's a doctor in Austria who writes about a complex, the Madonna Syndrome. I've read about it in medical journals."

"Madonna Syndrome? What is it?"

He lights the kerosene lamp beside the bed and sorts through some publications on the table. When he finds what he's looking for, he opens it and reads aloud:

"Some men are able to love one woman and yet not desire to have sex with her. For satisfaction, they must go to a woman who can be debased."

"Debased?"

He takes me in his arms and whispers very softly, "Some men, abused in infancy by a cruel or distant mother, are unable to have sex with a woman they perceive as good. They marry the good girl and then look for a tramp. I imagine such a thing would be exacerbated in a man brought up in the Catholic faith. All that virgin birth and Mary, the unstained mother."

"That's blasphemy. Mother Mary really was impregnated spiritually."

He leans up on one elbow in reply.

I've struggled with my faith over this very matter and also that nearly all the female saints are virgins. Surely some of them were not. Then, I remember Sean's birth.

"What if the man's mother died at his birth?" I ask him.

"I don't know, but such a trauma *could* impact a boy's brain. Perhaps he blames himself."

As he drifts off to sleep, I think about what he's told me. Some of the young women I've delivered have come back to me in tears, wondering why their husbands no longer desire them. I tell them to give it time, but perhaps there's truth in this theory that some men think a woman is either a saint or a whore. *And if she's both, they are frightened.* Does Sean think Nellie is too good to touch? It seems terribly perverse to me and certainly not in keeping with what's right or true, but human beings are a strange lot and not at all dependable to do what I think is normal. What an awful irony. And how difficult that makes marriage if the husband is so afflicted.

In my forty-five years, I'm blessed to have been deeply loved by two remarkable men, both faithful to their cores. That is what I've always wished for my sweet Nellie. Perhaps this baby will make a difference in Sean. Perhaps he'll see how fortunate he is to have Nellie and this tiny baby to love. *Please God, let this be the case.*

I remain here for a long time, drifting in rhythm to his steady sleep breathing. What a lovely man he is. How fortunate a woman am I to have him beside me at this advanced age. Some women never have such a blessing.

I roll over to look at him. Though his hair is now white, he still looks like the boy who saved me on that coffin ship all those years ago. Dark, strong, and handsome. He's one of the few Negroes who has thrived in this country. And that was through his intelligence and perseverance. When he first concocted Dr. Kamua's African Love Tonic and took off in his loaded wagon to sell it around New England. Kathleen and I doubted people would buy medicine from a colored man, but the apothecarist who employed him said it would be a success. Full of African herbs like yohimbe bark, which has restored desire in humans for centuries, Mr. Mendel said it was a solid formula and not just quinine and alcohol like many of the traveling medicine men were peddling across the country. Kam had learned such formulas from his father, an African medicine man who died while saving the Irish indentured servants on the sugar plantations in Louisiana when traditional medicines had failed to help them.

Kathleen recognized Kam's genius early on and taught both of us to read and write. We devoured knowledge like starving children. When Kam's Harvard friend gave him a copy of *Quain's Anatomy*, we spent day and night trying to broaden the knowledge learned from my Irish mother and his African father.

When I started practicing as a midwife, pregnant women died in droves from an illness called childbed fever. Scientists thought there was something in the air killing them, but common sense made me question the fact that a physician went from a surgery or an autopsy to a birth with the same unclean instruments. I began sterilizing instruments at Kathleen's Haven and mortality rates among my patients improved so enormously that the doctors became threatened. Though some of them still look at me with a skeptical eye, others now seek my counsel.

Louis Pasteur has seen with his microscope tiny organisms that exist on surgical instruments. Pasteur calls his discovery the germ theory. Could it be my common sense caught this years ago? I think perhaps so.

I must get some sleep. Another full moon is coming, so there will be three or four births for me to attend to tomorrow. I close my eyes.

CHAPTER TWENTY-SEVEN

MAY 1880

7:00 AM

Throwing a shawl over my nightgown, I hurry to answer the early morning rap at the front door.

Molly.

"Mary, get dressed. Dr. Forsythe sent a messenger to my house. Nellie's water broke."

Confused, I stammer, "N-no, not-not yet."

She grabs me by the shoulder. "I said her water broke."

We tie the horse to the wagon and race to the hospital, heading straight to the birthing floor. The elevator is slow in coming, so we take the two sets of stairs on foot. Molly knows her way around since she trained here. When we arrive on the third floor, we see Sean, looking haggard.

"What time did her water break?" Molly asks.

"About an hour ago. At first, I thought she'd peed herself, but she's in labor now. Will the baby be all right?"

Molly tries to reassure him but I wonder why this baby is coming early. *Stress? Alcohol?* She's gained only ten pounds, and

I worry things may go poorly for the wee one. Tiny babies often don't survive infancy. I mustn't voice my fears, though, because speaking them might drive me mad.

Molly seeks to reassure her brother. I tell him sometimes these things happen and that everything will be all right. Praying as I say the words that they will be true.

We are not allowed in the birthing room, so we wait and watch the minutes tick by on the round clock on the wall. How I yearn to be with Nellie right now; to breathe with her; to rub her back.

Morning becomes afternoon, and then evening, and still no word on her condition. Dr. Forsythe darts in and out, nodding silently as he goes. Finally, Molly scribbles a note and asks a nurse to take it to him. Again, we wait.

Twenty minutes later, the nurse returns. "Dr. Forsythe says that Mrs. O'Halloran is doing fine. He will allow Miss O'Halloran to come in for a few minutes, but no one else."

Molly rises and says, "I'm sorry, Mary. He's a stickler for protocol. I'll come back when I know something."

I sit here with Sean, feeling awkward as always. He takes out his pocket watch repeatedly and checks the time.

Finally, the silence between us defeats me. "Are you supposed to be somewhere, Sean?"

"Yes, I promised to meet the aldermen at eight for dinner at the Club."

"I'm sure they'll understand your absence when they find out why."

He doesn't answer, just looks at his watch again.

The silence continues until Molly comes out of the confinement area. "She's fine. Dr. Forsythe just gave her laudanum." Though her words are reassuring, her expression is not.

"Well, how long is it going to be?" Sean asks impatiently.

"There's no way to know that, Sean. Babies don't honor schedules."

He looks angry and huffs, "I need to get a cup of coffee."

When he leaves us, I turn to Molly. "Tell me what's happening."

Her forehead creases in a frown. "Forsythe doesn't know crap. I asked to check her for dilation, but he refused. I don't think he even knows the process of dilation."

"Is he getting her up to walk around?"

"No, he just wants her to lie flat in bed."

My nerves scream. She should be moving, walking, squatting, getting onto her hands and knees. If I were with her, I'd make her do that and try to open her up gently with oil. But I'm not with her, and the stupid doctor won't let me be there.

"Does he have ether or chloroform?"

"He doesn't believe in using them. Calls childbirth 'The Curse of Eve.' Damned fool."

"Is he using any scented oils to relax her?"

"No, Mary. He's doing nothing for her but the laudanum."

My child is suffering. I know ways to help her, but I am unable to use them. I start to weep. This hurts beyond physical pain.

Sean comes back in the room. He says, "I'm going to take a break for a bit. Meet the aldermen for dinner. Then I'll be back."

I will be glad for his absence because his presence makes me nervous. And although his words are a relief, I'm surprised at them.

Molly isn't. "Yes, go on your way. We'll stay here."

He strides off without another word. My shoulders relax.

Molly says. "I'm going to get us something to eat. We need our strength. This may be a long night."

"I don't know if I can eat anything."

"Mary, you must. I know you're worried, but you cannot go without food. Not tonight."

I nod, accepting her wisdom. She's right. I must keep my strength about me. As she disappears down the stairs, my thoughts turn dark. What if the baby is too small? What if Nellie doesn't survive? Many women die in childbirth. What if Nellie is one of them? How can I live with myself if that happens, knowing that perhaps I could have helped her? I want to storm in there, dismiss Dr. Forsythe, and take charge, but I cannot.

I stand and begin to pace. *Stop it, Mary. Such thoughts won't help anyone, especially Nellie. Pray. Just pray.* I fall to my knees and fold my hands. *Dear God, don't take my daughter away from me. Protect her and ease her pain. Mary, please intercede for me with your son, Jesus. You know the pain of childbirth. Help my child, please.*

When Molly returns with sandwiches and coffee, she finds me composed.

At ten thirty, we hear the elevator door open and hear someone whistling a familiar tune from a Gilbert & Sullivan operetta that recently played in Boston. A male voice sings "Dear Little Buttercup." Sean plops down on a couch near us, reeking of whiskey and cigars. "Anything yet?" he asks, unable to rightly focus.

We shake our heads.

He puts his feet up on a table in front of the couch. "Then I'm glad I went. The boys laid out the strategy for getting me elected Mayor. It'll be at least ten years, but the plan is solid."

We both nod.

Molly says, "Well, that's just splendid, brother dear."

Missing the sarcasm in her voice, he lies back on the couch and goes to sleep.

Molly and I wait quietly. It is after midnight when Dr. Forsythe comes out of the birthing area. "She's had a girl. A big girl! Eight pounds and screaming like an Irish banshee."

I nearly collapse in relief, and Molly starts to weep.

Sean wakens. "A girl?" His disappointment is obvious. "Oh, well. Next time," he slurs and crosses the room to shake Forsythe's hand.

Dr. Forsythe wraps his arm around Sean's shoulders. "Not sure there'll be a next time, lad. She's quite torn up."

My heart catches in my throat. "What? How is my daughter?"

"She's sleeping. Lost quite a bit of blood. We'll need to give her some." He turns to leave us.

I grab his arm. "Wait!" I say, startling him. Once in Ireland, a midwife gave the blood of a horse to a woman who had hemorrhaged during childbirth. The woman seized and died. It was a terrible and painful death. "Where will you get the blood?"

"From a person who recently died. It's common practice." His attitude is dismissive.

"Doctor Forsythe, I want to give her my blood," I say. "Take it from my arm and put it into Nellie's."

He stumbles over his next words. "A-hum, I've never done that."

Molly jumps forward, offering, "I'll do it, but I won't use your blood, Mary. There's a new technique using a saline solution that's been successful." She turns me away and whispers. "Half of patients die after receiving blood from another human."

She's right. I've seen it myself.

While Dr. Forsythe adjusts his white coat, clearly resenting the intrusion of two women, Sean agrees to let his sister do the saline treatment, and we are all allowed to see Nellie. She is pale as parchment, but smiles when we enter the room. "Mam, I have a little girl."

"Yes, love, and I cannot wait to meet her."

After the saline procedure, we leave Nellie to sleep. Sean had gone home earlier. My daughter looks so worn that I hate to leave. But then, Molly suggests, "Let's go to the nursery."

Tiny baby girl O'Halloran lies there behind the glass, her miniscule chest rising and falling rhythmically under the blanket. She is perfect, just perfect, and her color is good. Molly and I clutch each other's hands and breathe sighs of relief. There are two babies in the nursery, one a big, hearty boy. Suddenly, he screams and Kathleen starts a little, opening her wee mouth as if to protest but then falls back asleep. She is beautiful in a new-baby way . . . and the spitting image of Derry O'Byrne.

The next morning when I visit Nellie, she's holding her baby, trying to force her breast into the miniature rosebud of a mouth. Nellie's cheeks have pinked up reassuringly. She is very sore and tired, but I have grand hopes she will recover. *Thank you, Mary, Mother of God.*

CHAPTER TWENTY-EIGHT

After a long lying-in at the hospital, now early June, Nellie and her infant go home. Sean agrees to let me stay and help her with the baby. Especially since that dour Mrs. O'Keefe tells him she cannot take on the extra work of a newborn.

I know I'm prejudiced, but that baby girl is the prettiest newborn I've ever seen. And I've seen a lot of them. Light brown fuzz covers her head, and her heart-shaped face and pursing mouth speak of beauty down the road.

For once, Sean and I agree on something—the baby's name. Baptized at six weeks, weighing nearly ten pounds, she is called Kathleen after Sean's mother, my beloved friend. Oh, Lord, how I wish dear Kathleen was here to see this child. She's perfect. And what a scream on her! With the banshee blood in my family, I do worry a bit about that. But it makes me grin. Truly, I relish that loud wail; one of strength and good solid demanding. Something every woman should learn how to do.

Nellie, on the other hand, remains listless. The birth was diffi-cult, and I agree with Dr. Forsythe that perhaps it should be her last. I'm so grateful she survived it and that Molly's saline solu-tion worked.

* * *

On the first Tuesday in October, while removing my cloak after a long day at The Haven, a knock comes at my front door. I'm not expecting anyone. A young postman stands there, a letter in his hand. I grab my bag and give him two cents for the delivery. As always, he says it's not necessary to pay him, but mail delivery is a luxury I've enjoyed since the War Between the States, and I do appreciate not having to make a trip to the post office.

I take the letter and wish him a good evening. The envelope is tattered and torn with a return address of London's HM Prison Brixton. I don't recognize the handwriting on the envelope and am confounded for a moment, but only for a moment. It is addressed to Miss Nellie Kelly. *Oh, God.* My head swims and I clutch at the doorframe to steady myself.

After fixing a cup of tea, I sit down, the letter in my hand. *What should I do?* Logic tells me to give it to Nellie, but my heart says no. She wants to learn to love Sean. I sit there for a long fifteen minutes pondering. Finally, I open the letter.

Nellie, my dearest love,

I was drugged on the ship by the English and kidnapped to London by lifeboat. I tried to write sooner, but had to bribe a guard to get this letter in the mail. I am in Brixton Prison in London, awaiting trial for treason against Great Britain. They stole all the money. This place is a hellhole. I have no idea how long my sentence will be.

Nellie, please know how much I love you. I always will and pray we will be together again someday.

Yours forever,
Derry

As I read his words, tears flow for dear, desperate Derry. This is what I feared might happen to him. Irish Americans know about Brixton. It's a crater of English cruelty. A friend of Daniel's died there of the dysentery a few years past. He was arrested and tried for calling Queen Victoria a homely goat. God only knows what they might do to Derry. As I weep for the happy young Irish lad I'd come to love, I think of Nellie. *Good God, how can I tell her of this letter? How can I tell her that this man she loved with all her heart and whose baby she bore is in Brixton Prison?*

Stop it, Mary Kelly. Destroy this letter. Let your daughter fall in love with her husband. Let them live together in peace with the wee babe he believes is his. Yes, that's the right thing to do.

At the stove, I light a kitchen match. I hold it until it burns down nearly into my finger. Feeling the pain, I blow it out and stand there with the black stub staring at the letter. Why didn't I burn it? I'll do it later, I tell myself, after I talk to Kam. I carry the letter to my bedroom, then walk to Daniel's desk. I can almost see him sitting there working on a brief. After he died, the nuns cleaned the desk out for me. I just couldn't stand to open it. Startled, I hear his voice. *"Mary, do nothing now. Wait until your mind is clearer. No rash decisions, love."*

My eyes dart around the room. Did I really hear him? It sounded so clear, and the words were those he would have said. I know that. Breathing deeply, I open the front of the desk and see an old tintype. It's of me and Daniel on our wedding day. I hadn't seen it in years. Perhaps Daniel kept it there to look at when he was working. The nuns must have saved it, knowing that someday I'd treasure seeing it again. Tears fill my eyes. We look so young, so happy. Him with the starched collar he hated and me with a crown of wildflowers. So much love. I find a blue ribbon that Daniel used to tie in my hair and wind it around the picture and the letter. Before I close the desk, I kiss the picture and whisper, "Daniel, my love, please help me decide what to do."

* * *

For the next few weeks, I stew about my decision, then determine I need to talk to Kam about it. We sit together on the loveseat in his parlor sharing a pot of tea. Logs blaze in the hearth. His arm encircles my shoulder and his fingers caress my arm. It's mid-November, cold in Boston, and the warmth of the fire bolsters my courage to share my dilemma.

"Kam, I need your counsel."

"What is it, dearest?"

I hand him the letter. He reads it slowly, looks down at me, and reads it a second time. Finally, he folds it and hands it back to me.

"What should I do with it?" My eyes search his. "I tried to ask the same of Daniel, but . . ."

"I think if Daniel was still alive, he'd say this. 'You must tell Nellie. It's her right to know.'"

"I don't think I can. I want her marriage to work out. This could wreck everything."

His dark eyes turn angry. I haven't seen him look so harsh since he told me to stop crying on the coffin ship when I was thirteen. He was right then. Weakness could have gotten both of us killed. Now, I'm not sure he understands.

I touch his cheek to deflect the irritation on his face. "She wants to love her husband. She says he's kind to her, but I'm not sure she's telling the truth. He appears to worship little Kathleen. I fear if Nellie knows Derry's alive, it could destroy this marriage, Kam."

He shakes his head, frustrated, and removes his arm from my shoulder as he turns to face me. I shiver in the sudden loss of his warmth.

"You're making a bad mistake, Mary. I feel it in my bones.

You can't play God with another woman's life, and Nellie *is* a woman, not just your daughter. She deserves to know the truth so that her life decisions are hers alone."

Although I somewhat anticipated this response, his words anger me. "And if she decides to leave Sean and wait for Derry for the next ten years? The court will take Kathleen away from her. And even if they don't, how's she going to support herself and a baby?"

He begins to pace the room, his hands clasped behind his back. In spite of the warmth of the fire, I tremble from the cold. "You know that I will support your daughter and be happy doing it. You should have told me about her pregnancy. Instead, you and Molly ginned up this sham of a marriage. Sean O'Halloran is not a good man. He may be ambitious, but he's not good enough for Nellie, and you know it."

Of course, I know it. In spite of her grand house and adorable baby, she hasn't the look of a well-loved woman; that radiance that comes from satisfaction and knowing you're in exactly the place you're meant to be and with the person God intended for you. In all my years of attending young mothers, I've learned to recognize that look. And when it's there, it is beautiful to behold. Can things change with Sean? Will Nellie ever be happy with him? I don't know, but I must not destroy that chance.

My decision comes swiftly now. I will not show her Derry's letter. My fear of what might happen to her eclipses all logic. When Nellie came to Molly and me looking for a solution, I thought of Kam. I knew he'd help us, but some perverse stubbornness stopped me from confiding in him. She's my child, after all, not his. Mine and Daniel's. I deliberately ignored all Kam had done for us through the years—keeping Kathleen's Haven afloat in financially difficult times, buying Nellie's first horse and carriage, teaching her all he knew about African medicine, loving her as much as any father could. I had shut him out although I knew he would have helped us. And I know this was because of my perverse envy of him. *Yes, envy.*

I became jealous soon after we got off the coffin ship in Boston. Kam was able to get a job quickly because Mr. Mendel, owner of the apothecary, thought that having a polite, handsome Negro driving his delivery truck would appeal to the fake abolitionists living in Beacon Hill mansions. He was right. And that's how Kamua Okafor got his start to becoming a millionaire.

Meanwhile, I walked the streets of Boston begging for work. Until Kathleen O'Halloran hired me as a barmaid, all I was offered was prostitution. I felt Negroes were valued more than the Irish in Boston, and I was bitter. Now it's men who are granted all the favors. Many of them have their boots on their women's necks, and it's wrong. Women are smart. I see that every day. But we can't vote. We can't own property without a man to sign the lease. We can't even keep our children if the marriage doesn't work out. I know I shouldn't take my frustration out on Kam. He's not responsible for a society that still suffocates women. But I'm sick of being a second-class citizen.

My resentment exploded when the 15th Amendment was ratified. Kam was over the moon with elation. He had anonymously assisted his friend, Frederick Douglass, in getting the amendment passed. When Susan B. Anthony expressed a sense of betrayal that Douglass hadn't included women, I felt the same. Douglass took a one-thing-at-a-time attitude, and Kam fully supported his thinking. But I didn't and don't to this day. When Kam went to the polling station and cast his first vote, I sat at home weeping with resentment. In my deepest heart, I am a suffragette but won't wear the ugly bloomer outfit.

"I'm going home, Kam." My voice is hard.

He stops pacing. "Are you angry at me? I thought you'd stay the night."

"No, I'm tired." I sweep through the back hall and slam the door on my way out.

Wind has picked up, and it's a frigid night. I tremble with the cold. My shawl is not heavy enough for winter, and I make a mental note to get my warmer one out of the mothballs in the closet.

As I untie my horse from the hitching post behind his house and climb up into my wagon, he comes to me. "Mary, tell me what's wrong, please." His face is plaintive and confused, and I know my anger is misplaced but just don't care.

I put the whip to my horse and pull away without a word. Looking back, I see him still standing there, shivering. As we round the corner that takes us out of the colored neighborhood, candles blaze in some of the Beacon Hill windows. People already have lit them for Christmas and it's not yet Thanksgiving. *What a ridiculous waste of tallow.* Riding along, I start to chide myself for being a witch to Kam. It's not his fault. He's a good man. Someday, things will be different. But when? I whip the horse again.

Leaving the north slope of Beacon Hill, which everyone calls Nigger Hill, I am struck by the modesty of the homes, except for Kam's mansion. Negroes employed by the Brahmins on the south slope live here. What a difference these few blocks display. Nellie lives just a short way from here, and yet it seems another world altogether.

I decide to ride by her house. If I see light inside, perhaps I'll drop in and see her and the baby.

My journey takes only ten minutes. There it is, the white mansion. A perverse pride assails me as I look at it. Silk Stocking Irish now outnumber the Shanty Irish. We have come quite a way in this one generation. Sugar maples and red oak trees surround the sides of the house and a sweeping lawn flows up to the delightful rocking chairs on the front porch. Light twinkles softly through the leaded windows, making this place the image of elegant living.

How can I interfere with all this? And that's what I'd be doing if I tell her about Derry. Should I go to the door? I'd love to peek in on baby Kathleen, but I don't want to intrude. Nellie says Sean's gone to political meetings most nights, so maybe she'd welcome my company. Silently, I pull my wagon up to the front hitching post. It looks ridiculous in these grand surroundings, but people will likely think it belongs to a servant.

I tie up the horse and step down to the street. I'll just go up and look in the window. If Sean's home, I'll leave and they'll not know the difference. Trembling as I open the gate, I pull my shawl tighter around my shoulders. Silently creeping like a burglar, I walk up to the porch. The lawn under my feet feels springy and cushioned. The house towers before me, beautiful and inviting, a glorious place for little Kathleen to grow up in. When I think of the hovel I left in Ireland, I am proud that my daughter and grandbaby have come to such luxury. America is truly a magical place.

Almost at the house, I pause to enjoy the vision once again. Startled suddenly, I hear sounds familiar from my childhood. *What is it?* I remember. Moans like a woman keening. It takes me back to funerals in Ireland and a familiar sense of despair. *Should I leave?* Just as I turn to go, the weeping begins again, soft and lamenting. I follow the sound to the porch. Peering through the ornate balustrades, I see Nellie.

She sits in the rocker nearest the steps wearing only a dirty white nightgown. Her dark hair is tangled and unruly. Her head is in her hands, and the sound of her desolation rends my heart in two. I run up the stairs and kneel before her. "Nellie, love, what is it? You'll freeze out here."

Startled, she turns her tear-stained face up to me. She doesn't look like Nellie any more. Gaunt and blotched, she is a caricature of her former self.

I smell liquor.

"Tell me," I say earnestly.

"It's nothing, Mam."

"What do you mean, nothing? Tell me. I mean it."

She stands, swaying like a sapling. "I've got to check on the baby."

She turns to go inside, and I follow her, closing the door behind me.

"The baby's fine. She's asleep. Nellie, what is it? What's wrong with you?"

She hesitates, weighing whether to answer. I almost expect her to dash away to the foyer and up the stairs to get away from me. Her face finally eases into repose. "It's Sean."

I knew it even before she says it, but need to hear the truth from her own lips. This time, platitudes won't work. I want facts. "You told me he's good to you; that he loves the baby."

She lets loose a funereal cackle. "He loves the baby all right! It's me he can't stand!"

I put my arm around her waist and lead her to the living room. "Is he home?"

"Nah, he's never home."

"Sit down here," I say, as I place her in a comfortable chair. "I'm going to check on Kathleen."

I run up the staircase to the nursery. There she lies, all pink perfection, her mouth moving in a sucking dream. So dear, so sweet. I want to pick her up to cuddle, but I have a different girl to protect this night. I close the door to the nursery softly behind me and go down the staircase.

"She's fine, sound asleep," I say to the wreck known as my child limp in the chair. "Now, tell me what's going on."

For a minute, I see the fire of the old Nellie. There's anger in her eyes. "It's not your business, M . . . a . . . m." Her last word sounds like a slur, which enflames my Irish temper.

"Yes, it is, Missy," I say, kneeling before her. "You will always be my business—and don't you forget it—just like that baby upstairs will always be yours."

She looks toward the staircase. "Are you sure she's alright? She doesn't usually sleep this long."

"I'm sure. She'll soon be sleeping through the night, that's all. Count your lucky stars."

Nellie relaxes back in the chair.

"Now tell me. What's going on with Sean?"

"Ha! What isn't?"

"Other women?"

She smirks and gives me the "What do you think?" eye.

"Maybe you're mistaken. He seems enamored of you."

Eyes wide, she exclaims, "Oh yes, in public! If he is enamored of me, why did he move out of our bedroom? Why does he say I'm no longer pretty? Why does he never touch me unless he's drunk?"

I want to scream *That bastard!* But I must help this situation, not worsen it, so I swallow my true feelings and calm my racing heart. "Well, darling, there could be another reason. Sometimes, after a woman has a baby, the husband is afraid he'll hurt her or get her pregnant again." Even as I say the words, I don't believe them. Sean is not that sensitive.

Nellie cocks her head and places her hands on her hips. "Then how did I get a venereal disease?"

Oh, blessed saints! No! Please God, don't let it be syphilis. I had a patient last year who died of mercury poisoning after she contracted syphilis because some quack told her mercury would cure her. I must know. I take her hand. "Is it syphilis, Nellie?"

"No, just a nasty disease that itches like crazy and embarrassed me half to death when Dr. Forsythe diagnosed it. He actually asked if I'd had other partners than Sean since our marriage. Didn't even flinch when I said it must be Sean." Her head wags side to side. "Have you noticed how men excuse tomcat behavior in each other? Puff each other up and act like it's sort of a badge of honor?" She shudders still ice cold to the touch.

Yes, I've noticed. Some men, though, not decent men. Not men with any sense of honor about themselves. "What do you intend to do about it, love?"

She stands up and goes to a whiskey decanter on the table, pours a glass and swallows it quickly.

I bite my tongue.

"Mam, it's my word against his. I need proof. No court in this state would believe me. They might take Kathleen."

"Where is Sean now?"

"At his club, I think."

"Let's go there."

She jumps like a startled animal. "We can't do that. They wouldn't let us in. And, I can't leave the baby." She settles back in her chair like a cowed dog, which really raises my temper. Where did my spunky daughter go? The girl who'd tell a gobshite like Sean to hit the bloody trail.

"If I can get Kam to come here and watch the baby?"

I can see her mind working. Fearful but a stitch more lucid. "Would Uncle Kam do it?"

"Ah, yes, my girl. I think he'd love the opportunity. Can you squeeze him a bottle of milk in case she awakens?"

"And how I can! Right now, I'm full to bursting."

Relief flows through me like the Shannon itself. Maybe it's not too late. Maybe my Nellie will find a way out of this mess. That would help the guilt I feel, knowing I was part of plotting it. I should have known better. I did know better but took the coward's way out.

I just wish I hadn't left Kam in such a pissy huff. Now I'll have to make up with him first. To tell the truth, I'm grateful for an excuse to go back there. Already, I miss the man.

Standing at his front door, I arm myself for rejection. Why did I have to be such a snot when I left earlier?

The door inches open, and there he stands, arms crossed over his chest. "Yes?" is all he says.

I push past him into the foyer, relishing the firmness of his arm under the soft velvet evening jacket. In spite of my worry, I think, If this visit wasn't urgent, I would get that jacket off of him in a flash. Maybe later.

"I know I was rude before, and I'm sorry, Kam. I'm so worried about Nellie that it's turning me into a nasty *soith*."

His forehead creases in confusion. "*Soith*?"

"Sorry, that's Irish for bitch." He knows that when I'm rattled, I confuse what language I'm supposed to be speaking. I take his hand and lead him back to the study. Then, sitting beside him on the settee, I rest my head against his shoulder. I look up at him and whisper, "I'm truly sorry, love."

He huffs, but his body softens some. "You should be. You acted crazy."

"I know. I know. I think that beastly attitude came from years of resentment."

"Resentment? Of me?" He pulls away from me and again crosses his arms defensively. "Why do you resent me? And why would you not tell me?"

Stuttering, I stammer a rush of words. "I didn't tell you because it was foolish. Jealousy between friends usually is. But, in truth, Kam, I have resented you. Like when you got that job so easily with Mr. Mendel and I had to ask you for rent money."

"And?"

My mind scurries for an answer, and when it comes to me, I get vexed again. "And when you came over and told me you'd voted for the first time. You were gloating. You and your good pal, Frederick Douglass, who knifed the suffragettes in the back. Susan Anthony could not forgive him for that, and neither could I."

"Frederick knew they'd never get both things through Congress. Women have to wait their turn."

Wait our turn? I feel the banshee in me wanting to erupt, so I take a deep breath and soften my tone. "Wait our turn? And when do you think our turn might come? Will I ever get to see it? All my life, I've prayed for my home country to win freedom from England. Now that I live in a free country, must I grovel to earn the right to control my life in it? It's wrong, Kam." I pause to swallow the tears threatening me. "I know you're not responsible, but sometimes it's hard not to resent you." By the end of my diatribe, I can scarcely breathe.

He uncrosses his arms and leans toward me, dark eyes blazing. His voice is soft but dangerous. "Did you resent me when I was nearly hanged by those pale-assed murderers following the fucking white man's Fugitive Slave Act? When you and Kathleen had to dress the wounds from their whips? Did you resent me then, Mary Boland? You with your snowy white skin and red hair? Were you jealous then?"

My mouth falls open, shocked. Kam never uses profanities, but now I realize he, too, has deep resentments. And hatred. His vehemence releases my tears. As they course down my cheeks, I say, "Kam, I'm sorry. I truly am. I'd forgotten what you've had to endure in this country. I've been so busy feeling sorry for myself I ignored the pain your dark skin has caused you, even as I saw people rejecting you for it."

His eyes blaze anew and his response is through clinched teeth, "I love my dark skin. I come from a dark family with more pride in their heritage than any of these snobs on Beacon Hill or any red-haired mick." He is as close to screaming as I've ever heard him. The calm, reasonable Kam I love is gone. He storms over to the fireplace, standing with his back to me.

How could I have not known how damaged this man has been by the cruelty of prejudice? He'd put on such a good front all the years I'd known him. Filled with a pity new and devastating, I go to the fireplace and put my arms around him. Even as he twists away, I hold him firmly to my body. "I'm sorry, love. So sorry." As I continue to murmur words of love into his ear, I feel his rigid posture ease. When he stops trembling, I take his hands and look into his eyes. "I do love you."

After a long time of staring into my eyes, he puts his arms around me and whispers, "And I love you. I guess with all the excitement and passion of finding each other, we've neglected a much-needed conversation."

I nod. "And we'll have it, darling. But first," deep breath, "I need a favor."

My timing couldn't have been worse, but I had to get to why I was here, and fast. Nellie was waiting.

His body tenses up again. "What kind of favor?"

Kam is suspicious of the word favor because so many people have asked for them. Since he's one of the richest men in Boston, some social climbers, after snubbing him for years, have had the gall to request a loan during tough times. Though he often grants them the favor, I know he resents it. Even as he relishes his power over them.

"It's for Nellie."

He jumps. "Is Nellie all right?"

I hesitate and swallow my tears. "No, not really." I pause to calculate my words. "When I left here earlier, I drove by her house hoping to visit with the baby. I found Nellie sobbing on her front porch. No, she's not all right."

"Where was her husband?"

"God only knows. He might be at his club, but she isn't sure. Apparently, he's rarely at home."

He rubs his temples but does not say he told me so. "So, how can we help?"

His inclusive pronoun warms my heart. "I want her to know where Sean is. It may help her decide what to do, and it will definitely help me decide whether to tell her about Derry's letter."

Disapproval clouds his face. I know he thinks I should have already told her. Finally, though, his concern for Nellie wipes away the frown. "All right, let's go. We'll talk about the details on our way." He goes to a nearby cabinet, bends, and retrieves a large box.

"What's that?" I try to peer around him.

"My newest toy. It came out this year from a company called Kodak. It's a camera with film inside."

"How does it turn into a picture?"

"There's one place now in Boston that develops the film. It takes about a week, and the pictures are splendid."

"Why would you want a camera now?"

"Not sure, but it might come in handy tonight."

We hurry from his house and climb into his carriage. Careening through the dark streets to Nellie's, we make a plan. It starts with Kam saying, "I think I should go with Nellie while you mind the baby. These streets can be dangerous at night for two unescorted women."

I bite my tongue to restrain from saying that it might be dangerous for him to be seen alone at night with a young white woman. In New York, a lynching happened for less reason just last week. Everyone was shocked that such a thing could happen in the northeast.

"Maybe it would be best for the two of us to go, Kam."

He thinks about my suggestion and then responds, "Yes, you're right."

When we arrive at Nellie's, I see that Kathleen has awakened and is finishing her feeding. "Please, let me hold her," I plead. As I cradle the six-month-old infant to my heart, I am overcome with a love unlike anything I've ever felt. She is so soft, so innocent, and smells of cornstarch and that wonderful scent that only emanates from a tiny baby. I never want to let her go until Kam taps my shoulder.

"May I hold her, Nellie?" He has yet to have been allowed to.

"Of course, Uncle Kam. I've told you before I want you to be the grandda she doesn't have."

With reluctance, I release Kathleen into his arms, and the minute I see his face beaming down at her I fall in love all over again. With the baby and with the man. She is so small and white nestled in his strong dark arms, and his face radiates such intense caring for this child it takes my breath away. Family comes in all shapes and colors, and this man loves this baby like a true grandchild.

"I always wanted a little girl," he says. "But after we had Neo, Amani was not able to conceive again. We tried every herb from

Africa and consulted with the finest doctors in this country to no avail. Now I know how that would have felt, and I'm at peace."

I hated to break this lovely spell, but I said, "Nellie, we think it would be best if Kam and I go look for Sean. Is that all right with you?"

She hesitates for a second but answers, "Yes, though I don't know what you'll say if you find him."

"We'll tell him you're not feeling well and that he should come home." The answer had come to me in a flash, and when she nods, I know it was sent by God.

"I am a bit tired," she says "Thank you, Mam, Uncle Kam."

And so it is decided.

We kiss her and the baby good night and return to Kam's carriage. "Let's drive by the club first," I say. "Nellie says he might be there."

CHAPTER TWENTY-NINE

We pull up in front of the Somerset Club. Soft lights beam through leaded windows and the sound of male voices drifts out to the street. It is nearly eleven o'clock now, so the gentlemen inside are probably enjoying an after-dinner cordial in the library.

Kam says, "I can't go in there."

"Nor can I, and we needn't go in. Let's go to the back and see if Sean's carriage is there. I'd know it anywhere." It is an ostentatious solid black four-seater with a huge green shamrock on the side. Although the man disparages his heritage every chance he gets, he knows his future career in politics depends on appearing to embrace it. Ironic, isn't it? My eyebrow arches.

Of the seven carriages behind the Club, not one of them Sean's.

"Now what?" I ask.

"I know a few other possible places he might be. We'll just browse them."

Our journey takes us to neighborhoods I've seldom visited. Boston is a clannish town. The Italians live in the north section, the Poles in a small triangle between Boston and Dorchester

Streets, and the Blacks, of course, on Nigger Hill. The West End is a melting pot of Jews, Lithuanians, Greeks, and every nationality, with a smattering of Blacks, Italians, and, of course, Irish. In truth, the Irish are everywhere now.

As the clock nears one a.m., I see it. There it sits, black as the devil's soul. I look around quite confused. Some houses here are quite grand while others look shabby.

"Where are we, Kam? I've never been here before."

"I would think not, sweetheart. This is Pawnee Street, the red-light district. Many of these places are brothels. See the red lanterns in the windows?"

The number of red lanterns on this block surprises me, especially since the place where Sean's carriage is parked has the brightest one on the street.

"So . . . that means. . . ?"

"It means that your son-in-law frequents a house of ill repute."

So that's how Nellie got the venereal disease. I want to kill her bastard husband. But murder won't solve Nellie's problem. "What can we do?"

"You can't do anything, Mary. But I can."

"How?"

"Let's just say I know some people here. Frankly, my love, you are a liability in this neighborhood. I can't leave you outside while I confront Sean. It's too dangerous. I'll take you to a house in the next block that is respectable. I have friends there."

I begin to protest but stop quickly because he's right. I can't walk into a brothel. He whips the horse gently. and soon we are on the next street where no red lanterns blaze. We pull up in front of a brownstone and Kam goes to the front door, rings the bell, and waits. The Negro man who comes to the door has clearly been asleep, but when he sees Kam, the door opens wide. Kam gestures for me to come to the door.

When I get there, I apologize for disturbing this man at such an ungodly hour, but he is gracious and welcomes us in. A stately black woman comes down the stairs, tall and elegant. She carries herself like a queen. Kam introduces the couple to me and explains the urgency of our visit. Her name is Marion.

The woman, whose hair is wrapped in a purple turban, takes my arm gently and says, "Do come in, Mary. I could use a cup of tea. Will you join me?"

"Indeed, I will, Marion. I've never needed one more than this night."

Kam takes my hands. "I'll be back as soon as I can, Mary. Try not to worry."

Then he thanks his friend and goes back to his carriage.

Marion and her husband, Raymond, could not be more kind. They act as though it is perfectly normal to have their sleep disturbed at such a ridiculous hour; that it is not at all an unusual occurrence. As we drink strong black tea and eat her delicious oatmeal cookies, I feel obliged to explain the situation to them.

Raymond says, "Don't let this whole thing trouble you too much, Mary. Lots of politicians frequent that neighborhood. Not that it's right, but it happens."

His explanation is not comforting. "Perhaps they do, but only one of them is married to my daughter—only one is destroying her health, mentally and physically—and that one is the father of my adorable granddaughter." Even as I say the words, I think, *Not the real father, thank God.* "So, how do you know Kam?"

Raymond answers, "Mr. Okafor loaned us the money to buy this house. We bless him every day."

"Yes, we do," Marion says. "And pay him back a little each month, just like clockwork."

She is such a proud woman. I like her immensely. "Do you know how Kam and I know each other?" *Might they suspect we're lovers?*

Raymond chuckles. "Yes, we do. He talks about you a lot. About how you met as children on that coffin ship; how you saved each other's lives back then. The best story is about how you turned yourself into something called a banshee and scared the pants off those sailors. Lordy, how I'd loved to have seen that."

In spite of my worries about Nellie, my eyes crinkle at the thought. "Truth be told, I think I scared Kam as much as the sailors. You should have seen his face. He nearly turned white with fright."

Although I can see from his raised eyebrows and the upward tilt of her head that they are uncertain how to respond to my joke, it does eventually set the three of us chortling like old friends.

After we finish our tea, they place a pillow and blanket on a couch in their front room.

"Now you just get yourself some rest," Marion says. "You've had a tough time tonight, and it's not over yet. Save your strength."

She covers me with the blanket and tucks it around my shoulders. Before she leaves, I take her hand. "Thank you, Marion. You've been a real friend. And so very kind."

"Well, I should hope so, Mary. I like to take care of people. I was a field nurse in the war before I married Raymond. Now that the children are older, I'm interviewing to go back to work. Besides, any friend of Mr. Okafor's is my friend, too." She pats me on the shoulder and goes up the stairs.

I know I won't sleep, but feel warmed by the kindness of this couple I'd not have met were it not for the awful situation of this day. *Life is strange.* I must remember that. In the midst of our worst times, there are blessings to be gleaned. Friends to be made.

CHAPTER THIRTY

As the grandfather clock strikes twice, a knock at the front door rouses me from my dozing. I jump to my feet and hurry to open it. It's Kam. One look tells me what he saw in the brothel.

"What happened?" I ask, fearful of the answer.

"He's there. The madame told me which room, and when I quietly cracked the door open, I saw them."

My heart beats so fast I can hardly ask, "Them?"

"Yes, he was in bed with a girl named Carla. I've heard stories about Carla. She's well known in Boston for the spectacular prowess of her tongue."

The image of my son-in-law enjoying that prowess sickens me.

"Were they startled? What did they do?"

"Both were sleeping, but the smell of sex in that room nearly sickened me. Because of Nellie. I tiptoed to their bed, threw off the covers, and snapped a picture of their naked bodies."

"Oh, my god, Kam."

He grimaces. "You should have seen Sean's face when he realized what was happening. He was dumbstruck and mad as hell. He jumped out of bed and tried to wrestle the camera away from me . . . unsuccessfully." He takes me into his arms. "But Carla just stretched and invited me to join them."

"And were you tempted, Kam?" In spite of everything, I am jealous.

"I declined. But you know what? I think what they say about white men is correct."

In spite of myself, I laugh.

Marion and Raymond come quietly down the steps, and we break away from our embrace. "Need any help, Mr. Okafor?"

"No, no, folks. We'll be on our way now. Thanks for taking care of Mary."

Marion comes over and kisses me on the cheek. "I wish we could meet sometime for a cup of tea, but that wouldn't be proper, would it?"

"I suppose it would raise a few eyebrows in Boston. But maybe that's just what this town needs. Let's have tea at the Clarke Tea Room in Quincy Market. How about Wednesday?"

Genuinely sincere, she says, "I'll be there. Three o'clock, all right?"

"Should be, unless someone at The Haven is in labor. If that's the case, I'll send you a note."

The ride to Kam's is quiet, both of us mired in our thoughts. I wish I could check in on Nellie, but Kam had told Sean to high-tail it home immediately; that Nellie wasn't feeling well. After being caught in such an embarrassing situation, I think Sean is probably afraid to disobey Kam's directive. And besides, I certainly don't want to see Sean tonight, if ever again.

When we arrive at his place, he invites me in, and I accept. The comfort of his arms is a healing balm to my heart and soul.

When our passion is sated, I say, "I so needed you tonight, my love. Some things must remain normal lest I fall into hopelessness over what's happening to Nellie."

He cradles me and exhaustion finally lulls me to sleep, but two hours later my eyes fly open, my brain racing with images of Sean and his harlot. For all I know, he might be giving her another, possibly deadly, venereal disease right now. I truly hate the man. If I tell Nellie what Kam saw or show her the pictures, what could she do about it? Perhaps have the sacrament of marriage nullified in the Church. Sean never intended fidelity even as he pledged it on the altar of St. Augustine's. And though Nellie has tried to make her marriage work, it was an act of desperate deception from the start, so she shares some blame, too. As do I.

If she files for divorce, the Massachusetts courts will certainly side with Sean, no matter the evidence of the photo. He's politically well connected. He'll have every Democrat who owes him a favor swearing to his sterling character.

Five years ago, my patient, Mamie Connelly, sued to divorce her drunken, abusive husband, James. The Boston court granted the divorce but awarded the husband custody of their five young children. Because she loved her children, she stayed with James. He murdered her three years later in a sottish rage. Today, James is free as a bird, buying drinks for all his boy'os in the local pubs.

And those five children are without a mother.

My eyes don't close for the rest of the night, but when Kam wakens and tries to kiss me just before dawn, I pretend to sleep. As the sun rises, I climb quietly from the bed, trying not to wake him, then go into the bathroom where I wash up. When I walk back into the bedroom, dressed, Kam is awake and leaning on one elbow.

"What do you intend to do, Mary?" he asks.

"Nothing, until I see the pictures. Then, I'll decide."

He eyes me warily. "Are you stalling?"

Am I? "Maybe. But without evidence, it would be our word against his, and you know how that would turn out. I want to see those pictures."

"All right. But I cannot get them developed in Boston. Someone would spread the gossip. I'll take the train to Pittsfield. There's a developer there, too." He beckons me to come back to bed.

"I can't, Kam. I must get to The Haven. Molly will be there today, and maybe she can help me decide what I should do."

He stands, naked and beautiful. For a moment, I want nothing more than to walk back to him, but he destroys the moment. "Isn't Molly the one who dreamed up this horrible marriage in the first place?"

"That's not fair. We all decided we had no other option."

"Like coming to me?" He pulls on a pair of pants, glaring.

"At the time, that didn't feel like a possibility. I was wrong, but it was my decision. Molly had nothing to do with it."

He buttons his pants, stretches, then comes over and takes me in his arms. My desire to stay with him returns as I share his need for closeness. But he backs away, saying, "Very well. But promise me you'll let me be part of any actions going forward. You know that I love Nellie like a daughter. Please allow me to help with your decisions about her."

He is so dear, so steadfast that, as I pivot to leave, I rush back into his arms and say, "I do promise that. I need your wisdom. I've tried so hard to be independent all these years, and I must loosen those stubborn reins when it comes to you. I trust you, Kam, and love you with all my heart."

CHAPTER THIRTY-ONE

The next week lasts forever. Insomnia plagues my nights and my busy hours at The Haven drag by in a torpor of exhaustion and indecision. I must do something, but what that should be changes faster than the weather in Ireland. I haven't seen Nellie since that fateful night. Nor have I written to her. She must wonder where Kam and I found her husband, but is probably fearful to ask. What cowards we women are! What fools! And I am the worst of them all. After Kam shows me the pictures tonight, I'll know what to do. But will I do it?

What happened to that brave young girl who saved herself from starvation? Who got herself onto a coffin ship out of Ireland? Who survived rape and discrimination and built The Haven against all odds? What happened to her?

She had a child, that's what.

And as wonderful as that was, I can't find the good in it now. I must talk to Nellie, but what I say to her may destroy her life. There's no good way she can handle this situation. If she divorces him, he'll take Kathleen away from her. If she doesn't divorce him, her life will be a living hell. *Damn him. Damn men. Damn Boston.*

The one bright spot of my week comes when I meet Marion at the appointed time for tea. I arrive early at Clarke's and find a table smack dab in the center of the elegant tea room. Perusing the place, I spot Anne Longfellow holding court with several other Brahmin wives, little fingers suitably cocked from their cups and minks draped oh-so casually over the backs of their chairs. Anne is doing all the talking. I cock my ear and overhear what she's saying.

"White phantom city whose untrodden streets are rivers and whose pavements are the shifting shadows of palaces and strips of sky . . ."

With a burst of prideful joy, I recognize it. It's from her husband's recent poem, "Venice." I read an excerpt of it in *The Globe*.

The tearoom hushes. I spy Marion at the reception. She enters the tea room looking pretty but uncertain. As she tucks an errant piece of hair up into the bun at the nape of her neck, whispers break the quiet. Every perfectly coiffed head turns in shock as I rush to greet her with a hug and guide her to our table. Gratitude shines in her eyes.

Women's heads touch as they murmur to each other. I imagine what they're saying: How dare that Irish immigrant bring a colored woman here?

I've never felt prouder in my life. "How's Raymond?" I ask.

"Just wonderful, thank you. He has a new position as a butler for Governor Oliver Ames."

"Marion, that's wonderful! You must be thrilled."

"Yes, I am, Mary. He takes the train back and forth every day to North Easton, looking ever so handsome in his black uniform. He says Governor Easton is a real gentleman and treats him well."

"When did Raymond learn to be a butler?"

"Back before the War. He was the head butler of a big planta-tion in Virginia. He always had a way of carrying himself that appealed to white folks."

"Like Kam," I say, smiling.

"Yes, exactly like Mr. Okafor. I think that's why they became such good friends."

She looks around the room, saying softly, "Mary, this place is so stylish, and so . . . so *white*." We squeeze one another's hands in solidarity.

When the waitress arrives, I order high tea for two, then she asks, "How is Mr. Okafor?"

"He's good. I'll see him this evening and tell him you asked."

"Thank you. He's such a fine gentleman, isn't he?" Her eyebrows rise in an unspoken question. It's clear she's curious to know if Kam and I are more than friends.

"Indeed, he is, and I love him very much."

At first, her eyes widen in uncertainty, but then she takes my hand in hers and says, "I'm happy for you, Mary . . . and for him."

As we sit chatting comfortably about her children and everyday life, I am aware of the gawking women around us and am happy to realize I just don't care. They remind me of clucking chickens, whereas Marion appears as an African Queen with her mocha skin and long neck. She is elegance personified. A swan among the hens.

"How did you get to be a field nurse in the War, Marion?"

She holds her hands together in her lap, back straight, and begins, "Well, when I was a girl, my daddy insisted I learn to read and write, so I wouldn't be illiterate like most Negroes back then. I grew up in Pennsylvania, so we weren't a slave family. He worked as a janitor in a hospital there, and when he retired, doctors and nurses held a party to honor him." As she says these words, her face glows with love and pride. "He was a very special man. My mama adored him, and so did all us kids. When I was eight, he got me this book on Florence Nightingale, and I fell in love with her. So, when the war broke out to free the slaves, I wanted to do my part. There was no formal training, but I loved taking care of the poor wounded soldiers, black and white."

I reach across the table and take her hand. "You might have cared for my husband, Daniel Kelly. He was injured in the battle of Shiloh."

"I don't reckon I nursed him, Mary. I stayed mostly in Northern Virginia."

"You must have seen awful things."

Her eyes cloud with memories. "Yes, I did. But I felt I was doing God's work and doing it as well as anyone could, so that made it bearable."

Our tea arrives at our table and is served with aplomb by a handsome young waiter. There are platters of shaved ham and chicken, scones and berry preserves, as well as a brimming bowl of clotted cream circled by tiny cubes of sugar. The waiter pours two cups of strong, dark tea and leaves the table.

"Oh my," Marion says, "isn't this wonderful?"

"It certainly is," I answer as I pick up a scone and ladle on a large spoonful of the cream. "I'd like to do this frequently, Marion. I could use a new friend."

She reaches forward with her hands to grip mine and says, "Me, too, Mary. Me, too."

When we part, we set another date for next month and I hurry back to work.

At six o'clock, Kam pulls his carriage up to the front of The Haven. I say goodnight to the evening staff and climb in, not caring if anyone sees us together. The hell with propriety and

Yankee judgment. In the eyes of Boston, what Sean is doing is sowing his oats while my love for a fine black man like Kam is a scandal. Society's idea of morality is a cockeyed farce, and I'm sick to death of it.

We don't speak until we get away from the busy Boston downtown. As the carriage approaches Beacon Hill, I can stay silent no longer. "Do you have the pictures?"

He gives me the eye.

At the curb of his house, he helps me from the carriage and we walk in the front door together as if it is the most natural thing in the world. I think we are both tired of hiding, of not living our truth.

He pours me a glass of wine in his study.

"Do you think I'll need this?" I ask.

He doesn't answer but takes a packet from his jacket and hands it to me. I take a large sip of wine and slowly unwrap what's inside. There are two pictures. Both are clear as Waterford crystal. In one of them, Sean lies next to a pretty girl, both of them asleep. Their bodies are covered by a blanket. But in the second picture, they are uncovered, their mouths open and eyes wide with shock. And they are naked as the days they were born. In this picture, a used prophylactic is visible on the table next to the bed.

Though I'm somewhat relieved to see the it, I fight the urge to throw up.

"Sean must have lost his mind when he realized what you were doing."

Chuckling, Kam says, "He jumped from the bed and tried to wrestle the camera out of my hands, swearing a blue streak, but I held on to it and shoved his skinny ass right to the floor." His grin is smug. "Then I told him to high tail it home before I called the police."

"Oh, Kam, thank you. What would I do without you?"

"That's something I hope you'll never have to find out, Mary."
He rises and walks across the study to the fireplace where he
stands with his back to me, hands clasped behind his back. For
some reason, his posture unnerves me.

"What is it, Kam?"

He turns to face me. "There's something I haven't told you
and you need to know." As my shoulders stiffen and my breath
grows shallow, I brace myself for another catastrophe.

"Don't look stricken, my love. This isn't bad news. Take a
couple of deep breaths and try to relax." He comes back, sits
down, and kneads the knot between my shoulder blades.

As he feels me ease, he says, "Neo knows everything that has
happened here. Both Nellie and I have written him regularly and
kept it secret from you. He and Angelique have visited Derry in
prison several times and told him what's happened to Nellie."

I whip around, back straight, at first riled that the two most
important people in my life have kept me in the dark about all
this, but then sweet relief washes away my dander. I don't have
to worry about writing to Derry. Neo's taken care of that for me.
Keeping Derry's letter from Nellie has troubled me. "I'm glad
they know."

"Thank God you see this as a good thing, Mary. Neo and
Derry are close friends, you know, and Neo loves Nellie like a
sister. He's a good intermediary for us across the pond, so you
needn't feel the weight of this problem rests on you alone."

"You're right. I need all the help I can get right now. Please
write Neo and thank him for what he has done and whatever he
can do." I sit back and take a sip of my wine. "By the way, how
are he and Angelique doing in Ireland?"

"Great, I think. They're happy as can be and they've made a
good deal of money with the magic show. They bought a house

in Galway and are talking about expanding their family once Neo finds a girl to take Angelique's part in the act. If she does get pregnant, neither of them wants her to continue on the road."

The good news restores me. At least one of our children is having good luck; the luck of the Irish, so to speak. Lots of people worried when the two of them decided to live in Ireland, but I knew it would be all right. I never heard the word "nigger" spoken in Ireland.

"Neo is also busy volunteering with a man named William O'Brien on something called Home Rule."

"How wonderful! That cause has been going on for years. My da was a Fenian, and their goal was to kick the English out of Ireland, too. I wonder how they're doing with it. I'm afraid it's going to take a long time for my country to be free of those limey bastards."

"They're taking a slow, smart approach. Neo helped O'Brien organize a rent strike last year. More than eight thousand Irish tenants rose up against their English landlords, demanding their homesteads be returned to them. They're making progress, one step at a time."

"Good for Neo. Sometimes, I wish I were there helping out with the cause. England has had their heels on Irish necks for centuries. It's time for change." I slap my thigh and guffaw.

"What's so funny?" he asks.

"I guess Neo brings new meaning to the term 'black Irish,' doesn't he?"

CHAPTER THIRTY-TWO

I don't see Nellie for twelve days. In truth, I can't imagine what we'll say to each other, her knowing what I know about her husband. Surely, Sean must have told her. He'd be afraid of me telling her first. Finally, the need to see my girl forces me into my carriage. I pull it in front of the big white house and tie up the horse. It's a Wednesday at one o'clock, a time Sean will typically be in court or at a business lunch.

Mrs. O'Keefe answers my ring in her typical stiff-necked manner. I stand very straight and glare right back at her. "Is my daughter at home?"

"Yes, ma'am. I'll take you to the parlor and tell her you're here."

Her back is ramrod straight as she goes up the stairs. Even from the back, I feel a certain disapproval from the woman. *To hell with her.*

I sit there studying the elegant room for fifteen minutes. It's quite grand, but I question whether Nellie had any part in its decorating. It doesn't look like her taste. Maroon silk covers three of its walls and the floors are a rich mahogany. The fourth wall is lined with bookcases, and books fill every shelf. I hope someone in this house reads them, and they're not there just to impress Sean's important visitors. I walk over and study the spines. There are two books by Henry James and one called *A Doll's House* by Henrik Ibsen. I pull a volume from the shelf that features on its cover a stuffy, mutton-chopped old man. It's called *An Introduction to the Principles of Morals and Legislation*. Must be Sean's. I figure it's there for show. Principles of morals certainly don't appear to be his cup of tea.

As I return the heavy tome to its place on the shelf, Nellie opens the door. "Mam!" she calls out as she comes to me and holds me in a long embrace. She is so thin that I feel her ribs through her day dress. When she finally pulls away, I notice dark circles under her blue eyes that were not there before.

I vow to not dwell on these changes today. I'm so happy to see her again, and I shan't say anything that might ruin this time between us.

She takes my hand and leads me to a settee. "Mrs. O'Keefe is bringing us tea," she says. "I'm glad to see you."

When we're seated, I ask, "How are you, love? And how's that beautiful baby girl? Will I see her today?"

"She's wonderful, Mam. Asleep right now, but should be waking soon. You'll hear her when she does, trust me. I think Miss Kathleen will either be an opera singer or an auctioneer someday. That girl has quite a mouth on her. And she's stubborn as can be. Surely, she gets that from her grandmother."

My brain scrambles ways to navigate the imposing issue I'm certain we're both aware of. Sean. I'm certain she knows where Kam found him. And if so, does she care? *Again, mind your tongue, Mary Boland.*

After Mrs. O'Keefe leaves us a tea tray, we busy ourselves with pouring and sugaring our cups, then sitting back to sip them. It seems a good time to ask the question. "And how's Sean?" Certainly, that's a simple, logical inquiry. She is his wife after all.

She peers over her cup at me before answering, "Same as ever, Mam. Busy as a beaver and charming as a serpent."

My breath catches in my throat, and a choking sound escapes my mouth.

"Are you all right?"

I wipe around my chin with a napkin and answer. "Why, sure I am. Just swallowed wrong or something." I guess I can't ignore the issue after all. "Why do you say that, Nellie?"

Mirthlessly she says, "Mam, I know where Kam found him that night. He told me lest I find out from you. But, of course, he had an excuse for being there. Said he was canvassing for votes. That he'd never been there before, but that the other Aldermen told him that part of town is ripe with new potential voters." Sarcasm flows. "Isn't that rich? Especially since none of them want women to ever get the vote."

Her bitterness breaks my heart. "Nellie, I'm sorry."

"Don't be, Mam. It hurts less every day. Sean's evil stripes are soul deep, and he's not going to change them."

Does she really mean to stay here? With such a vile excuse for a man? "Can you leave him?"

"And lose Kathleen? I think not."

I shake my head in frustration. "Damn him."

She shrugs and we stare at each other in defeat. Finally, I pull myself away from the hopelessness of the situation. My daughter needs to hear something that will lift her spirit. "Nellie, Kam learned something from Neo that you should know."

She stares at me, then clears her throat. "That Derry is alive and in prison in London?"

She knows. "How long have you known?"

"Neo writes to me pretty regularly. He told me last month in one of his letters."

"And you never told me?"

"No. What's the point? Derry managed to get word to Neo but not to me." She pulls at her wedding ring, running it up and down her thin finger, thinking of the one that should be there. "Obviously, he cares more about Neo than he does me. I guess our great love affair was a figment of my imagination or he's angry that I married Sean. I tend to believe the former." Her face darkens with resentment. "They're all the same, it seems; looking for sex and then abandoning you once they've had it."

A loud cry comes from upstairs. "Well, Miss Kathleen is awake and hungry again," Nellie says as she stands to go to the staircase.

When she's gone, I muddle about the bitterness that has overtaken her. Where did my sunny girl go? Nellie even looks different because she's so hurt. Her face has taken on an acidic expression that wasn't there before. She looks older than her twenty-three years and harder as though she's daring anybody to bother with her. I've seen such changes in women when their hearts are shattered. I never expected to see it in Nellie.

She comes back into the room carrying the squalling baby. Settling onto a divan across from me, Nellie unbuttons her bodice and puts Kathleen to her breast. Immediately, the sound of voracious sucking replaces the baby's loud wailing.

Nellie whispers, "That's how it is each time. She's so desperate you'd think she's starving. I cannot wait until she can eat soft food."

"That will be next month, I'd imagine. She's growing fast."

As I watch my child feed her child, I am nourished by a continuum of life so beautiful it brings tears to my eyes. If nothing else makes women equal to men, the act of mothering should. But I hate it that this beautiful young mother is so disillusioned by love.

Nellie raises adoring eyes from her baby. "She really is cute, isn't she, Mam?"

"Cutest baby I've seen since you, love. And you know I've seen a lot of them."

Nearly fifteen minutes or more passes—both of us gazing at the content Kathleen—before Nellie finishes nursing the baby and hands her to me to burp. I cuddle her close and say, "Hey, Miss Kathleen. How are you doing? Your grandma loves you, you know?"

Do I imagine her laugh? No, it's not my imagination. Her toothless chortle enchants me. "Nellie, she laughed at me."

"I thought she did yesterday at the doctor's office. But I've read it's a little early for that."

"Well, see then, she's not only beautiful but smart, too. Way ahead of her time. Just like you were."

Her eyes cloud. "Was I?"

How can she doubt that? "Of course, you were. Don't you remember? Always top in your class. First in your family to graduate from college. A great teacher. Nellie, you were extraordinary and still are."

"I guess I forgot."

As sadness returns to her face, I make my decision and reach for my drawstring bag. I've carried Derry's letter all this time trying to decide whether I should show it to her. Now, I know I must. I pull it out.

"Sweetheart, I got this a month ago and have been trying to decide how to go about giving it to you. I think you need to read it."

She takes the letter from my hands, studies the envelope, then looks at me, her mouth agape. "Derry?"

I motion for her to open it. "Read it."

As she reads, tears course down her cheeks. Soon, her breath comes in gasps and halting sobs. When finally she can speak, she says, "Why didn't you tell me?" Her eyes are wide with shock.

By now, I am weeping, too. I pull a handkerchief from my bag and wipe the tears away. "I didn't know what to do," I choke out. "You were trying so desperately to make your marriage work, and I was afraid this letter would ruin that."

She stares at me, her eyes incredulous. Instantaneously, anger replaces grief. "That was wrong. Not your place. Terribly wrong. I have been in hell thinking Derry didn't love me; that I was just a plaything to him." She jerks Kathleen from my arms, and the baby whose eyes were closing bellows in anger. She comforts the infant with soft coos and whispers. Raising her eyes from her baby to me, she says, "I don't know if I can forgive you."

My mouth falls open unable to bear the pain her words cause. "But you must, Nellie. I'm your mam, and what I did was out of love and concern for you. You know that."

Her face remains cold. "I think you'd better leave. Now."

CHAPTER THIRTY-THREE

FEBRUARY 1880

That night, when I tell Kam what happened, he shakes his head and says, "I'm not going to say 'I told you so.'" His tone provokes every murderous impulse in my brain, but I bite my tongue and stay silent. I cannot fight with Kam right now. Besides the fact that I love him, I'm going to need his help to figure out how to make things right with Nellie—if I can.

In the next weeks, Kam and I send flowers to her along with my notes of contrition. This goes on for over three months with no word back from Nellie. In one note, I ask if I can babysit Kathleen and still get no response.

Kam comes up with an idea. "Mary, your birthday's coming up, isn't it?"

"Next month," I say. "March seventeenth, St. Patrick's Day. Lord, Kam I'll be forty-six years old. Will you want to trade me in for a newer lady?"

He squeezes my hand. "Never. Don't forget, I turned forty-nine on my last birthday. I don't think I could handle a younger woman, let alone a young version of you. You're quite enough for me, my dear."

His words thrill me. I anticipated this response from him, but it's always good to hear. My hair has a bit of silver in it now, and that's all right with me. It tones down the flaming red that used to embarrass me as a girl. And though my body has changed some, most of its parts remain reasonably close to where they used to be. I'm grateful to have not gotten the middle-aged spread like many women my age. I have Kam to thank for that. I've observed that a well-loved body tends to keep itself up.

"Anyway, the reason I brought up your birthday is that I'd like to arrange a small dinner party for you at Hibernian Hall. To avoid gossip, I'll ask Molly to extend the invitations. Of course, we'll invite Nellie and Sean and, surely, she won't stay mad at you on your birthday."

I am so pleased with the idea I reach over and kiss him, all the while praying his plan works.

Every day I wait for responses to Kam's invitation. They arrive from my next-door neighbors, Father Ruzzo, and four people Kam invited from St. Augustine's, as well as from a few of his friends. I'm delighted to get a note from Marion saying that she and Raymond will be honored to attend. And, of course, Molly—ever dependable Molly—is coming.

But nothing from Nellie.

On St. Patrick's Day evening, I don my Kelly-green church dress and wait for Kam to pick me up. When he arrives, his carriage is bedecked in green ribbons. Even the horse has a bright green halter around his neck. And in comes Kam, looking handsome in his black evening trousers and frock coat and sporting the most brilliant green ascot I've ever seen.

"Kam, I must say you look Irish as Paddy's pig tonight."

"Everyone's Irish on St. Patrick's Day. You've said that every year, and in Boston, I'd say it's truer than any place East of Dublin."

I close the front door and he takes me into his arms. "You look beautiful, Mary, and not a day over eighteen."

I snuggle into his embrace and poke him. "And they say Irishmen talk blarney. Listen to yourself, mister."

"I mean it, Mabo. Happy birthday."

His using my old nickname from the coffin ship warms my heart. His English was so poor back then, and Mabo, a combination of my two names was easy for him to say.

"I have your birthday gift, love. I'd like to give it to you now." He hands me a tiny box tied with lavender ribbon. Engraved on its top is E.B. Horn.

"Pretty fancy there, Mr. Okafor. The priciest jewelry store in Boston."

"Open it, Mabo."

I untie the lavender ribbon and open the small box. When I see what's inside, my breath halts. "Kam . . . That's the most incredible thing I've ever seen." It's a gold ring with a large green stone in its center encircled by diamonds.

"That's an emerald, Mary. And though we must hide our love right now, I want this ring to be an engagement ring between us. Because one day, I *will* marry you."

He takes the ring from the box and places it on my finger, the one that held Daniel's plain gold band until I buried it deep in the earth over his coffin.

"It fits perfectly," I whisper.

"Yes, I measured that finger one night while you were fast asleep. I wanted it to be just right."

On our journey to Hibernian Hall, I can't take my eyes from the ring. It sparkles like the stars as we ride along. "This is the most beautiful piece of jewelry I've ever looked at. Prettier than any of the ads in the *Sunday Globe*. But it must've been frightfully expensive."

He is so proud as he says, "Don't worry, my love. I can afford it."

When we arrive at the hall, he makes quite a show of helping me down from the carriage. Even bowing at the waist to me. I look around, hoping that no one sees him, but in some perverse corner of my soul, wishing the whole world could observe his courtliness. I do so love this man.

Spritely Irish music wafts from inside, and its sound sets my heart beating like a bodhran. It's a jig. And I realize I haven't danced a jig in years, not since Daniel died. The music lifts my Celtic heart to the heavens as I do a few steps up the stairs.

When we find the dining room, all crisp linens and fine China, I am wrapped in embraces by Molly, Father Ruzzo, and everyone else. Marion, looking gorgeous in a blue silk gown, whispers in my ear, "You look beautiful, just beautiful, Mary. I'm proud to be your friend. Happy birthday."

The warmth, the music, and the fellowship stir my heart deeply. But as I look around for Nellie and Sean. I don't see them. "Did you hear back from Nellie, Molly?" I ask.

She shakes her head sadly. "No, but I'm still hopeful they'll just turn up. They probably think an R.S.V.P. is unnecessary for family members."

I taught Nellie better than that. But I refuse to allow poor manners to spoil my party. When the champagne toasts commence, I drink heartily from my glass and grab hold of Marion for a spin around the table. "Mercy, Mary, I can't do Irish dances," she pants.

"Of course, you can. Just listen to the beat and let loose with all your heart. Irish dancing is more about joy than perfection."

She proceeds to dance as the others circle us and clap; her husband and Kam the loudest of anyone. Soon, she moves like a born and bred colleen. We finish the jig, both gasping for air but laughing our heads off.

But then, the clapping stops and a hush comes over the room. When I follow the gazes of the guests, there's Sean at the door. He's dressed formally and wears a white ascot covered with shamrocks. He looks handsome as the devil himself.

I walk over to give him a hug, but he steps away from me and looks down his nose as if I were nothing but trash. My blood runs cold. Kam is immediately at my side. His body tenses like a coiled animal waiting to pounce.

"I'm here with the Aldermen, Mary. I just stopped here to tell you neither Nellie or I will be attending your little soiree."

I am so shocked I don't answer, but Kam does. "We're sorry to hear that, Sean. Is Nellie all right?"

"Oh sure, she's fine. Just not in the mood to celebrate." He walks away to shake Father Ruzzo's hand. When he returns, he says, "My wife sends her happy birthday greetings."

The snide sound of his voice tears me from my silence. "I haven't seen Nellie in six months, Sean. I miss her and the baby so much. *Please* . . ." I am begging, but he remains disdainful and looks at me as though I am beneath his contempt.

When he does answer, he says in a soft voice that only Kam and I can hear. "And don't think you'll be seeing them any time soon, Mary. We feel that our lives will be better without your meddling."

I start for him, my Irish blood boiling in my veins, but Kam holds me back. Sean cockily turns his back on us, then commences to circle the room, greeting and shaking hands with everyone there, except for the coloreds.

I cannot move. This can't be happening.

Suddenly, sensing trouble, Molly is with us. "What did he say?"

My words stumble, so Kam puts his arm around me before he

says, "He said Mary can't see Nellie and Kathleen; that their lives will be better off without her meddling."

"That bastard," she says, heading for him.

Kam grabs her arm. "No, Molly. He's angry because Mary and I trailed him on one of his late nights, and I caught him in a house on Pawnee Street."

A light of understanding dawns on her face. "Oh, no."

Kam nods.

When Sean returns to us along with Father Ruzzo, Molly can't hold her tongue. "What's wrong with you, Sean? You're acting like a real *cunus* to Mary." She turns to the priest, "Sorry, Father."

Father, not understanding Irish, starts to speak, but Sean interrupts him. "Pardon me, sister mine. Who are you to call me names? You with your shabby clinic in the slum district. You who can't get any gentleman in Boston to take you out on St. Pat's Day because you stink of disinfectant." His lip curls. "You disgust me."

The party guests, sensing an argument is occurring, whisper nervously among themselves.

Sean notices and says loudly, "That's a good one, Molly. You always were the joker, weren't you?" At that, he leaves the four of us standing dumbfounded and joins the others, shaking hands and smiling like he's the happiest man in the room.

Kam starts toward him, but Father Ruzzo grabs his shoulder. "He's not worth it, Kam. Leave it be."

Sean now moves to the center of the room and, lifting his hands up into the air, says, "Well, I must leave you now. Duty calls. But I want to wish all of you a most joyous St. Patrick's Day. Your next drink is on me."

The guests cheer their thanks while I resolve to try one more time. Walking to him at the door, I touch his arm and whisper,

"Sean, you don't mean this, do you? Please don't turn Nellie against me. She's my only child."

He shrugs my hand away, all the while smiling to the crowd. Then, he bends down as if to kiss me on the cheek, but instead whispers in my ear, "You should have thought of that before you sicced your nigger boyfriend on me, Mary Kelly. If I have my way, you'll never see your daughter *or* your granddaughter again." He turns his back and swaggers out of the room, waving all the time.

When my guests begin singing "Happy Birthday," I burst into tears.

Chapter Thirty-Four

JANUARY 1883

NELLIE

Everything in this place is a dingy gray. The walls, the cots, the floors, the sheets, even my nightgowns are so gray they look dirty though everything gets laundered weekly. Why is there no color here? I yearn to see the green grass outside and the blue of the heavens, but all the windows are shuttered and sealed tight. There are seven other women in this cramped room though it's more a cell than a room. Across the hall is a tiny bathroom we share. We are divided from other cells by locked gates and sometime we hear screaming from an adjacent room.

This place is called Danvers, and it's an insane asylum. I never complain about the awful food or cry and scream like the others, though sometimes I'd like to. They mustn't think me mad or they'll never let me out. Sean says that I'm to have no visitors, but Mam has been here. When I saw her in the visitors' lounge, I cried with pure joy. She's been here twice. The first time, she burst into tears at the sight of me. That broke my heart because

I haven't seen her cry that hard since Da was killed. She's very strong, and says I am as well. I hope she's right.

Two of the women in my room are mongoloids. They are sisters and very sweet, short and stout and have slanted eyes. Their names are Sarah and Susan. Though their speech is unintelligible, they sometimes babble to me and I pretend to understand. The other four are named Hezbolah, Charity, Emily, and Constance.

Constance is a tall middle-aged woman who moans and cries pitiably, and not much of what she says makes sense. It's awful in the dark of night to listen to her woeful wailing. Hearing her moans, my heart feels leaden.

I'm not certain how long I've been here. Sometimes, I think it's days and sometimes months. Needing to mark passing days, I asked the doctor for dried beans, but he refused; said I might choke on them. If I just had beans, I could hide one under my pillow each night at eight o'clock when they turn off the gas lamp. But I have no way to mark time, and the days and nights just pass and pass and pass.

Emily sleeps most of the day and all of the night. She is able to speak but seldom does. Just lies there in her bed, her long gray hair fanned out on her pillow, staring at the ceiling. Every day, she asks the nurse for more pills, but the answer is always the same, "You're at your maximum dosage, Emily. I've told you that a thousand times."

I can't tell how old Emily is. She could be any age from forty to ninety. All I know is she's been here for a long, long time and never has a visitor on monthly family day.

Hezbolah, a pretty girl in her twenties, says she's here because her mother wanted her out of the house. "My mam runs a high-priced gentlemen's house frequented by doctors and lawyers from Northampton. It's an hour's train ride from Boston. They come over here so as not to be suspected at home." She grins wickedly at my look of shock.

"They tell their offices and wives they are attending a conference somewhere but spend the weekend in my mam's house." Hugging herself, she shudders slightly. "One man thought me one of the whores, and I set him straight right quick. My mam prides herself on running a sanitary establishment and has her girls tested for diseases regularly. Clean outside, clean inside is her marketing slogan, and she's fierce about it.

"Last year, though, a client took home a dose of syphilis. When his wife caught it, he called her a whore and had her committed here at Danvers." At this point, her face changes from sarcastic to despondent. "A judge ordered me to testify, and I told him the husband was infected first at my mam's house. A week later, she committed me."

Sean went to court to have me declared insane. When the doctor told me that, I was furious. He told a judge I'm a danger to myself and to him. "Doctor, I never hurt my husband, even after he tossed me down the stairs that time. If I had raised my hand to him, I think he'd have killed me."

Things between us got worse after Mam's birthday party. Sean was angry that I wanted to attend it and locked me in my room with Mrs. O'Dwyer on guard outside the door. I begged her to let me out, but she wouldn't budge.

I was drinking too much and knew it, but never until the baby was sleeping. Sean ignored that until one night at a political rally when I performed an Irish jig on the dance floor of his club, his precious club. I did it because the music made me happy and reminded me of when I was little and did Irish dances with my da. And I was drinking.

All us girls visit Dr. Abernethy once a week. He's a psychiatrist. My time is Tuesday at eleven in the morning. Though it gets me out of this room, it's a waste of time. The first time, when I tried to tell the doctor that I'm sane, he said, "Now, now."

"Now what?" I said, keeping my voice calm.

He became clearly annoyed with me, and I learned to play the game his way. After that, I stopped telling him anything. He asks how I am, and I say, "Just fine."

Then, he says, "Good. Good. Your medication is working."

"Yes, doctor, indeed it is."

What a joke. My medication does nothing except make me sleepy, but I smile, nod, and agree with him. Because I must get out of here and see my little girl. She'll be three this summer. Sean thinks Kathleen's his child, but she's not. Derry, darling Derry, is her da, though he has never laid eyes on her. If he could see her, he'd fall in love with her. She is the spitting image of him. After her bath, I swear she smells like heather. Like Ireland.

Last week, nurse Rebecca snuck me outside for a few minutes. That was so kind. Though it was cold, I breathed in deep that day, hoping to remember forever how fresh the air felt in my lungs, how warm the sun was on my face. Under the snow, I saw patches of grass and remembered the green grass in Ireland.

Ireland. Yes, I was there, but that was long ago, and sometimes I forget. The pills make me question things. When I try to spit them out, nurse Rebecca catches me and holds my nose until I swallow. Then she checks my mouth to make sure they aren't hidden in there. Twice a day, they bring the pills in their little white cup. I hate them.

Yes, I was in Ireland. That's where I met Derry. Back then, he was simply a lovely boy with a fiddle who walked me home from a pub in the rain. I felt so cared for, so safe. He kissed me, and I fell in love.

"Good morning, Mrs. Nellie," Nurse Rebecca says as she bustles into my room. "I've brought you breakfast. Same old oatmeal, but at least it'll fill your belly." She comes to my bed and puts down the tray. Then, she brushes the hair hanging down in my face and ties it up for me. "If you're a good girl and eat all this, maybe I'll take you out in the sun for a bit."

As she takes trays to the others, I gobble the cereal so quickly it chokes me. I mustn't miss the chance of going outside. I've emptied the bowl before Rebecca finishes serving the other women. As I put the tray back on the metal cart, I hear a growl that sounds like a rabid animal. I look around and see Constance on her cot, her eyes red and her pupils so large her eyes look black. When she catches me looking at her, she snarls and jumps on my back. "Mama! Mama!" she screams over and over while pulling my hair nearly out of my head. When she stops screaming, she bites my arm so bad I howl for help.

Nurse Rebecca runs toward us, blowing the whistle around her neck as she wraps a towel around my arm and pulls the snarling woman off my back. Before this moment, Constance was a skinny soul of a woman who did nothing but weep. Today, she seems powerful as an enraged wildcat. Andrew, a tall, burly guard, runs into the room and grabs her, then wrestles her into a straitjacket. She screams again, "No, Mama, not again. Please."

Another guard joins Andrew and they drag her, screaming, out of our room. Andrew shouts, "It's the restraint chair for you, Missy. That'll teach you to behave yourself." Her shrieks echo all the way down the hallway.

Blood saturates the towel on my arm, so I hold it high in the air. "Nurse Rebecca, what's the restraint chair?" I ask through tears.

She examines my wound and replaces the blood-drenched towel with a clean one, then answers, "You don't want to know, dear. You don't want to know. My, that's a bad bite. I guess

Constance truly is insane. She'll be in that straitjacket for a good long time, I wager."

As she ties a clean towel on my arm, I touch her hand. She jumps, startled, as if I'm going to hurt her. "Nurse, do you think I'm insane?"

She stops and stares into my eyes. I think I see compassion there. Her right eyelid quivers wildly. I'd not seen such a tic before. "I don't know, Missus. I'm no doctor, you know; let alone a psychiatrist like the one who admitted you. Several girls in here don't seem crazy to me, but who am I to judge? Doctor knows best, dearie. Doctor knows best. Here now, take your medicine."

She hands me the little white cup, and I swallow the three pills with one mouthful of water like a perfect patient. No hiding them in my cheek this time. I don't want to be denied my time outside.

But I don't get to go outside that day or the next or the day after that. They take me to the infirmary instead. Constance was found to have an infection of some sort, and since she had bitten me, they isolate me for a week to make sure I haven't contracted it.

Once back in my room, the days drag on in their usual interminable pattern. Sometimes, I try to read but soon find myself drifting off to sleep. Nurse Rebecca is soon gone and replaced by a Negro nurse called Marion. The woman seems nice enough and is the prettiest colored woman I've ever seen. Not that I've seen many, except for maids in Sean's friends' homes. I do hope Rebecca wasn't let go because of what happened to me.

Constance has been moved to another part of the hospital; one they call the containment section. It's for the violent crazy people. I wish I knew what caused her to turn on me that day. Though she is a pitiful creature, she was not vicious before to anyone. I was the only one in this room who treated her with any kindness. The other girls made fun of her for crying so much, but I never did. She was sad, but not mean, not till that day.

They give her cot to a new girl named Hannah who, like me, seems confounded to find herself here. She readily admits having an affair, which at first shocked me. I've not known a woman to do such a thing, though many men do. Hannah and her husband live on Beacon Hill near Sean's house, but I didn't meet her until now. When she arrived, her face was bruised and swollen and she rarely ventured off her cot. I feared we had another silent, sad creature here, but after a bit, she settled in better. Now, she wants to be my friend; says because I'm in her social strata. *Strata.* I've not heard that word used in regular conversation, and certainly never in this place.

Hannah comes to my cot each night after the others are sleeping and shares whispered secrets. "I was a virgin when James and I married, and I thought I loved him. Though he was slight of stature, he was very handsome and quite wealthy."

She looks around to make sure no one is listening. "Well, on our wedding night, I put on my lacy white nightgown and reclined on the bed. I had put perfume behind my ears and even down my belly."

Hannah is a pretty redhead, and the picture of her in my mind's eye is quite vivid and certainly seductive.

"So, he comes out of the bathroom wearing a purple dressing robe with blue pajamas underneath. I could tell they were blue because the pant legs hung below the robe. He looked quite dashing, I must say. I was nervous as could be, of course, since I'd never been alone with a man before."

"And what happened then?"

She grimaces. "Absolutely nothing."

Surprised, I exclaim, "What?!"

"He leaned down and kissed my cheek, said good night, and went to his own room."

"No," I whisper.

"And I thought I must look ugly or that my perfume was too strong and sickened him. I climbed out of bed and ran into the bathroom where I washed myself, again, all over. I stared in the mirror and didn't think I looked ugly at all, but how could I know how he saw me? Then I tiptoed over to his room and slipped inside. He was sitting up in bed reading. I approached his bed and said, 'James, have I done anything to displease you?' He then said, 'No, Hannah. Why do you ask?' just as plain as can be. What was I to say? I didn't know then how men acted when they desired a woman. Maybe I expected too much. Maybe he was just nervous."

I understood her feelings. When Sean lost his desire for me soon after our marriage, I questioned everything about myself, my looks, my mind, and yes, even my scent. Fortunately, I'd been intimate with Derry and logic dictated that the problem didn't lie with me. Possibly, the difficulty was with my husband. Poor Hannah had no such experience or knowledge.

Now she looked as if she could cry. "That went on for two years, with me trying to be my most alluring and James never touching me and never telling me why. I was confounded."

"What did you do?"

"I began talking to women who were married to his friends and asked how their husbands behaved. I didn't tell them my concerns with James, just that I wondered what their daily life was like as a wife. I never complained or shared the fact that I was still a virgin, but one of them figured things out and told her husband. Who told James."

"Dear me. What did James say?"

"He didn't say anything at first, but after thinking about it, he was beyond furious. He said I had broken the cardinal rule for a wife and made him look small. That's when he started screaming at me and calling me a nymphomaniac and a whore. And then, the beatings started."

Shocked to silence, I felt such pity for Hannah at that moment I cried with her. "Why didn't you leave him?"

"How? I'd lose everything—the house, my maids, the chauffeur, all the luxury in my life. No, no, I wouldn't leave him."

"So, you continued being miserable?"

She grins. "Not for long. James sent me to a doctor in Cambridge who treated hysterics in women."

"Hysterics?" Then, I remembered. Mam had told me about a patient of hers who'd disobeyed her husband and was diagnosed as hysterical.

"Yes," she answered. "The term applies to women who are unreasonable, demanding, and miserable in their marriages. In other words, they nag. After visiting this doctor once a week for a month, I felt much better."

My mind spins with possibilities. *What could this doctor do to a woman to make her less unhappy?* Finally, I can contain my curiosity no longer. "Why did you feel better? What did the doctor do?"

She hesitates for only a moment. "First, he gave me some wine to relax me. Then, he put on his surgical gloves and started examining me."

"Where?"

"In his office."

"No, I mean where on your body?"

"All over really. First, my breasts. And then . . . down there. He found a certain spot and rubbed it and kept rubbing it until I was overcome with . . . something I can't describe."

Embarrassed by my own memories, I say, "Never mind, Hannah. I think I understand."

But she's not finished. "After a month, I started going to that doctor three times a week because I felt so much more relaxed and James and I were getting along better."

How sad. How desperately sad.

"But after a year of this, I wanted more. I was still a virgin after all, and I wanted to change that."

I dared not ask, so I didn't, but she continued anyway.

"We had an Italian gardener. His name was Matteo, and he was quite handsome. I began talking to him in the garden. About flowers and trees . . . at first. We became friends, and he shared with me that his wife had gotten quite fat after her third child and he was unhappy. I said I understood; that I, too, was unhappily married. It didn't take long until he was panting with desire for me. So, he became my lover. It was perfect."

"Did James know?"

"Not for more than a year. But then, our butler figured us out and told James. That's when he committed me here." Silent tears coursed down her cheeks.

Hannah speaks often of her servants, and the other women in our little room dislike her for acting superior to them. For me, her stories pass the time, and thanks to her, my head got clearer. Because, clever girl that she is, Hannah teaches me to swallow the pills and then go immediately to the bathroom and throw them up by sticking my finger down my throat. At first, it felt awful, but after a while, I did it easily and was no longer tired all the time.

Now, Marion, our new nurse doesn't check my mouth, so I no longer take those trips across the hall. I just hide the pills in my cheek and then toss them out.

CHAPTER THIRTY-FIVE

MARCH 1883

Two weeks after Nurse Marion takes over our care, she asks me to meet her in the hall privately.

"Nellie, I'm a friend of your mother's, and I want you to know I tell her every week at tea how you're doing here. I hope you don't mind."

This revelation fills me with more joy than anything that's happened over the past several months. Though I've seen Mam twice, I worry about her. I know she's devastated at what's happened to me.

I take Marion's hands in my own and say, "I cannot express how much I don't mind, Nurse Marion. My husband keeps my mam away from me, and I know how that hurts her. Realizing that you can tell her I'm all right lifts my spirit more than any pill they can give me. Thank you, thank you, for telling me."

Her lovely face softens as she replies, "I'm glad you feel that way, dear. I love your mother like a sister. My husband and I owe a great debt to her friend, Mr. Okafor, who lent us the money for our first house and to educate our son and daughter. My girl is about your age, and I'd hate to see her in your situation."

"How did you and Mam meet?" I ask.

She hesitates. "Mr. Okafor introduced us. She's actually been in our home."

Something in her manner tells me she knows more than she's saying. I wonder if she knows Uncle Kam found Sean in that awful place that night. I shake the thought from my head. *What does that matter? What matters is I have a friend here, someone who will keep my mam aware of what's happening to me. That's what matters.*

Hannah begins to suspect something. "You and Nurse Marion seem to be thick as thieves. Did you know her outside?" she asks one day. I wish I could tell her the truth, but caution prevents that. It cannot leak from this room that our nurse is a friend of Mam's. If Sean somehow learned of it, he'd make sure she was fired.

After that day, Marion and I talk frequently, often when the others are visiting with callers in the meeting room. Marion says that Kathleen will start nursery school next year at the exclusive Bradwell School and that my Aunt Molly says she's smart as a whip. When I last saw her, she was eighteen months and just beginning to talk in sentences. I can't dwell on all I've missed with Kathleen because it would break me. I swear to make it up to her one day.

Marion says Mam will make her uniform for school, though Aunt Molly will tell Sean it is store bought. I'd love to see her all dressed up. I wonder if her hair is long now and still that color she inherited from Derry. I wonder if it's unruly as his was and needs to be tied up in a ribbon to keep it off her forehead. A pretty green ribbon to match her eyes. When I think of all the things I'm missing, my heart aches. Someday, I will be with her again, and I must focus on that lest I really do go mad.

I wish she could attend St. Augustine's as I did, but I can't expect that to ever happen with Sean in control. Status is so important to him, and he wants bragging rights to impress his friends and other politicians. I wonder how his political climb is progressing. If I know Sean, I'd wager, swimmingly. That's what drives the man, after all; status, money, and ambition. If he wants to be mayor, there's not a doubt in my mind that he will be mayor.

I am so grateful to have a friend like Nurse Marion in my corner here in this place.

CHAPTER THIRTY-SIX

APRIL 1883

MARY

I gaze up at her. The statue is so beautiful, wreathed in peace and loveliness. A ray of sunshine drifts through the stained-glass window and lights her face. I'm alone in the church. It's Tuesday at four o'clock, and I'd walked to church from home. I planned it this way so I wouldn't be bothered by any nun or priest or a parishioner there for their daily communion. I only want to speak with Mary.

"Remember, oh most gracious virgin Mary, that never was it known that anyone who fled to thy protection, implored thy help, or sought thy intervention was left unaided." Sitting in St. Augustine's and whispering the old prayer makes me think that anything is possible. Mam and Da only used it in times of severe trouble because they didn't want to waste the magic of the *Memorare* on anything trivial. I feel the same.

I know Mary will understand the pain I'm in over my girl because she went through it with her son. Watching your child flogged and crucified would be the worst torture on earth for a mother. And I still have hope that I'll get Nellie back whereas Mary watched her son die before her very eyes. The pain must have been unbearable, but then he made good on his promise by rising from the dead. He must have been a corker as a youngster. Imagine raising the Son of God.

I finish the prayer. "Mother of the Word Incarnate, despise not my petition, but in thy mercy, hear and answer me. Amen." Tears run down my cheeks.

I gaze up at her again. Her face glows like no woman I've ever seen in my life. I guess that's because she's the mother of Jesus. Ordinary women don't glow. Well, maybe except for Nellie when she was with Derry. She had a radiance about her then, for sure. And God knows it wasn't from being a saint.

When I've said my piece to the Blessed Mother, I stand and genuflect, then turn and walk back up the center aisle. At the end, I bless myself with the holy water thoroughly. I figure I can use all the blessing I can get right now. Then, I turn back. "Dear Jesus," I whisper. "I'm sorry about having sex with Kam. I would marry him in a leprechaun's minute, but you know that's impossible in Boston. Please forgive our sin until we find a way."

Leaving the church, I wrap my shawl around my shoulders. The fall wind that blows off the Charles makes me shiver. The older I get, the harder such cold feels on my bones. As I start trudging home, I hear my name.

"Mary," a deep male voice calls out. When I turn to see who it is, there stands Neo. I'm shocked for a minute because I still think of him as a young boy and not possessed of such a grownup voice and commanding physique. But there he is, over six feet tall, and handsome as his father. A man, grown and smiling.

"Neo!" I exclaim. "How did you get here? No one told me you were coming." I run into his extended arms, not caring a whit if some gossip spreads a tale about me embracing a young, colored man.

"Mary, dear Mary," he says. "I am so happy to see you. They told me at the clinic you might be here. I came right over."

Sputtering with shock and delight, I say, "Does your father know you're here?"

"Yes, yes, I arrived last evening on *The Mara*. Da picked me up at the dock, but swore me to secrecy until I found you. He wanted to surprise you."

"Is Angelique with you?"

"No, she couldn't come. But the reason is a joyful one. She's expecting our first child, and her doctor didn't want her to travel so far away at this time. But she sends all her love and good wishes to you."

"Neo, how wonderful! A baby! When's she due?"

"In about three months. She wants you to come to Ireland to attend her birth. She likes her doctor but wants the presence of an experienced woman there, too. Her mother is no longer alive, and she felt so comfortable with you when you were at our wedding that she'd like you there. My father will make all the arrangements for your trip over if you agree."

My heart swells with love for Neo, the boy with the beautiful dark eyes who was brilliant even as a child. He inherited his father's brains and his mother's compassion and I love him like a son. "Well, that lifts my spirits, lad. Going back to Ireland and helping deliver your first child is just about the best tonic I can think of right now." Even as I say the words, I wonder how I can leave Nellie. "But you haven't told me what brings you to Boston."

The two of us climb into his carriage and he takes the reins. As we ride along, he says, "I'm here to get Nellie out of that place, Mary."

For a moment, my heart almost stops beating. Joy fills me to the brim, but it is tempered with fear, too. "But, Neo, how? Security there is tight as a bodhran, you know."

"So I've heard, but I have a few tricks up my sleeve and think I can do it. Father and I have been planning this for the past several months. He didn't want you to know lest you get your hopes up before our plan was complete. Now it is. Father is taking us to dinner tonight at the Claddagh Restaurant. They allow coloreds. Some other friends will be joining us as well."

I stare at the young man driving the carriage. Such a fine man. Just like his father. His profile looks chiseled from a perfect brown marble, and he's handsome as any statue of David or Adonis I've ever seen. Now, he looks as powerful as St. Mauritius, the Negro saint Father Ruzzo told me about. Mauritius led a division of the Roman army, and when the Roman Emperor ordered him to murder Christians, he refused and was then martyred himself. Looking at Neo, I have no doubt his resolution is as strong as was Mauritius's.

We arrive at the Claddagh at five-thirty and Neo ties up the horse and helps me down.

"I've never been here," I say. "But I hear the food is good."

"Yes, so do I. And I'm starving for the biggest steak they can come up with. Along with a dram of Irish whiskey. I've learned to love Jamison's in Dublin."

"Ah, yes, my Daniel loved it, too, but I've never developed a taste for it. And your father seems to prefer American bourbon. I'm a glass-of-wine person. And usually only one. I've seen too many drunks in my life, especially when I was a barmaid at O'Halloran's."

He grins. "I've noticed that some Irish men can't stop after one or two."

"Indeed, it's the curse of living in a cold-water country."

When we walk into the private room in the restaurant, I am surprised that several friends are assembled there: Kam, Molly, along with Marion and Raymond. Kam rises from the table and greets me with a kiss on the cheek. "Here, Mary, sit down here beside me."

A Negro waiter dressed in black pants and a crisp white shirt approaches the table. "May I take your order, sir and madam. The others have already placed theirs."

Neo orders his drink and a sirloin steak as Kam pours me a glass of wine from the carafe on the table. "I'll have fried chicken," I tell the smiling waiter, "and mashed potatoes, please."

"Very good," he says, bowing slightly, and leaves the table.

"Well, my dears, this is quite a surprise. I had no idea you'd all be here. Nor that Neo was here from Ireland." I poke Kam in the shoulder. "What's with you, mister, keeping secrets from me?"

He lifts my hand and kisses it. "When you learn why, I'm certain you'll forgive me, Mary."

His gallantry, as always, melts my heart. What a dear gentleman he is. Black or white, every woman should have such a man in her life. I've been blessed with two of them.

"So, speak up. Who's going to tell me why we're all here?"

"Let me begin," Kam answers. "Everyone here loves you, Mary. And we love Nellie as well. I know—we all know how devastated you've been during her two years at Danvers. Her being there is an abuse of justice, perpetrated by her husband. Although he tells everyone he was devoted and had no part in it—another lie—we intend to do something about it."

The four other people at the table are each nodding.

"But how?" I ask, almost unable to breathe.

"We'll all have a task in freeing Nellie. And *we will* accomplish our mission," Neo says. His tone is resolute.

In spite of, or because of my nerves, I shiver. "This sounds like an invasion or something. Are you serious?"

"Serious as a heart attack, love," Molly says. Her mouth has lost its customary devilish grin. "What Sean has done to Nellie is unforgivable. It must be fixed, and him along with it."

I study each loving person around this table. All good people, all dear friends. All as determined as I've ever seen them. My heart lifts with possibility. "I love every one of you for trying to help, but how in the world can you pull off getting her out of there?"

Marion takes my hand. "As Neo said, we each have a role to play, Mary. Each role is important. First, Raymond, please tell her your part in this."

He stands, impeccable in his black suit and white shirt. I cannot imagine how he can help with getting Nellie out of Danvers, but I remain quiet. Marion said each of them has a role to play, and I trust her implicitly.

He clears his throat. "Mr. Okafor is why I'm here. He's been very good to me and my family. It's time to return the favor." He turns and shakes Kam's hand. Sitting down, he says, "Mary, six months ago, I became the head butler at the Oliver Ames mansion. Mr. Ames is an abolitionist and knew of my slave work for the master of a Virginia plantation before the war."

"As you probably know, Oliver Ames is the newly elected Governor of Massachusetts," Kam says.

Everyone nods their heads.

"Yes," I say, "and a great philanthropist. He's donated to Kathleen's Haven more than once."

Raymond continues. "In my position, I'm privy to a good deal of political talk as you can imagine." He takes his wife's hand who grips his in support. "At first, when Mr. Okafor asked me to help, I felt it was disloyal to Mr. Ames. But since none of this relates to my employer's political life, I'm comfortable in helping Nellie any way I can. Because Mr. Ames is a Republican, there's sometimes discussion about ways to keep political power away from the Democrats."

Molly speaks up, "I'm sure. Politics is a nasty game."

Raymond agrees, "Yes, it is, but Mr. Ames is an honorable man. Everyone knows that."

No one disagrees with his statement. Oliver Ames is known as a fair and decent gentleman.

I speak up, "But Raymond, what does this have to do with freeing Nellie?"

He turns to face me. "Quite a lot, Mary."

Confused, I shake my head.

"When the talk turns to Democratic candidates for Boston's mayor, the name spoken often is Sean O'Halloran." Raymond shakes his head. "As I said, I've struggled with sharing information because I like Mr. Ames and feel great loyalty to him. However, it could be helpful in getting Nellie out of Danvers, and it's mainly gossip, certainly nothing to do with governing."

"Go ahead, Raymond," Kam says.

"One of the damning criticisms about Mr. O'Halloran is that he's a scoundrel and that his wife is in Danvers. She's considered a great political liability."

Good. I'm happy Nellie has a part in keeping the bastard out of office. He'd be a terrible mayor anyway. "Go on, Raymond."

"That's really all I have to say. I believe—considering Mr. O'Halloran's ambition—knowing his wife is a detriment to his becoming mayor may be useful in some way. Whenever I hear more, I'll share it with you."

Molly interjects, "I'm already figuring out how to use this information. I know my brother very well. Just hearing that having committed Nellie makes him less appealing as a candidate will infuriate him. When the time is right, I'll have to share it with him," she grins, "as any good sister would." She turns to Raymond. "Don't worry, sir. He'll never know where I got my information."

"Thank you, Molly," Raymond says, open-palming his wife in an invitation to speak.

Marion's eyes rest on Mary. "I'm the nurse on Miss Nellie's floor. She clearly doesn't belong in Danvers. That's apparent to everyone there, but they're afraid of what her husband might do financially to the hospital if he becomes mayor. I know the place like the back of my hand—all its ins and outs and secret corridors. I know which guards are lax and some who drink on their shift. I'll do whatever I can to get her out. I owe this to Mr. Okafor and to my good friend, Mary." She circles the room with her dark eyes. "I need my job. My part in this must be kept strictly between us."

"As it will be," Kam reassures her.

Neo stands. "As some of you know, I'm a magician." My mind drifts back to when he was a child and fooling Nellie and me with his tricks while exclaiming, "A magician never reveals his secrets!" When asked how he did what he did, his reply was always the same. "It's pure magic."

"In Ireland, my wife and I have performed many illusions together; one of which involves locking her in a trunk and inserting swords through it. Such an act requires a girl who is extremely flexible. Nellie can bend herself every way possible, I remember. She's not only flexible, but quite athletic. That will prove to be helpful in accomplishing her escape."

"Except that she's been in Danvers for two years. Do you think she could still be flexible without exercise and stretching?" Molly questions.

Marion answers, "We exercise every day. Many of the girls won't, but Nellie always does."

"Good," Neo says and turns to Kam. "My father will work with me to free her."

"Confidentiality is critical to the success of our mission. Anything said in this room must never be repeated, even among ourselves." Kam stares everyone down until he sees a confirmation in their eyes. "Nellie's future depends on absolute secrecy."

One by one, each person at the table swears to keep every word said here strictly private to this group. Their dedication to freeing Nellie nearly brings me to tears. Tears of relief.

After the others take their leave, Kam, Neo, and I remain in the small room.

"Do you really believe we can do this?" Palatable fear makes my voice tremble.

"If I didn't, I wouldn't be here," Neo responds. "So, where can I get a trunk?"

"Do you need a special kind?" I ask.

"No, I can modify any of them to suit my needs."

"Then go to The Mercantile on Dorchester Street. They'll have one to suit you."

Kam pats his son on the back with great pride. "I'll take you there, Neo. I know exactly where it's located and, of course, I'll pay for any supplies you need."

"Kind of you, Da, but I'd like to pay my own expenses. I don't need money. I've been doing quite well in Ireland."

"So I hear," I answer. "Derry told us all about seeing your act in Dublin. Sounds as though you've combined your talents as a magician with a great sense of dramatic showmanship. How'd you ever learn that?"

"Believe it or not, I learned the acting when Nellie and I were in the circus. I was supposed to be a mind reader there and learned to study my audience carefully and act as though I really could read their minds. I was lucky more often than not."

"Don't remind me of that, Neo," I plead. "The two of you running away like that drove me and her da nearly out of our minds. We were so worried about you. You were both so young."

"I'm truly sorry for having done that to you, Mary. Nellie and I thought we deserved a great adventure like you and father had as kids on the coffin ship. Though we both learned a lot from our circus experiences, I now understand how frightened you and my parents must have been. Especially now that I'm to be a father."

"Do you want a boy or a girl, Neo?" I ask.

"I don't really care, though a little girl as pretty as Angelique would be quite magical."

"I remember. She is certainly one of the most beautiful young women I've ever seen."

"Yes, I miss her terribly. But she understands completely why I must help Nellie. After all, Nellie's like a sister to me." He turns to Kam. "So, the sooner we can pull this off, the faster I can return to my wife, and the happier I'll be."

Knowing exactly how he feels, Kam says, "We'll go to The Mercantile tomorrow morning at ten to get that trunk."

After that night, things move at warp speed. It takes less than a week for Neo to get the trunk and modify it to suit his needs. He will pose as an orderly in a uniform acquired by Marion and the trunk will be loaded with supplies for the hospital.

Marion and I meet regularly to discuss methods. We both enjoy plotting this clandestine mission and take to wearing black clothes when we do.

This day, we sit in my kitchen sharing a cup of tea. She pulls out a notepad, which has a detailed drawing of Danvers. "Here is the door for deliveries. This is where he should come with a trunk full of bedding, pillows, empty pill bottles, and syringes," she says, pointing to a place on her diagram. "Neo will need an identification tag for his uniform. I can get one and he can fill it out with whatever name he wants to use. He can buy the items at Webster's Medical Supply Store on Miller Street. He should say they're for Dr. James Malvern who's the Director of Supplies at Danvers. It's a fake name, but they won't question him further. The doctors at the hospital change frequently. He might want to wear a fake beard or something to disguise his identity to look a bit less elegant. We do have Negro orderlies at the hospital, but none as glamorous looking as Neo."

She's right about everything. Neo looks more like an African prince than an orderly.

"He'll have to bring someone with him to carry the trunk to the room where Nellie is held." She points to another spot on her diagram. It's on the third floor of the hospital. "This is Nellie's room. It's locked, but I'll be there to let him in."

Clearly, Neo will need another strong man to help carry that trunk up and down three flights of stairs. I know Kam would do it, but Kam is familiar at Danvers. He's a financial supporter of the institution. Also, it should be a white man. Two strange Negroes appearing at the hospital together could be suspect. When I mention this to Marion, she makes a note to get two uniforms and badges but offers no suggestions. Most of all, it must be someone I trust implicitly.

I ponder different people. There are neighbors, but I can't be sure any of them would be secretive. Mainly because many of them imbibe in whiskey regularly which tends to loosen their tongues and their brains. *I need a man I can trust to keep our plans under wraps. But who?* Suddenly, a face comes to me. *He's just the man. He's young, big, and looks to be ox-like strong. Thank you, Jesus, for divine inspiration. Now all I have to do is convince him.*

CHAPTER THIRTY-SEVEN

My sleep last night was fitful as I mulled over his possible objections in my head. He'll say it's unethical because he's a person of uncompromised morality. Or at least, I think he is. If he does say that, I'll remind him that sometimes one must weigh the common good of an outcome against the means used to accomplish it. I don't know if he'll buy that, so I'll have to come up with a second argument.

He's a very bright man, and kind, too, I think. We've met only twice, but I liked his eyes and his decidedly devilish grin. There's more to this man than meets the eye. He scarcely knows me, but the person who introduced us told him I am a pillar of the community and a true asset to the women of Boston.

Am I? And, if so, how did my own daughter get into this awful fix? Maybe I neglected her to establish my business. I tried so hard to be a good mam to her, but The Haven sometimes came first. The good Lord knows I did my best.

I asked Neo to join me at this appointment so he could meet the person with whom he'd carry the trunk. Mainly, I asked Neo because he's quicker than I am with a counter argument. If the man meets Neo, surely, he won't question his intrinsic honor. It's written all over the lad.

Unless he hates Negroes. But no, I don't think he does. Not with his job.

Our appointment is at noon at a small restaurant on the south side and it'll probably be an Irish restaurant since this is where had we all settled and live. Maybe I should have picked a restaurant on the north side, the Italian side of town. Oh well, too late to change the locale now. It's quarter till twelve.

As my horse pulls my wagon toward the restaurant, I again consider possible objections. Will he feel he's lying? No, of course not. He needn't say a word. Neo will handle all the talking. Will he think we're exaggerating Nellie's plight? I'll tell him when he meets her, he can see for himself how unjust her commitment was. Then, if he thinks she's really insane, he can walk out the door.

But he won't, as long as I can convince him to help us today. Please, Father, let him help us. I'm out of options on who I can trust to keep things confidential. He's good at that. His position demands it.

I arrive at the restaurant and say a quick prayer to the Blessed Mother. Then, I cross myself and climb out of the wagon and tie up my horse. Taking a deep breath, I approach the front door. Irish music is playing inside. Good sign or bad? I'm not sure.

Then, I see him. He's standing near a table bouncing up and down and clapping his hands. He's a large man with shaking jowls and a protruding belly, but his girth doesn't seem to slow him down. A waitress joins him on the floor and they commence to jig. He whirls her expertly around the tiny floor for several minutes until they both stop, panting from lack of breath.

My mouth hangs open as I watch them. An Italian who can dance Irish?

I walk across the room and take his hand. "Come now, you need to sit down," I say.

"You are absolutely right, Mrs. Kelly, but only till I catch my breath. If that fiddle starts up again, you're going to join me on the floor."

The thought pleases me. He looks to be a fine dancer, and it's been a long time since I've done a jig, but is it proper?

He walks me to the table, pulls out my chair and seats me like the appropriate gentleman that he is. I pour him a tall glass of water from the pitcher on the table and he gulps it down ravenously. "Thank you, Mrs. Kelly. I needed that."

"Please call me Mary, won't you? Most everyone does."

"Very well, I will. And you call me Frank." He crosses himself. "Dear Lord, thank you for what, from the smell of things, I think will be a delicious lunch of corned beef and cabbage. And for the fellowship of my new friend, Mary Kelly. Amen." Again, he crosses himself and settles back in his chair. "Now, Mary, tell me why you invited me here. Can I help you in some way?"

It's only now I notice his Roman collar. Watching him dance, I'd almost forgotten he's a priest. Father Ruzzo introduced us before he went on sabbatical two months ago. Everyone at St. Augustine's is raving about Father Frank's inspiring homilies and down-to-earth attitudes. They call him a modern priest; not a fuddy-duddy like some of the old ones. Of course, many of the elderly people in the congregation complain that he's too modern; too young for the oldest Catholic Church in Boston, and that his decorum needs quite a bit of work. But when I go to Mass now, I see it crowded with young people and children. And that warms my heart.

"Father Frank," I say. "I do need a favor."

He raises one dark eyebrow. "Yes?"

I begin to ramble. "You see, my daughter's husband had her committed to Danvers two years ago, probably because she was getting in the way of his philandering. It's a dreadful abuse of justice. Everyone says so. Nellie's not insane. Not at all. She is unhappy, yes, but far from insane. But she's got a beautiful little girl, Kathleen, and misses her desperately. I want you to help me get her out of there."

"Whoa, Mary. I have no purview over Danvers. Nothing I do can change things for your daughter."

"Well, actually, I'm not asking you to pull any Ecclesiastic strings. I just need a strong body to help carry a trunk. And it looks like you have that, for sure."

"What?"

With that, Neo walks in the front door of the restaurant. He sees us and rushes to our table. "Sorry I'm a little late, Mary. The hardware store took longer than I'd planned." He turns toward the priest. "Please introduce me to your friend." Then, he gasps. "Frank?"

Father Frank gasps, too. "Omar?"

Neo is the first to recover. "I can't believe this. I haven't seen you in over ten years. Not since the circus. By the way, my real name is Neo." He turns to me. "Frank was a rigger and apprentice clown at the Costello Circus, you know, the one Nellie and I joined when we ran away. We were great friends back then." He reaches out and touches the Roman collar. "What's this?"

Still shaking his head in wonder, Father Frank replies, "Well, remember when Pierre fell and died from the trapeze?"

Neo searches his face. "Of course."

"I felt that it might have been a mistake I made with the rigging. The guilt was destroying me, so I sought counsel from my priest. It took about a year before I realized I hadn't rigged the trapeze he was on and that I needn't feel that way. By then, I'd gone back to church and had heard God calling me to be a priest. I finished the seminary last year and got assigned to St. Augustine's parish."

Lord, you do work in strange ways, indeed.

By the time our waitress brings our corned beef lunch to the table, Neo and Father Frank are jabbering like all old friends do after a long separation. Neo tells him about marrying Angelique, Pierre's daughter, the beautiful flyer on the trapeze, and that they now live in Dublin where they await the birth of their first child.

"I remember how infatuated the two of you were back then," Father Frank says. "You had stars in your eyes every time she walked in a room."

"And I still do, Frank. We are very happy."

"Good, good," the priest responds. "A happy marriage is a blessing on the world. Did you marry in a Catholic church?"

"Yes, we did; a very forward-thinking church in Dublin. She goes every Sunday, but I can't say that I do. Maybe when the baby is born."

"I do hope so, Neo. You must set a good example for your children."

"Yes, sir."

Father Frank catches Neo up on the happenings with the bearded lady and her husband, Tiny. He is still in touch with all the circus friends that Neo and Nellie loved, and I can't wait for Neo to tell Nellie in person about them. She so enjoyed her time there, though I'd like to murder her every time she talks about it. Her father and I both stopped sleeping until we found out she was all right.

As if Father Frank is reading my mind, he says to Neo, "Whatever happened to your friend, Felicity, the bareback rider? When Bianco threw her that time, I didn't think she'd ever get back up on him. All of us were pretty impressed that she did. That was a pretty bad concussion she suffered."

Neo sniggers. "Yes, it was, and she played it for all it was worth. Finally, I had to shame her into getting on that horse again. And by the way, her name is not Felicity. We made up our names. That's why you called me 'Omar.'"

"Oh yes, that's right. You did tell me you were really named Neo, but I forgot."

"Yes. I knew I could trust you to keep my secret. Felicity's real name was Nellie. We changed our names to sound more exotic."

Father Frank's face slowly lightens with awareness. "Nellie?" He turns to me. "Your Nellie?"

I nod rapidly, tears welling in my eyes.

The priest shakes his head. "There's no way that spunky, brave little girl is now insane. She was one tough kid. What happened to her?"

I wiped the tears that had overflowed and lower my misty eyes. "That is a very long, complicated story. Suffice it to say she fell in love with an Irish boy and got pregnant. The boy went to prison as a rebel against England and Nellie married a scoundrel in order to keep the baby girl. Advising her to do that was one of the stupidest things I've ever done in my life. I'll never forgive myself for it."

"Have you confessed it, Mary?"

"No, I was too ashamed."

"Well now you have. I absolve you of your sin." He crosses me with the ancient sign of absolution. "Make a good Act of Contrition and five Hail Mary's."

As always, after confession, I feel my guilt lift from my shoulders. I think to myself, once again, Confession is a truly magical sacrament, but do we really need to tell a human being, and a priest no doubt? Christ did not say that.

Neo redirects the conversation, "I can't believe we meet again, Frank. I've often wondered what happened to you, but after we left the circus, things happened so quickly I couldn't look for you."

"I feel the same way. You were a special friend to me all those years ago. Let's promise not to lose touch again."

They shake hands.

At that moment the fiddler strikes up another tune, and sure enough, Father Frank grabs my hand and we head to the center of the room. Just as I thought, he's a mighty fine dancer.

When we sit down again, both of us are huffing and puffing; me from age and him from the considerable heft of his belly.

Catching his breathing, he says, "So, tell me how I can be of help to you two. Don't make it sound immoral or illegal."

CHAPTER THIRTY-EIGHT

MAY 1883

MOLLY

Molly dresses carefully for the meeting with her brother. His law firm is considered the finest in Boston, and its red brick exterior and arched windows showcase its importance emphatically. Situated on the corner of Chauncy and Bedford Streets, it is one of the few structures that survived the fire that decimated Boston's business district in 1872.

The June day is glorious, and graceful flowering crab and jacaranda trees in full bloom line the streets and perfume the air. She takes a deep breath of their heady scent and finally feels ready for her difficult task. Wearing her new high-collared blouse and only bustled skirt, she stands on the side-walk and looks heavenward, saying a silent prayer that her words can convince Sean. Bless me, Father. Please give me the strength, wisdom, and knowledge to do what you have me do. If I'm unable to do that, all the rest of our strategies will fail. With resolve, she ascends the marble steps to the stately front door.

She has not been in this lobby before and its grandeur takes her breath away. Black and white porcelain tiles from China cover the floor, and the gracefully curved windows on the dark mahogany walls are draped with white curtains of the finest damask. A massive gold chandelier hangs directly in the hall's center over a cherry reception desk with a white marble top.

Seated behind the desk and typing rapidly sits a young woman wearing a deep purple dress trimmed with ecru lace at the collar and cuffs. When she stands to greet a client, Molly notes that the dress is cut close to her body and eschews the ever-present bustle favored today by Beacon Hill society ladies. Her dark hair is swept up into a simple chignon. Pince-nez hang from a nearly invisible chain onto her chest. Seated, she wore them, but rising, they are removed.

The sight of this young woman pleases Molly. Only recently, with the invention of the typewriter, have women escaped the kitchen or the role of governess when they need to earn money. Young working women are still few and far between in the business world, but there she is, in the lobby of the best firm in Boston, looking both professional and confident.

Molly approaches her desk. "Hello, Miss. I am Molly O'Halloran. I'd like to see my brother, Sean."

Did she just startle slightly? Certainly. there was an involuntary reaction that Molly's well trained physician's eye caught. *What did it mean?*

"Oh, yes, Miss O'Halloran," she says, regaining her poise. "Is he expecting you?"

"I don't have an appointment but was in the neighborhood and decided to stop in."

"I see." Rising from her desk, she says, "Let me check that he's available. Please have a seat over there." She gestures toward a brocaded settee.

As the receptionist walks to the back of the lobby and up the brass staircase to the upper floor, Molly notices a quite seductive swaying in the girl's hips. *Hmm, this young one is not without guiles. Inexperienced virgins never walk that way.*

Picking up a copy of *Popular Science Monthly* from an end table, Molly thumbs through it. An article on experiments being conducted by Louis Pasteur catches her eye and she is deep into it when the young woman returns. "Mr. Halloran will see you now."

Rising, Molly muses, *So, Sean finally dropped the "O" from our name. He's been threatening that for years.* Grinning, she follows the young woman up the stairs to a hall lined with eight offices, to Sean's; its wooden door closed. When they arrive at the second door on the right, there it is: *Sean Halloran, Esq.* in gold lettering.

The woman knocks, opens the door, and with a tinge of authority says, "You may go in."

Before the young woman closes the door, Molly catches the lidded look she and Sean exchange. Its meaning is clear.

Tucking that bit of knowledge away for now, Molly approaches Sean's desk. "Hello, brother mine. How are you today?" She sits in a straight-backed wooden chair across from him. There are no family photos on his elegant mahogany desk and few papers clutter it. Portraits of mutton-chopped old men hang over the wainscoted walls. *Probably founders and former partners.*

He opens a desk drawer and pulls out a cigar, which he promptly lights as he relaxes back into a butter-soft leather chair. "Very well, Molly. What brings you here?"

"I want to talk to you about your wife."

One blonde eyebrow shoots up. "What about her?"

"There are a number of people in Boston who feel that you railroaded her into that sanitarium with little or no cause . . . important people."

He bristles slightly, then chuckles it away. "Nonsense. Everything was done legally with a doctor's papers to support the fact that she is mentally unstable and a danger to herself and others."

"Yes, Dr. Wainscott, wasn't it?"

He flicks an ash into a heavy brass ashtray.

"He's very well known in the medical field as a society hack. How much did he cost you?"

"Sister dear, are you accusing me of bribery?"

"Probably, but I want to get to the point of this visit."

He's silent.

"Nellie is going to be freed from Danvers this week."

His eyes bug out slightly. "You're bluffing. There's no way she'll ever get out of that place."

"All right, believe what you wish. Just know that it's going to happen and that you will never see her again. She will disappear, and gossips will say she probably walked into the ocean and committed suicide. You can play the grieving husband for the newspaper and get lots of sympathy. Poor Sean Halloran, with a crazy wife who escaped an insane asylum and killed herself and possibly her child. The more you play it up, the sadder it will be. And, best of all, the publicity should help you with the election in four years."

She can see his mind working feverishly. The cigar is ignored.

"I've heard that the party feels that having a wife in Danvers will be quite a hardship during your campaign. A grieving husband is much more palatable to the electorate than a scoundrel who falsely committed his wife to an insane asylum, Sean." She crosses her arms over her ample chest. "Think about it."

Molly remembers now the sisters at St. Augustine telling her that her little brother was a very smart boy, but not as smart as she had been. She remains silent, waiting for his response.

"I need to think about this."

"There's no time. And besides, I'm not finished."

"What?"

"There's the matter of Kathleen. The little girl you're planning to send to boarding school next year to get her off your hands. It's common knowledge you don't see much of her."

"She's taken care of nicely by Mrs. O'Dwyer." An ash falls on the carpet unnoticed. "What about her?"

"You are to tell your housekeeper that a relative will pick Kathleen up at home on Saturday morning. It's her third birthday, lest you forget. Tell Mrs. O'Dwyer you'll be staying home that day and that she has the day off. Kathleen will disappear from your life that day, along with her mother."

Sean's face reddens with anger. "Are you crazy, Molly?"

"Not at all, Sean."

"She's my child."

"That's the thing, Sean. She's not."

As he hears the truth about Kathleen's birth and Molly's part in the deception, Sean visibly shrinks down into his chair.

"Did you never question the lack of resemblance to you and Nellie? Didn't you wonder, Sean, why Kathleen came so early and weighed eight pounds at birth? You were duped, dear brother, plain and simple. Happens all the time."

"You're lying."

"No, I'm not, and now you know it."

"I'll have you arrested, Molly. I'll tell the police you tried to blackmail me." His grin is nearly a snarl. "I'll close up your practice and Kathleen's Haven as well. You will never practice medicine in Massachusetts again."

"Well, there's one more thing, Sean. Do you remember that night when Kam caught you in the brothel? So embarrassing, wasn't it?"

His eyes flame pure hatred at her.

"Do you recall that Kam took pictures of you and a woman, not your wife, in what I must call a very compromising situation? You'll be pleased to know those pictures turned out very well; a bit comical, but clear as crystal. He still has those pictures and the negatives as well."

"You are blackmailing me." He viciously jams his cigar into the ashtray.

"Yes, I suppose I am, Sean. But it's better that you know all this now rather than right before election day when they appear on the front page of the *Boston Globe*, don't you agree?"

"I want those pictures and the negatives, Molly," he hissed through clenched teeth.

"I don't blame you. And here's how you'll get them." She hands over Kam's instructions.

In the lobby, Molly again approaches the receptionist's desk. "Mr. Halloran doesn't wish to be disturbed this afternoon."

As she walks back out of the law firm and into the sunshine, she is smiling. *Well, Sister Sarah Marie was right. I am smarter than my brother.*

CHAPTER THIRTY-NINE

JULY 1880

NELLIE

My eyes flutter open and at once fill with tears. Yesterday, I'd caught a glimpse of a calendar and realized that my baby turns three years old today, and I won't see her. *Will they bake her a cake? Will they put a pretty dress on her? Is there a party planned?*

I sit up, stretch, and wipe my eyes. I cannot be depressed today. If I seem sad, they'll take that as a symptom of a new kind of mental illness and give me a pill for it. I do not want another pill to hide and throw away. I must be strong and not think about Kathleen right now. I must focus on how to act so that I can be released and see her again. It's hard to be always cheerful when my heart is breaking, but if that's the price of getting out, that's what I will do.

As I dress in the clean grey shift they gave me yesterday, I look around. *Where is everyone?* The room is empty of all the women. *Even Nurse Marion isn't here. I must see if I can find anyone, although I'm certain that door is locked. It is always locked. But if I call out loud enough, someone will come and tell me where everyone is.*

I go to the door to call out and try the lock. Magically, the door swings open freely. Confounded, I go across the hall to wash up. If I'm clean, it's easier to act happy.

Back in the room, I hear someone knocking on the closed door. I call out, "Who's there?"

"Orderlies," a male voice answers.

I open the door and two tall men stand there, wearing scrubs and masks. One of them is a Negro who says, "Nellie."

That, that voice is so, so familiar.

Then, I notice it, a large trunk. They carry it into the room and open it. It's filled with what looks to be soiled linens and uniforms.

For just a minute, I think, *Am I going crazy?*

"Don't you recognize me?" The Negro lowers his mask.

I gasp, hands clasping over my mouth, and whisper in urgency, "Neo."

He gives me that grin that has always meant we are going to have an adventure. I start to grab him for a hug, but he stops me. "No time for that, Nellie. We're here to get you out of here."

"How?" Before he can answer, I get a better look at the white man. "Aren't you from the . . . circus?" I ask in disbelief.

"Sure am, Felicity."

"Who are you?"

"Frank, the clown."

Oh my gosh! The clown that all the children loved the most. He used to ride into the center ring on a mule-drawn cart and honk a horn at each child as he passed them. Even the most timid little one couldn't resist his joyful honks. Little arms would rise to him, wanting more. And he always gave it to them. "Frank, oh, Frank, I'm *so* glad to see you again."

"Yes, me, too, Felicity, but right now, you must get in this trunk. We'll talk later."

Because I trust these two with every fiber of my being, I obey and climb in. The space is tiny, and it makes me contort in a way I didn't think I could do ever again. Neo covers me with soiled linens and says, "I'm going to close the lid now and lock it. Whatever happens, don't move a muscle nor make a sound."

With that, the lid lowers and I hear a solid click. It's completely dark. My coverings stink of sweat, blood, and God knows what else, but I don't care. Anything's better than Danvers. I feel myself lifted and carried somewhere, but have no idea where. The trunk shifts and I am pressed against its wall. I think we are going down a flight of stairs. We stop and I'm set on the floor.

"Whatcha got in there, lads?" a male voice says.

"Just some dirty laundry," comes a reply.

Was that Frank?

The lid unlocks and lifts, but I remain covered; barely breathing; the stench horrid. I will my heartbeat to slow, thinking he might detect it. The man rummages through some of the linens but never touches me; appalled at the filth and goes no further.

"Okay, get," he says, cocking a thumb, then wiping his hands on his pant legs in disgust.

The lid closes, then immediately Neo and Frank lift me and start down another set of stairs. Again, I am smashed against the wall, but I do not utter a sound. After one more staircase, I see light through a crack in the trunk.

Are we outside?

I am lifted and thumped down on a hard hollow surface. We start to move, and I hear the clip clop of horses' hooves. I am banged from one side of the trunk to the other and just know my body will be covered with bruises.

And I have never been happier in my life.

We travel for an indeterminate time, but finally, the horses' hooves slow to a slow walk.

Where are we?

"Tie up the horses, Frank, then we'll get her out."

Muffled sounds come from outside as I am lifted once again and then banged down. I hear the key turning until the lock clicks. The lid of the trunk is lifted and sunshine pains my eyes. It takes me a minute to unwind myself from my pretzeled state. A strong hand takes hold of my wrist and slowly pulls me up and out of my confinement.

For a minute, I fear my legs will not support me, that they will buckle under me as I try to climb out, but then I am on a sidewalk, standing free, squinting in sunshine. "Neo, Frank, I love you and can never thank you enough for this."

Neo clamps onto his sidekick's shoulder with great reverence. "Actually, Nellie, it's Father Frank now."

"What? You're a priest?"

"Sure am, Felicity. Or should I call you Nellie? Seems Neo here was playing lots of tricks on me back in our circus days."

Each of them takes an arm and they begin to walk me around until I am steady on my feet and warming up.

"Where are we?" I ask, taking in a deep breath through my nose, detecting the scent of salt water.

"At a pier."

I take in my surroundings. "This doesn't look like Boston."

"No," Neo answers. "This pier is in Fall River, Massachusetts. We'll meet the others here later today, and tomorrow take a steamship to New York."

"Others?"

Neo says, "We're going to a boarding house near the pier. The lady there is an old friend of Frank's."

Father Frank guffaws at the thought. "Just wait'll you meet her. Maeve O'Brien, one of the saltiest saints I've ever known. The word corker was invented to describe Maeve. Her mouth might shock you, but her heart will win you over every time."

As we stroll through the sooty streets of Fall River, I remember, *The last time I was here was with Derry.* I tear up and realize that I'm as rumpled as all the other people on the road and draw no attention for my wrinkled gray shift, worn slippers, matted hair, and gray woolen blanket wrapped about my shoulders. *Oh, what would he think?* Then my thoughts go further back, *It was so different when Neo and I were in this town enroute to New York to join the circus. We were children, out for our grand adventure. Who knew how our lives would diverge back then?* He met a gorgeous French girl, Angelique. I worried then, because of their different color, that their love was doomed. I told Neo that. And now, here they are, happily married and living in Ireland. What a silly girl I was in those days. I actually thought I was in love with Sean O'Halloran and could imagine no future brighter than as his wife. *How wrong I was. How wretchedly wrong.*

But that was then.

Now, I really want to know how Neo got me out of Danvers. When I ask him, he commences a long tale that sounds like something concocted by Edgar Allen Poe; a story so complicated I can hardly believe it.

"Nurse Marion was a major contributor to your freedom, Nellie, along with her husband, Raymond, who is the butler in the house of Governor Oliver Ames. Raymond overheard Republican conjecture that having a wife committed to Danvers would be a distinct political liability for Sean."

That could explain a lot about Sean's motivation for not reporting my escape. *But I didn't even know nurse Marion, except that she was a friend of Mam's. And her husband? Raymond? Never heard of him. How can it be that two unknown Negroes helped free me? Did they know Uncle Kam? Was he the catalyst for their aid to me? If so, God bless him.*

Neo continues, "Mollie arranged to meet with her brother at his law firm where she pointed out to Sean ways that he could make your disappearance an advantage to him. She also told him that Kathleen was another man's baby. Your mam brought Father Frank on board. She felt he could be trusted with the secrets of your escape. And also," he says, patting Frank's belly, "we needed someone with the heft to help me carry that trunk. She had no idea I knew him from his clown days, let alone that he knew you."

As I listen to the machinations employed to get me out, I marvel at all the people who had helped free me. Most of all, I thank God for bringing them all together and making their efforts successful. Brushing the hair from my eyes, I look heavenward. *You really do work in strange ways, don't you?*

"Well, here we are." Father Frank points to a two-story brick home. "This lady and I go back a long way." He knocks on the front door.

When a woman opens the door, her brogue is so thick I struggle to understand her. "Frank, you guinea rascal, get your arse in here right now."

The foyer of the house is all shining wood and heavily scented with furniture wax.

Frank laughs and gives her a big hug. "Maeve O'Brien, you mick scamp, you never change, now do ya?"

"God love ya for being a liar, you big oaf you." She slaps him on the shoulder and turns to me. "So, this is Miss Nellie Kelly, is it?"

"Actually, Mrs. O'Brien, it's Nellie O'Halloran now. My maiden name was Kelly."

"Ach," she says, grabbing me in an embrace that feels like it might crack a rib, "once a Kelly, always a Kelly, I say. From County Kerry I'd wager. The O'Halloran name comes from County Antrim, hardly Ireland at all, at all. The Northerners are more Scottish by temperament, truth be told. Stingy bastards."

"Watch your mouth, Maeve, or I'll have to give you a penance," Frank says.

"Just you try it, Francis Cancro. I knew you as a squalling babe at your mam's breast, long before you became a high-fallutin' priest. Your mam taught me how to make Italian gravy, for Christ's sake. Don't you get all judgey about my language now. Louisa Cancro could outswear any sailor ever courted either of us. Gah, I loved that girl from the day we got off our boats, her from Italy and me from Ireland."

"And so did I, Maeve. So did I."

Do I detect a slight mist in Father Frank's eyes?

"Can you show us our rooms now?" he asks.

"Indeed. Just follow me up these stairs."

On the second floor of the house, I'm shown into a small room with two beds. "This will do for you and your mam, love?"

"Yes, indeed. It's fine." *Mam is coming? She's one of the others Neo spoke about?* My heart is full. *I'm going to see Mam again!* I follow Neo and Father Frank to the next room with its two small beds.

"You'll share this room with your da, young man." She points to Neo.

Uncle Kam is another other. "Where will Father Frank sleep?" I ask.

He answers, "I'm bunking at the rectory of St. Thomas Aquinas here in Fall River. The Monsignor is an old friend."

In the hall, Mrs. O'Brien opens a closet and pulls out a small cot. "This'll be for the little girl. I'll set it up in your room now."

Little girl? Can it be? My breath catches around my heart and I turn to Neo. "Is it?"

His eyes twinkle when he says, "Yes, Nellie, it is. Your mother is bringing Kathleen."

My joy exceeds my exhaustion. *I'm going to see Kathleen, my baby girl!* But just as quickly, my happiness is clouded by doubt. *How did they get her away from Sean? Does he even know she's gone?*

Neo, sensing my anxiety, says, "Don't worry, Nellie. He's agreed to let you have her. Mollie took care of that."

"But how? I can't believe he'd let her go."

"Once he learned he wasn't Kathleen's father, it seems he decided she was more trouble than she was worth. He needs to be free to campaign; to fabricate some story that will make him look good. You know Sean."

Yes, I know Sean. His ego is far bigger than his heart. Maybe he really will leave us alone now. My relief is quickly eclipsed by more questions. *Will she even recognize me? It's been over two years, most of her life. Where did they tell her I'd gone? Is she mad at me for leaving her? How will I ever explain to her that she won't see her father again?* My mind races with fearful possibilities.

Neo, knowing me so well, recognizes them instantly. "They'll all be arriving later today, Nellie." He turns to Mrs. O'Brien. "Would it be all right if the three of us had a cup of tea in your parlor, ma'am? I need to explain things to Nellie."

"Ach, sure! You boyos put the kettle on. Tea's in the small cannister. Sugar in the bowl and milk in the ice box. Help yerselves. I'm keeping this young lady up here to get her cleaned up some. She'll join you shortly." When we're out of hearing range of the men, she says, "Sorry, love, but you've the stink of three pigs about you, and that hair of yours is knotted beyond combing. Can't have you seeing your baby smelling bad and looking the banshee."

Though her words embarrass me, I know they're true and accept her hand as she leads me into a bathroom. There's a small heater thing attached to a bathtub and the water she runs into the tub quickly turns steaming hot. She opens a drawer and hands me a soft white towel and washcloth. "Soap's on the counter and here's vinegar for your hair. Soap it up and rinse it with the vinegar. It should take most of the dirt out of it."

She leaves the bathroom and returns in seconds holding a blue dress. "This one should fit you, dearie. It's from my skinny days. Maybe a bit old fashioned, but it'll suit you much better than the ugly thing you're wearing. I'll turn my back now. Take your clothes off and hand them to me. I'll take them to the back of the house for burning. You won't be needing them anymore." As she turns around, I strip off the gray shift from Danvers and hand it and the blanket to her; nothing else to give.

She opens the door, saying, "Now, give yourself a good, long washing, love. Take yer time."

My little girl. Kathleen. Soon, I'll be with her. I must make myself presentable. I lower myself the hot water and groan with pleasure. *How long has it been since I've bathed without a nurse watching me?* Bathing at Danvers was a bi-weekly event with only ten minutes allowed per girl. I soap up my hair and give it a good scrubbing, then rinse it with vinegar and hot water. My hair feels cleaner than it has for a year. *Such a luxury, clean hair and a clean body.*

When I'm finished, I pull myself up out of the hot water, wrap up in the soft towel, and rub myself dry, peering at my naked likeness in the mirror, something I had not seen in over two years. Feeling somewhat like my old self, I don the blue dress, which fits fairly well, and run the brush I find on the counter through my hair, letting its dampness hang down my back. Now, in the full-length mirror in the corner, there is a trace of old Nellie, me, clean and shining, not Ellen O'Halloran as Sean insisted on calling me. Twirling in the blue dress, I marvel that Mrs. O'Brien ever fit into it.

When I leave the bathroom, she greets me, "*Whoosh, mavourneen*! That dress never looked that pretty on me. You look grand, you do." She faces me away and lovingly braids my hair into one long tail; cinching it with a blue ribbon to match my dress. I pull it around my neck and finger it still in disbelief.

Reaching downstairs, the approving glances from Neo and Father Frank tell me the transformation is complete; the return of the woman called Nellie Kelly.

"I've got shopping to do," Mrs. O'Brien says, scurrying like a person half her age. She grabs her purse from a hall table and hurries out the front door.

We head into a spotless kitchen and, within seconds, boiling water is poured over loose tea in a lacy teapot next to the stove. Crisp, white curtains adorn the immaculate windows and the wood stove against the wall looks cleaner than most I've seen. When I open the icebox for cream, there it is on the top shelf in a pretty Belleek pitcher; its delicate white porcelain dotted with green shamrocks. A matching sugar bowl sits on a check-ered tablecloth nearby. Opening the cupboards, I pull out three green tea mugs and place them on the table. I am pleased that it's strong black tea, not the insipid brew they gave us at Danvers.

This feels so much like a dream. I pinch myself to make sure it isn't.

We gather in the parlor, carrying tea cups, the sugar bowl, and the cream pitcher on a tray left out for our use.

"I'll get the teapot after it's had time to steep a bit," Father Frank says.

Neo and I relax into two flowered chairs and gaze lingeringly at each other. I think neither of us believes we are here, together again.

When Frank goes to get the teapot, Neo says, "I want to tell you a bit more about how we got you here."

When he relates Mollie's meeting with Sean, I can't control myself. "I wish I could have seen his face when he realized he'd been bested by a woman, and his own sister at that. That would have been hilarious."

"So, Nellie, the plan is for all of us to go to Ireland. I've booked passage for us, under fictitious names to be on the safe side. I don't think Sean will try to find you, but we can't take any chances." He seems to fall into his own thoughts, then raises serious eyes. "Plus, there's one more thing for me to do, and I must do it from Ireland."

Though his somber demeanor intrigues me, I decide not to ask anything that might distill my delight. *Ireland. We're going back to Ireland. The place where I fell in love with Derry O'Byrne. Can it be I'll see Derry there? God, please let it be.*

Father Frank returns with the tea pot and sets it down on the table. Stirring cream into the hot tea, I question Neo further about Kathleen. He tells me that Sean angrily accepts that Kathleen is not his and probably has a plan to make her disappearance advantageous to his political ambition.

Poor Boston. What a scoundrel they will have as mayor. And there's not a doubt in my mind that he will be elected. It's what he's always schemed for after all.

The doorbell rings. Neo and I exchange an excited glance.

"Them, do you think?" I'm nearly bursting inside. *My baby!*

Father Frank rises. "Let me check. It could be someone for Maeve."

Neo takes my hand and squeezes it. My breath halts in my chest. Frank opens the door and I hear Mam's voice, "Hello, Father."

I madly dash to the door, my heart in my mouth. There they are, Mam, Uncle Kam, and, and my daughter, the most beautiful little girl in the world. They embrace me warmly. I want to grab her into my arms but see that she tries to hide behind Mam's skirt, so I restrain myself.

I gaze questioningly into Mam's tear-filled eyes. "Give her a minute, love," she says. "She's a bit scared."

Mam comes into the parlor, holding Kathleen's hand. She won't let go. "Sweetheart, now you can have the hot chocolate I promised. Let's find the kitchen," Mam said as she squats down to be on her level.

Oh, God, my child does not recognize me. A lump forms in my throat as I gently take Kathleen's other hand, and though she looks at me with suspicion, she allows me to lead her and Mam into the kitchen.

Mam takes a box of Van Houten powdered chocolate and a box of sugar from a drawstring bag. "Kam just found this wonderful chocolate. If we mix it with sugar and hot milk, it makes the most delicious beverage."

As Mam heats milk on the stove, I lift Kathleen onto a chair at the table. I sit next to her. "Sweetheart," I say, "do you know who I am?"

She shakes her head, her eyes large and suspicious. My heart breaks. Though she hasn't seen me in over two years, I thought she might remember me. I force the sadness away, telling myself with time she'll remember. She was only a little over a year old when I disappeared and God knows what Sean might have told her. I'm sure of it. And we have lots of time. All the rest of my life. "Kathleen, I'm your mama. I got sick and went to a hospital for a while, so I don't blame you for not knowing me."

"Mama gone."

"Yes, I know, darling, but now Mama is back."

Her eyes cloud with confusion. "No, no. Dada say Mama never come back. Mama in heaven."

So that's what he told her. Bastard. I hated him before, now I hope he burns forever in hell. "Did anyone ever tell you your mama is still alive?"

"Aunt Molly, but Mrs. O says she lies."

Mrs. O'Dwyer, Sean's devil housekeeper. May she rot in hell, too. "Honey, your dada and Mrs. O made a mistake. They probably thought I was dead, but they were wrong. I'm alive and right here beside you. And I'll never leave you again. Ever."

Her tiny forehead creases in doubt, but she looks closely at my face. Is there some recognition I see in her eyes? I want so much to take her into my arms and kiss her. I want that more than anything, but must be cautious and not frighten her further. So, I just squeeze her little hand and put my cheek against hers. "I love you, Kathleen," I murmur into her ear.

When I pull my face away from her, I see tears glistening in her eyes, but I can't tell whether they're tears of fear or recognition. I must and will give her time to remember me. As much time as she needs. And though she didn't see much of Sean when she lived with him, I must figure out some way to explain to her why he's no longer in her life. My child has been through enough confusion in her three years. I swear from now on my baby girl's life will be filled with love and security.

"Hot cocoa coming up," Mam says cheerily. "Who wants some?"

"I do," Kathleen says giddily. "Please."

"I just had tea, Mam, but thank you." It is all so surreal. My mam, my daughter, and me—all three generations—together again.

When she sets our steaming mugs on the table, she has tears in her eyes, too. And there's no mistaking them for sadness, they are pure tears of joy.

Just before she sits down with us, my mother reaches into her pocket and takes something out. I don't know what it is until she takes my hand and slips the *Claddagh* ring into my palm. I grasp it to my heart and rise to kiss her on the cheek. "Thank you, Mam. Thank you."

She kisses me back and sits.

Turning my attention to my little girl, I say, "Be careful, Kathleen, It's hot. Blow on it a bit, love."

The green eyes looking up at me glimmer with some faint remembrance. At least, I think they do.

CHAPTER FORTY

In the early afternoon, Mam and I decide to take Kathleen shopping. With money from Neo and Uncle Kam, we treat her to the best clothes we can find at Pilgrim's, the only store in Fall River. Since it is summer, we buy tiny cotton dresses with shirred bodices and petticoats and 'big girl' flowered pantalettes. I wonder who trained her to the chamber pot and hope it was done kindly. She wore nappies when I was taken from her. I just can't see Mrs. O being gentle nor kind.

Our last purchase for her is a velvet coat with a bunny fur collar and matching muff. Ireland can get cold when Autumn comes. Wearing the coat, she pirouettes and rubs the muff all over her face. She wants to wear her new coat home, but I say, "It's still summer, sweetheart. You must wait until the weather cools."

I almost expect a tantrum at this refusal, but she accepts my decision with only a slight pout. We stop at a tea room where she sits in a tiny highchair. Ladies around us murmur she is the prettiest little girl they've ever seen. And, they are not talking blarney to my child. Her golden-brown hair falls in delicate waves beside a face that is a perfect oval, with large eyes and a cupid's bow mouth. She really is a beautiful little girl. If she weren't mine, I would turn my head to look at her on the street. Kathleen seems embarrassed by the attention, but I love it. My chest may burst through my bodice with pride because she is a feminine replica of her handsome father, even to that stubborn forelock that insists on falling onto her forehead.

Upon our return to Mrs. O'Brien's, we find Neo pacing across the front porch. "Thank God you're home, Nellie. I received a wire changing our plans. Our ship to Ireland on Friday was cancelled. Now, we must leave New York tomorrow. So, this evening at six, our steamship to New York leaves Fall River. That trip is eight-and-one-half hours, so we'll get to New York in time. It's now after five, so we must gather everything and get to the dock immediately."

We hurry to our rooms to pack things up with thoughts flurrying through my head. We're going back to Ireland. Though I have many questions about citizenship and where we'll live, I brush them aside. I am with Mam, Uncle Kam, and Neo and I have my little girl beside me. What more do I need?

As I leave her house, Mrs. O'Brien again gives me a bone-crushing hug and makes me promise I'll toast her with a Guinness in Killarney one day. "That's my hometown, Nellie Kelly, and the place I vow to visit again before I push up daisies." She looks heavenward. "Ah, Killarney, how I miss you."

Saying farewell to Father Frank saddens me, but he wipes my eyes with a handkerchief that smells of fresh soap and incense.

"Kneel down all of you," he says.

We comply, even little Kathleen.

"I bless you on this journey in the name of the Father, and the Son, and the Holy Ghost. And now, for an old Irish blessing: May your lives be like good wine, tasty, sharp, and clear. And like good wine, may they improve year after year."

Amid hugs and kisses, we all climb into Mrs. O'Brien's wagon where her husband awaits to drive us to the pier.

At exactly ten minutes till six, we board the *Priscilla* and scurry to find our state rooms before we leave Fall River. I unpack the two dresses, shawl, and undergarments Mam bought me during our shopping trip with Kathleen. Although Mrs. O'Brien had kindly provided me with a dress, Mam insisted that it wouldn't be enough to carry me across the Atlantic, and she was right. Though my new dresses are far from fancy, they will do for this journey.

At bedtime, Kathleen cries a little until I rock her to sleep and tuck her into my bed, snuggling in next to her. Though I am assailed this night with fear about Sean not keeping his word and about how I will manage to earn our living, I hold her all night long, kissing her silken hair and whispering how much I love her, and praying, *Dear Father, please watch over us and keep us safe. Thank you for giving me back my daughter and my whole family. Amen.*

When I waken in the morning, she is staring at me with large, magical eyes. "Good morning, sweetheart. Did you sleep well?"

She nods and snuggles against me contentedly. "Yes, ma'am."

In time, she'll call me Mam. In time, everything will be all right.

We sail out of New York Harbor without incident, though I find myself constantly looking over my shoulder to make sure Sean's not behind me. All day, Kathleen is a whirlwind of questions. She asks often about her father. I lie to her because I don't want her traumatized further. "You'll see him again someday, baby girl. We're just going on a vacation with Grandma Mary and Uncle Kam. And Neo, too. You like Neo, don't you?"

She giggles. "Yes, he's funny and plays the best tricks."

"I know he does, sweetheart. He did when we were children, too. And he loves you very much. Everyone loves you."

A dark cloud descends upon her precious face. "I don't think Mrs. O loves me. She's mean. 'Specially when daddy goes away. Which is a lot of times."

I pull her into my arms. "You won't have to see Mrs. O ever again, my darling. Not unless you want to."

"I don't want to."

"Then, that settles that. Never again. Now, let's get dressed and go to breakfast."

"Can I have pancakes?"

"You bet you can, with maple syrup and butter."

CHAPTER FORTY-ONE

Our eight-week journey is blessed with mild weather and balmy skies. Though Kathleen sometimes erupts into a stormy tantrum, I am always able to calm her. Mam assures me this behavior is normal for a three-year-old, especially one whose life has been so disrupted by change. Her support calms me so that I am able to quiet Kathleen's fears and wait for the tempest to pass. Thank God Mam is here, experienced and mature.

It is nearly August when we spot the green of Ireland's shores, and my brain quivers in remembrance. As we near the harbor, passengers crowd the rails of the ship, excitement building as each minute passes. Once again, the heady scent of heather and the slower pace of the people moving along the verdant countryside brings a gentle relaxation I'd forgotten. I feel I can breathe again, without fear, without restraint.

As we disembark, Angelique runs up the gangplank to embrace Neo. Her beauty, as always, stuns me, and then I notice the new swell of her belly under the pink dress. She is radiant with joy and good health. When she reaches Neo, their kiss makes me long for Derry. He holds her away from him and caresses her stomach gently. "She's growing nicely, isn't she?"

"Ah, *ma chère,*" she pouts. "What if it's a boy? Will you be sad?"

"Of course not, love. I'm just hoping it's a little girl who looks like you." He opens his arms to the rest of us, and we all walk into the circle of their embrace. There are some tears but, mostly, there is joy. As we set foot on the Dublin dock, I notice a tall, dark-haired man standing next to a large carriage. For no reason I can decipher, his stern demeanor causes my happiness to darken.

Angelique introduces him as the husband of the house where we'll be staying. "Everyone, meet Thomas O'Neill. He'll be driving us to the cottage." As the others climb into the carriage, Angelique takes my hand and pulls me to the side. "Nellie, I need to talk to you."

Her urgent tone alarms me. "Are you all right, Angelique?"

"Oh, yes, it's nothing serious. I am just terribly frightened of childbirth. I know nothing about it and have no one to ask. Since you've experienced it, I hope you'll talk to me."

Remembering the pain of my long labor with Kathleen, I embrace her before speaking. I mustn't tell her how painful my labor was, so I stall with this excuse. "As soon as we settle in, Mam and I will talk to you about it." As we join the others in the carriage, she wraps an arm around my shoulder.

Her obvious relief makes me feel as though I've deceived her, and that troubles me.

"Dear Nellie, I am so happy to hear this. You are like a sister to me, and I need you. My baby is due in six weeks, and I've been so worried."

I touch her child mound and lean down to kiss it. When Mam sees me, she bends over it and makes the sign of the cross. "All blessings to this wee baby. As its Celtic godmother, I pray that the luck of the Irish will abide with it all the days of its life."

Angelique has rented a house for us near where she and Neo

live, in a lovely neighborhood only ten minutes or so from the port of Dublin. It's a pretty stone bungalow with buttercups and clover covering a trellis in the front yard. A well for water lies to the right side of the house tells me the Irish have not the luxury of running water that many in America have enjoyed for some time. *That's fine with me. I'll trade away convenience for safety and peace any day, especially after what I endured as the mistress of Sean O'Halloran's fine house.*

Angelique says our landlady is out shopping and that we're to let ourselves in. So, I find the key under the rock on the top step and open the front door.

Kathleen runs in and says, "It's so pretty . . . and little." The parlor is painted a cheery yellow and its main wall is a large stone fireplace. In a copper carrier next to the fireplace are pieces of brown slag where I would expect to see coal.

Mam explains, "'Tis peat, Nellie. Turf the Irish dig and use for heat. When I was a girl in Kinsale, my mam and I would take a wagon to the bog and dig out the bricks of peat, then set them to dry in a cave nearby. Because of all the rain, it took nearly half a year before we could use them to heat water in our one-room cottage. But the burning of the peat was truly a heavenly scent. And one I wager you'll experience soon."

Between the parlor and a bright kitchen, a wooden staircase leads to a second floor. Upon ascending it, I find two bedrooms. Turning, I see Uncle Kam and Mam going into one of them. I figure he's helping her with her suitcase. But when they come out of the bedroom, both of them wear expressions that confuse me. They look guilty.

"What's the matter?" I ask.

"Why don't you put Kathleen down for a nap, Nellie. We'll wait downstairs. We want to talk to you." Uncle Kam's tone is serious.

Nodding, I take Kathleen into the other bedroom. The large bed is topped with a downy white coverlet that beckons me to lie down. I undress Kathleen and put her into a pink nightie we'd purchased in Fall River. Its soft flannel is covered with sleeping lambs. When she has it on, I tuck her under the downy coverlet and lie down with her until she is fast asleep. My urge is to stay there with her and sleep a bit myself, but the whistle of a tea kettle from downstairs beckons. I close the curtains against the late afternoon sun and tip toe out of the room, leaving the door ajar for hearing.

In the parlor, I find Mam and Uncle Kam sitting together on a small sofa. Three tea cups filled with black tea sit on top a small table centered between the couch and two matching chairs.

I take one of them and gratefully lift a cup to my lips. "She's sound asleep. It's a relief to not feel the rolling of the ship. I'm pretty tired myself."

Mam clears her throat and tucks a tendril of her red hair back up into the bun at the back of her head. Her gesture seems self-conscious, something unusual to her normal no-nonsense manner.

"What's wrong, Mam?" I ask.

She stammers some nonsense about being relieved to leave Boston behind; that she's happy to finally be home in Ireland. But her tone is hollow and nervous. Then, Uncle Kam takes her hand.

I'm surprised at his gesture. In all the years I've known him, I can't recall ever seeing him touch her before. And there is a certain familiarity with the way he cradles her hand in both of his that startles me. *What's going on?*

"Nellie, we've wanted to talk to you about something for a while now but the time was never right. First, there was your obvious unhappiness in your marriage to Sean. And then, of course, Danvers. We just couldn't find the proper occasion for telling you our relationship has changed."

"Changed?" I look from one to the other, totally confused.

"You know that Kam and I have been like a brother and sister since our time on the coffin ship? That your da and Aunt Imani were dear friends as well?"

"Of course, I know that. The Okafors have always been family to me. Some of my happiest times happened at their house on holidays. What's changed?"

Uncle Kam says, "Do you recall the night you went off to New York with Derry."

I nod, feeling my face grow warm.

"That evening, after we put the two of you on the train, I invited your mother over for dinner. She sorely needed a distraction from her worries about you. After dinner, we went into my study for brandy. As we sat there, I could see her trembling."

"I was terrified at what people would say, Nellie," she interjects. "It wasn't that I didn't trust you. But if our neighbors or parishioners at St. Augustine's learned that you traveled alone with a man to New York, the gossips would go crazy. I feared their silly chatter might negatively impact your teaching position at Girls High. You know how people are."

I nod my understanding. *Oh yes, Boston loves a good scandal more than most towns. Dishonor satisfies its puritan sensibilities.* I don't blame her for worrying. I'd feel the same if Kathleen decided to pull a trick like I did when she's grown. As I think of Kathleen off with a man, my stomach tightens. *What if she inherits my lustful nature? I'm the one who climbed up into Derry's berth on that train, who spent every possible minute of that weekend in his bed. He tried to protect me, but I wouldn't allow it. Even now, my body heats in remembrance. What if Kathleen is like me?*

Kam's voice interrupts my thoughts. "As we sat there that evening, your mother started to cry and, in an effort to comfort her, I sat next to her and put my arm around her shoulder. I hated seeing her so upset and wanted to calm her."

Calm her?

She sighs, smiling. "After a while, I settled myself, but when I looked up into his face, things were different."

"Different?"

"Yes."

Is she avoiding my eyes?

"Kam was still my friend. Would always be that, but in that instant, he was something more."

The meaning of her words startles me. *Is she in love with Uncle Kam? Surely not. They're so old. He's fifty now, and she's only a few years younger. How can they experience love at this age?* Though he's like a second father to me, it's impossible to think of the two of them as lovers. *He's a Negro. It was hard for me to accept such a relationship between Neo and Angelique, but with my mam? Impossible.*

"Nellie, I love Kam. Along with your da, he's the finest man I've ever known."

So, not impossible.

Unable to speak, I stand, excuse myself, and go upstairs to bed. When they think me out of earshot, I hear her say, "Kam, do you think I should go up and talk to her?"

"No, love. Let Nellie work through this by herself. When she's mulled over what we told her, we'll both talk to her. But not tonight. She needs sleep after all she's been through."

I close the bedroom door behind me and climb into bed next to Kathleen, fully clothed. My mind whirls with questions. Why did they keep their secret from me all this time? According to Uncle Kam, their love affair, or whatever it is, began during the week I was in New York City with Derry. And that was nearly four years ago.

Derry. Memories flood my senses. His scent, his eyes looking down at me, the feeling of his skin pressed against mine. The joy of him finally inside me, undulating like an ocean wave. taking me to heights of feeling I never knew existed. People's gossip didn't matter a whit to me then. What mattered was me and Derry. Falling deeply and forever in love with each other. It was the happiest time of my life. As I look at my ring, I ponder, *Can that be how Mam feels?*

No wonder she worried about me. Though I wouldn't change one minute of my time with Derry or one day of being Kathleen's mother, I didn't show good sense back then. Then, I compounded the foolishness by lying myself into a marriage with Sean.

But can they enjoy making love as Derry and I did? At their age? The thought of it embarrasses me. *Maybe it's just a deeper friendship for them. Companionship.*

Does Neo know? Oh yes, of course he does. Perhaps he encouraged them to come to Ireland to protect them, where they would be better accepted. His hero was Frederick Douglass who said he was happier and more welcomed in Ireland than anywhere in the world. No one in Boston would accept miscegenation. *But is that what this is?* On the ship, Kam slept in Neo's cabin and she with me and Kathleen. But now they're together in the bedroom right next to me and Kathleen. But perhaps, just as friends. I snuggle next to the child sleeping beside me. A rush pours over me like an ocean of love. She is so perfect in her slumber, so innocent. *When she gets older, will she understand her grandma sleeping with a Negro? Will her friends make fun of her because of it?*

Would she have been better off if I'd stayed with Sean, living in that mansion on Beacon Hill? As a child, I envied the girls at St.

Augustine's who lived there. I was jealous of their clothes and the fancy carriages that dropped them off at school. I coveted their crustless sandwiches cut into perfect triangles by their maids. Mam calls people with maids "silk stocking Irish." I so wanted to be one of them and live on Beacon Hill.

And then, I did. *Did that make you happy, Nellie Kelly? No. What made me happy was time with Derry and life as a teacher.*

So, Uncle Kam's a Negro. As a scientist, I know that his dark skin is because he came from the sun in Africa. When I was little and asked why some people had dark skin, Mam used to say that people were like puddings . . . some white and some dark. Both wonderful, depending on whether you liked vanilla or chocolate. Now that I'm educated, I know full well that a Negro's heart has ventricles just like mine; that they bleed red blood just as I do; that his bones break as painfully as do mine. I'm a scientist because Uncle Kam taught me science. It's because of him that I was the first science teacher at Girls High.

I think back to holidays with him and Imani. His maid, Martha, made the most delicious cookies I've ever tasted and taught me how to make them, too. And when, years later, I felt guilty about nighttime raptures, it was Martha, with her dark skin and divinely wise heart, who told me that my dreams were just God's way of preparing me for marriage.

I learned with Derry that she was right.

I must accept them, whatever their relationship. I love them both so very much. God, please help me. With that prayer ricocheting in my brain, I fall asleep.

CHAPTER FORTY-TWO

I am awakened from a delicious dream of Derry by Kathleen's persistent tapping on my shoulder. "Mama, I smell breakfast. I'm hungry."

What did she call me? Mama? Yes, she surely did.

As I kiss her good morning, memories of that dream bring heat to my body. Without warning, a strange question enters my mind. *What if Derry were Negro? What if his skin was black, like Uncle Kam's? Perhaps I would never have been attracted to him, but what if I were? Could I have given him up? Would it have mattered if I were twenty or fifty? Did God send me that dream to remind me of how it feels to be loved and the power of passion?* I have no answers to these questions, except I know I would still love Derry, no matter what. Perhaps that's how Mam feels about Uncle Kam, even at her age.

A water basin filled with warm water sits on the floor outside our room. After we both use the chamber pot tucked under the bed, I wash Kathleen and myself and get us dressed to go downstairs. Sun streams through every window, and I am struck once again with how clean Irish women keep windows and how perfectly ironed every lace curtain is that covers them. For some reason, this makes me happy.

Everyone sits at a large breakfast table, including Neo and Angelique. Two mixed couples happily enjoying and loving one another unconditionally. Although my stomach still clenches at the sight of Mam's and Uncle Kam's happy faces, I tell myself it's time to be practical, if not understanding quite yet.

"Good morning, Nellie, Kathleen. Did you sleep well?" Neo asks.

Kathleen burbles giddily, "Yes."

A large woman wearing a homespun house dress comes in from the kitchen to greet us. Her hair is red and curly, and her eyes, clear as blue crystal. "Good morning, good morning. I'm Mamie O'Neill, your innkeeper. Sorry I wasn't here to greet you, but my sister next door had the woman troubles last night." She shakes her head. "She's better today. I'll be cooking your break-fast now." She goes to Kathleen. "So, tell me, darlin', what can I get you?"

"Pancakes?"

"Yes, indeed, love. With butter and syrup? And a glass of milk?"

Kathleen glows as she politely says, "Please." I can tell from the look on her face that she likes this woman, and so do I. She's jolly and seems to understand little girls, and maybe big girls as well. She taps my shoulder. "And you, Mama?"

"The same, please. And perhaps a fried egg? And coffee, Mrs. O'Neill."

"Please call me Mamie, won't you? It's simpler. When someone calls me Mrs. O'Neill, I think they're talking to my mother-in-law, God rest her soul." She lets out a loud guffaw. "Though I question whether the woman got past the pearly gates at all, at all. Don't tell my husband, Joe, I said that, okay? He's something of a sourpuss."

So, the dour man who drove us here is married to this cheerful soul? They seem an even stranger pair than Mam and Uncle Kam.

Mamie is clearly playful and funny like many Irish women, and I do like her. Sean would have called her vulgar, but I think she'll be a friend. Perhaps our time in this charming stone cottage will be lovely. It's sure to be full of laughter. And perhaps, love. Uncle Kam's eyes glow with adoration as he gazes at Kathleen. No one at the house on Beacon Hill looked at her that way. Certainly not Sean or Mrs. O'Dwyer. It's good for a child to see faces filled with such love. Whatever their color.

When did I begin to judge anyone for the color of their skin? When did I allow the word nigger to be said in my presence? How could that have happened when both my parents despised prejudice and all the other snobby beliefs surrounding us in Boston? Then, I remember Sean sneering at every Negro on the street. He would scarcely allow Uncle Kam in our house. Called him a nigger. Same with Neo. *Am I becoming like Sean?* I cringe. *Dear God, this I swear: Katheen will be taught acceptance, not bigotry.*

I take Mam's hand. Her eyes turn to me, frightened, which breaks my heart. "I'm sorry, Mam. I was being a brat."

Her hand relaxes under my touch. "Yes, you were, Nellie. But that's all over and done with now. Water under the bridge."

After we've eaten, Neo asks me to come outside for a minute. The sun is now covered over with clouds.

"Irish weather is so unpredictable, Neo. From one minute to the next, you don't know what's coming. I need to get a shawl. Be right back."

When I return, he's sitting on a swing on the porch. When he sees me, he pats the space next to him. "Come, sit with me Nellie."

I do, and he commences to swing us gently, then angles his body to face me. "Do you remember when I told you there's another thing I must accomplish before our baby is born?"

"Yes, I do, Neo. And I wondered what you were talking about."

"I leave tomorrow for England."

My breath catches in my throat. "Derry?"

"Yes, I have a friend there who will help me get him out of Brixton. It's going to be tricky, but I think our plan is sound."

His plan is sound. Neo doesn't do anything unless that is the case. That means that soon I'll see Derry again. In my excitement, I grab his hand. "Can I come with you?"

"No, Nellie, and I can't even tell you how we'll do it. Nobody knows that but my friend in London. And Derry. He's aware we're on our way to him, but the fewer people who know about this, the better. Trust me."

"You know I trust you. More than almost anyone. If you say I can't know what you're doing, that's all right. Just bring him back to me."

The door opens, and Angelique comes onto the porch. "Do I interrupt?" she asks in her heavy French accent.

Neo rises from the swing and takes her in his arms. "Of course not, sweetheart. You are always welcome. But now, I must excuse myself and prepare for tomorrow's trip."

She raises an eyebrow in curiosity but doesn't ask the question. She knows her husband well. If he keeps his destination secret from her, she appears to recognize that it's all for the good. "Just travel safe and come home to me, Neo."

He kisses her and goes into the house.

She stares after his departing back wistfully. "May I join you on the swing, Nellie?"

Patting the spot beside me, I answer, "Of course, Angelique." When she sits down, I put my arm around her shoulders and squeeze. She turns her face to me, and I see consternation there. "Are you all right?"

"*Oui*, I mean, yes. It's just what I told you about. I'm frightened of childbirth. And I wish my mother was alive to explain how to manage the labor."

"Oh, yes." I'd forgotten for a minute or deliberately put it out of my mind because of the labor I'd experienced with Kathleen. "Let me get Mam out here, if that's all right with you. Although I've had a baby, she has the experience of being a midwife. She can help you better." Maybe help us both. Birthing Kathleen was so difficult for me, and perhaps Derry will want more children, so I need reassurance as much as Angelique.

I rise from the swing and kiss Angelique's cheek. "I'll be right back with her."

I find her in the parlor playing with a giggling Kathleen. "Mam, Angelique is on the porch. She's concerned about labor and birthing her baby. Can you come out and talk to her?"

She stands immediately, looking around, then sees Uncle Kam on the staircase. "Kam, could you come here and stay with Kathleen for a few minutes. I need to go outside."

He comes into the parlor and picks up Kathleen. "Hey, little missy. Wanna play hide and seek?"

Kathleen giggles and nods her head.

On the porch, Mam sits down beside Angelique on the swing while I take a nearby chair and sit facing them.

"So, tell me, dear. What is your worry?"

"So many things, Mary. Will my baby be healthy? Will I love it enough?" Her face contorts in fear. "And the pain. I'm so afraid of the pain. A friend told me it feels like your back is breaking. I've never had pain like that. I don't want to embarrass myself by screaming, but I fear I will do that."

"Angelique dear, look in my eyes, please." The girl complies. Mam takes her face into her hands. "I'll be this close to you all through your labor and delivery. This close. I won't leave you. There may be pain, but I'll help you through that. I have *many* techniques to relax you. Tension and fear are the things that cause the most pain in labor. Plus, I brought laudanum with me from America. If necessary, I'll use it. But I bet you won't need it. You're a healthy, strong young woman. Your body was created to birth babies."

Angelique begins to cry softly. "But what if I'm too weak?"

Mam chuckles a bit before speaking. "Aren't you the girl who used to fly through the air on a trapeze? Do you remember the first time you did that?"

Angelique straightens up slightly. "Yes, I was eight. And terrified."

"Of course, you were, dear. Just a little girl with big courage. But you did it, didn't you? You sailed through the air, trusting your father or brother to catch you? Do you realize how brave and strong you must have been to do that? Think about that first time and what a wonder you were."

Angelique has a faraway look in her eyes and I hearken back to when I climbed back up on Bianco, my circus horse, after he had thrown me and given me a concussion. Come to think of it, I was courageous enough to run away to that circus when I was only thirteen. Foolish maybe, but brave and strong, too. How much better my birthing of Kathleen might have been had my mam attended me and not the man who refused her admittance to that awful white room where I labored alone.

"And you'll do this, too, Angelique. And end up with a beautiful baby to show for it."

Chapter Forty-Three

MARY

Four days have passed since Neo left for London. Every time the doorbell rings, Nellie jumps to answer it, hoping for a wire. Each time, she is disappointed. Kam and I reassure her that all is well and that Neo will write when he has news. But honestly, that's mostly blather. In truth, I'm as nervous as she is. So many things could go wrong. If the limey jailers get a hint of a plot to free Derry, they'll not hesitate to shoot him and Neo both. It's happened before.

Although Kam repeats that no news is good news, I can tell he's beginning to share my concerns, and that really frightens me. Kamua Okafor does not worry without cause. I go to early Mass at St. Brigid's every day and pray for their safe return. There's little else I can do. Sometimes, I ask Daniel to intervene with God on Nellie's behalf. I know he will, if he can. The nuns always told us that those in heaven who loved us on earth can intercede with God for us. *But, please God, forgive my disbelief.* Sometimes, I wonder if there is such a thing as heaven or even God. Even as I think such a thing, I curse myself for having such weak faith. *If there's no God to help, what chance do poor mortals have on this melancholy earth?*

Something happened that troubles me deeply, so deeply I've not even told Kam about it. Three nights after Neo left for London, when everyone was sleeping, voices awakened me; hushed but angry. I snuck from our bed without waking Kam, wrapped a shawl around me, and crept to the steps. I descended them until I settled in a crook on the staircase where I was invisible to the downstairs. Mamie and Joseph O'Neill were seated in the parlor arguing in voices tight with control.

"How dare ye let a nigger darken the doorsill of this house, woman?" he snarled.

"Lower your voice, Joseph. You'll wake the dead."

"'Tis disgraced, I am. The Yankees at the pub call me a coon lover because you allowed that darkie under my roof. Are ye daft, woman? You didna ask my permission to do such a thing."

"Since when do I need your permission to rent a room in this house? It was willed to me by my parents long before you came into my life."

"You're me wife, and you'll do what I tell you. Especially since the governor under the direction of Queen Victoria herself appointed me landlord. Not you, Mamie. Me! I don't care whose name this house used to be in. Now, it's mine to manage for the Commonwealth of Great Britain."

"Which makes you a traitor to Ireland. Your family was nothing in this town and hadn't a farthing to their name. The only way you got the license of landlord was by marrying me two years ago. And we both know that's what this unholy union is all about, don't we? You never lift my covers, though every gossip in Dublin knows about your whoors. When I get my annulment, now won't you be ashamed once your pub pals learn you've never consummated your marriage to me?"

He stands and towers over her, but she doesn't cower a bit. "Sit down, fool."

"That annulment you're always spouting about only applies to our standing in the Catholic Church. 'Tis not legal in the courts."

A gallows cackle escapes her as she states, "Just wait till all of Dublin knows you've betrayed Ireland to become a cuckold to Victoria. Your pals will ride you out of town and right into the Irish Sea, boy'o."

He jumps to his feet and storms out the front door. When she's certain he's gone, Mamie cries softly into her kerchief. Do you wonder that I've not told Kam about what I heard? He'd never stay in this house if he knew Joseph O'Neill called him nigger and is a traitor as well. My heart breaks for poor Mamie. Married to a bastard *quisling*.

'Tis eight days later when the doorbell rings, and the postman delivers the wire Nellie's been living for. Her face beams radiant as she reads it aloud, "'We've departed London and will arrive at Dublin Harbor on Friday.'" She whoops for joy. "Thank you, Jesus! Thank you! Friday! That's in two days." She lifts Kathleen into her arms and smothers her face with kisses.

When Nellie finally sets her down, the little girl dances around the room, singing "Jingle Bells." Mamie O'Neill, coming from the kitchen, joins right into the song and grabs onto the child's hands for something resembling a jig. They joyfully twirl around the room.

Mamie pants, "Though 'tis only August there is a Christmas feeling in the air today. What is it?"

"My love is coming back to Dublin on Friday." Nellie takes the older woman into her arms and joins the dance, all three of them singing, "Dashing through the snow on a one-horse open sleigh, o'er the field we go, laughing all the way," louder and sillier with each verse.

As I watch them, my heart nearly bursts. My beautiful girl, so happy. The daughter I feared might never laugh again, and there she is singing and dancing for joy. I tell you this moment makes the pain of watching her misery with Sean, the shock when he admitted her to Danvers, and the helplessness I felt because I could do *nothing* to save her—all of it almost washes clean in this one minute in time. *Almost. 'Tis moments like this that make motherhood worth it.*

"What'll I wear when we pick him up?" Nellie suddenly halts in a dead stop. "I must look pretty for him, and I fear I've grown too thin."

Indeed. Though the hollows in her face have begun to fill in from Mamie's good cooking, she still looks fragile as a willow branch. *Love will fatten my girl up.*

Mamie tips Nellie's chin up. "Miss, you're the prettiest girl I've ever seen in all of Dublin. And there's lots of beauties here. And thin is fashionable, you know?" She chortles. "Would that I could get myself down to your size. Aye, but I love me potatoes too much, I fear." She pats her ample hips. "As to a dress, perhaps you could get your sweet friend, Angelique, to take you shopping this afternoon. I wager she knows just the places to take you."

Kam, hearing the commotion, had come into the parlor and taken in all the conversations. "That's a good idea, Mamie. Have you a cart or carriage I can rent for the day? We'll pick up Angelique, and you girls can have a day of shopping on me while I look around the city of Dublin properly. I've been wanting to explore its apothecaries."

Within the hour, we're on our way. Angelique takes us to Wicklow Street, where a French designer friend owns a small shop.

"Grafton Street is where most women shop for clothes," she explains, "but Wicklow is more modern."

My da, Sean Boland, came monthly to Dublin from our home in Kinsale for meetings of the Fenians. That was more than forty years ago. Sometimes he'd bring me along to the meetings, wanting me to understand the importance of the fight for Irish independence. "Ireland is a proud country, Mary," he'd say. "And the limeys from across the pond have plundered us for more than five hundred years. They took our trees to build their ships and our food to fill their fat bellies while we stayed behind, starving." I can almost see him again, shaking his head. "They stole homes our ancestors built and appointed thieving landlords to collect rent to enrich the Crown; places the Irish have owned forever. A place in Kinsale was named Boland House before they stole it and renamed it Victoria Manor. Bolands fought with the great kings of Ireland for centuries. Now I will continue that battle until we are once again free."

"But, Da, when will that ever happen?"

"Ach, maybe not in my lifetime, girl. But hopefully, in yours."

And now I'm living in the house of one of those thieving landlords. Joseph O'Neill who became a traitor to Ireland and a lackey to England. And did it all by marrying poor Mamie, a woman he cares for not a whit. I despise the man, skulking around and looking down his nose at Kam and Neo, men whose boots he's not fit to polish.

It was important to Da that I love our homeland. It broke my heart to leave it as a young girl. But leave it I did. Now, I'm back.

On one of our trips to a Fenian meeting, Da told me, "Dublin is in County Wicklow, which is called the Garden Center of Ireland." On that same trip, he took me to the Wicklow Mountains, the majesty of them stirred my consciousness for months. Beautiful granite monoliths that seemed to soar all the way to heaven. Daniel once promised to take me to the White Mountains in New Hampshire. He'd seen them once as a boy fresh out of Ireland and yearned to revisit them with me. We never made that trip, though. He died too young. Too young.

All these memories rush back to me as we turn from Grafton to Wicklow Street. 'Tis sure this street reveres its namesake. Trees line the boulevard and every store front boasts a wooden box filled to overflowing with blossoms. Purple and green bells of Ireland entwine with white roses, thistle sprigs, and ivies I've never seen intermingle their fragrances all the way down the street.

Nellie, drawing in a breath, says, "This is what heaven smells like, I bet."

When Kam pulls the carriage before number 57 Wicklow, Angelique, Nellie, and I eagerly scramble to the cobblestones.

"I'll leave you ladies to shop and have lunch and pick you up at four o'clock. That should give you plenty of time to damage my bank account."

I kiss him on the cheek and am pleased to see Nellie do the same.

We ascend the stairs of the brownstone with Celine tastefully lettered on its awning. As we enter the shop, Angelique is greeted by a pretty young woman, the proprietor. Angelique introduces me and Nellie to Celine Allard who promptly breaks into excited French-tinged English. "Yes, this is my shop. I came here three years ago with my husband, a barrister. I had studied dress design in England before I met my Pierre. The dear man suggested he buy this shop for me. He's very modern, my Pierre, and wants me to be happy." She runs her finger through a rack of gossamer gowns. "My dresses are modified Regency styles, no corsets needed. Soon, I think, women all over the world will embrace them." She takes Nellie by the hand and turns her around and around, studying her physique with the trained eye of the skilled designer. "Ah, you, *Mamselle*, have the perfect figure for my styles; *elegante* with just a hint of the *demimonde*. Now that Angelique can no longer model for me because of her condition, maybe you?"

Nellie, clearly flattered, responds, "No, *madame*, my future is in such a flux right now, but thank you for the compliment."

"Well, if you ever change your mind, I would love to have you."

Nellie gives me a delighted wink over her shoulder as Celine takes measurements.

"Perfect, utterly perfect," she exclaims. "Now, please take a seat here and I will bring you some things to try."

We sit down on luxurious velvet tufted settees in shades of lavender and pink. When Celine returns with an armful of pastel confections, she holds each color close to Nellie's face. "Beautiful. Mmm, maybe not yellow. Your coloring requires rich jewel tones to set off the contrast of your dark hair and fair skin." Finally, she selects a blue dress made of a fine batiste and an emerald green silk gown as delicate as a whisper and takes Nellie into a dressing room.

In minutes, Nellie comes through the diaphanous curtain in the emerald dress. Angelique and I gasp at the vision of her. She wears small satin heels and short white gloves, and Celine has pulled her hair up into a tumble of dark curls that fall down her back.

"Beautiful," Angelique whispers as Nellie stands on a small platform in front of three mirrors, and twirls to see all sides of the dress."

Celine says, "It would require only a small alteration to be *parfait*, and I can do it tonight." She tightens the dress slightly through the waistline.

"I'd like to see the blue dress, too," I say.

"*Certainement.*"

"It's going to be hard to outshine that green dress, but blue has always been Nellie's best color. Because of her eyes," I tell Angelique.

When Nellie and Celine return to the parlor, there is no question in my mind that this is the dress she must wear to meet Derry. The slightly empire waistline and scooped neck show just a hint of bosom, and the color perfectly enhances her eyes. When Angelique emits an audible sigh, Celine and I look at each other in a silent conspiracy to convince her to take this dress, without any alteration. As it turns out, no convincing is necessary. My girl has already made her choice.

"This is the one, Mam."

So, dress in hand, we go to a nearby restaurant to celebrate our purchase.

"Do you think Derry will like me in this dress?" she asks.

Angelique pipes in, "If he doesn't, he's dead. If I wore that dress, Neo would make sure to remove it quickly." Blushing, she turns to me. "*Pardone*, Mary. I didn't wish to offend you."

"Offend? Hardly, girl. Don't forget, I was young once and my memory is very clear about how young men react to a woman like Nellie in a pretty new dress. Especially, young Irish men, whose horns seem to be more fully developed than some other nationalities, like the English."

Angelique says, "I wouldn't know about that. I met Neo when I was so young, and since then, I've had no interest in any man but him."

"And why would you? Look at him. He's a big beautiful panther of a man, I'd say. His father was the same when he was young."

"And now?" Angelique teases.

"Older and wiser," I answer but say no more lest I embarrass my daughter. I know Nellie has trouble accepting that Kam and I have any kind of physical relationship, and I understand that. Let it be our secret. Mine and Kam's. Our sweet, wondrous secret from the world.

After a lovely lunch of salmon fresh from the sea and strong black Irish tea, we head back to meet the man himself.

"Uncle Kam," Nellie says. "Thank you for everything. When we get back to the rooming house, I'd like to show you the dress you just bought me."

My dear man, happy to be back in her good graces, says, "And I'd love to see it, Nellie. Though I can't imagine you looking anything other than beautiful, whatever you wear."

At that, I let out a hearty *HA!* "And they say the Irish are full of blarney. Listen to himself, will you?"

"Let's just call me Black Irish, sweetheart."

Catching my breath, I glance at Nellie to see how she received the endearment. I'm relieved to see her smiling ear to ear.

CHAPTER FORTY-FOUR

MARY

On Friday morning, I wake to the sound of water being poured into the tub in the bathroom next to our bedroom. I nudge Kam awake. "Nellie's up early. She must have risen at dawn and drawn water from the well to heat for her bath."

"It's a big day, sweetheart. She wants to be sweet smelling for her lover." He pulls me over to him and nuzzles my neck. "I bathed yesterday for the same reason but fell asleep before you came to bed. Stay here a bit with me. We don't want to waste bath water, now do we?"

I don't resist his invitation. Stay I do. By the time I awaken again, I hear her footsteps going down for breakfast. "I'm up, Kam." I nudge him. "Want to be with my girl this day. I'll see you at breakfast." Wrapping a robe around my naked body and raking fingers through my tangled hair, I kiss him quickly and head downstairs.

"Good morning, Mam," Nellie says brightly. Sitting at the table with rags in her still-damp hair, she looks so like the little girl she was and my heart swells remembrance. I tied up that long, dark hair in rags for every special occasion of her childhood.

That's when I notice it—on the third finger of her left hand. "Nellie, love, you're wearing the Claddagh . . . for Derry."

"I never told you the whole story. Derry gave it to me when we were in New York. It was his mother's. I'll never take it off again."

I take her hand in mind. "'Tis beautiful, love. Wear it with pride."

Mamie brings us a tray full of pancakes, syrup, and butter, then fetches a pot of coffee and pours me a cup. "Mind if I join you?" she asks. This has become an every-morning experience of late and one I enjoy because of her marvelous sense of humor and good nature.

Sitting, she pulls at one of the rags in Nellie's hair. "So, going for curls, are you? Today is an important one, I guess?"

Nellie pours herself a second cup of coffee, grinning like a schoolgirl. "Indeed, yes, Mamie. A very important visitor sails in this afternoon." As she adds cream to her cup, she casts a devilish grin at me.

"I see. Will you be wanting Joseph to drive you to the harbor then? Just so long as he's able to meet his chums at the pub for supper, he'll do it. Who's coming in?"

Nellie pauses and her neck pinkens. "A young man named Daire O'Byrne. Someone I knew in the past and haven't seen for over four years. I call him Derry. We met when he was singing and playing his fiddle at The Brazen Head back when I came to Ireland for Neo and Angelique's wedding."

"The Brazen Head, was it? He must be very good with that fiddle. Only the best get hired there. When I was a young wan, my family had supper there once a month. Me da so loved the music. The Brazen Head has the best corned beef I've ever tasted. Haven't gone back since I got married. Where's Mr. O'Byrne playing now?"

"Nowhere right now." She takes a sip of her coffee and gives me a quick glance. "That was before he graduated from Trinity Law School and got deeply involved in the home rule movement. I doubt he has time to play his fiddle much anymore."

"Musical and principled then. I look forward to meeting young Mr. O'Byrne."

"And meet him you shall. May I invite him to join us for dinner tonight?"

"Surely you can. I've got a beautiful leg of mutton ready to cook. Plenty big to feed a crowd if you want to invite Angelique and Neo."

"Brilliant. Derry was Neo's groomsman. Yes, I'd love that, Mamie. Maybe we can convince Derry to play us a tune."

Mamie claps her hands in joy until footsteps on the stairs make us turn and look.

"Good morning, ladies," Kam, looking fresh and handsome, pulls a chair up to the table. "Sleep well?" He kisses me on the cheek and I catch the distinct scent of mint toothpaste.

"Not really. Scarcely a wink," Nellie says.

"Excited? I can understand that, dear," he says.

"Pancakes all right, Mr. Okafor?" Mamie asks, rising from the table.

"Perfect."

"So, where's young Mr. O'Byrne coming in from?" Mamie asks as she ladles pancakes onto Kam's plate.

"London." Nellie doesn't explain further and Mamie seems content not to ask.

"When's his ship expected?"

"Around two this afternoon, though it could be earlier or later, depending on the tides."

Mamie returns to the table, coffee pot in hand. Kam and I

accept a cup, but Nellie shakes her head. "So, is this Mr. O'Byrne a special friend, Nellie?" Mamie asks.

Nellie lifts her eyes, then, blushing a most becoming shade of pink, says, "Yes, special indeed."

As she carries dishes to the sink, Mamie begins to hum "The Rose of Tralee" in a lovely, throaty alto, then adds the lyrics, "She was lovely and fair like the rose of the summer, but 'twas not her beauty . . ."

At that moment, Joseph O'Neill stomps down the staircase and out the front door, slamming it behind him. Mamie shakes her head and sings no more.

Kathleen sleeps till nearly ten. After Nellie gets her washed, dressed, and fed, she cradles the child onto her lap in the parlor with a book. I join them; touched to see my daughter reading to her child. As she opens the cover, Kathleen asks, "What's this book called?"

"*Grimm's Fairy Tales*, honey. It was one of my favorite books when I was a little girl. Lovely stories. We'll read one every day. The first one is *Hansel and Gretel* about a brother and sister in Holland."

"I wish I had a sister, no brother."

This thrills Nellie. "We'll see."

Katheen's forehead puckers in a frown of remembrance. "Nobody ever read to me before. Mrs. O. couldn't read, I think. Will I learn to read someday?"

"Yes, you surely will, sweetheart. Actually, I'll begin to teach you now."

The little girl opens the book and finds a picture of *The Hare and the Hedgehog*. Delighted, she points and says, "Bunny."

"Yes, a bunny. Have you ever seen a real bunny?"

Kathleen lifts her eyes to the ceiling, then glowers and shakes her head. "Once, in our front yard, but Dada shot at him. That made me sad."

Nellie darts a worried look across the room to me, and I say, "Honey, I think Dada was just playing. Did the bunny run away?"

"Yes."

"See," I say. "The bunny was fine. Dada was just trying to make him run."

Nellie's eyes shine with gratitude.

At one o'clock, Nellie, looking lovely in her blue dress, says, "It's time to go. In case his ship is early."

Kam has agreed to stay home and help Mamie with Kathleen. As I kiss him goodbye, Mamie tugs on my sleeve. "A word, please?" I follow her into the parlor where no one can hear her. "Miss Mary, I need to tell you something." Her brow furrows with worry.

"What is it, Mamie?"

"My husband got wind of the fact that this gentleman coming from London was in prison for conspiring against England. I don't know who told him such a thing, but just be mindful."

"What might he do?"

"Nothing." She shakes her head. "He's mostly blather, but Joseph O'Neill is forever trying to impress the British Peelers. Makes him feel important. Just wanted you to know."

"Thank you, Mamie." *How sad this woman is married to such a blackguard.* Before I join Nellie at the door, I take Mamie into my arms for a hug.

"What's that all about, Mam?"

"Mamie just told me her husband learned that Derry was in prison." I climb into the carriage beside her.

Joseph O'Neill comes striding toward us, clearly intending to climb into the driver's seat.

"Joseph, you needn't come. Nellie can take us."

Nellie moves like the wind and beats him to the driver's seat to take the reins. "Don't you worry, Mr. O'Neill. I drove a carriage like this all over Boston. I'll be sure to tie up your horse securely."

His mouth gapes in protest, but Nellie brings the reins down on the horse's back and we trot off with Joseph scampering behind. When we are a good distance apart, I yell, "Whoa, Nellie. Slow down."

"Sorry, Mam, I needed to get away from that bastard as fast as I could. I don't like him."

Relaxing back into the soft seat of the carriage, I muse, *My girl is definitely getting a good share of her pluck back. She's going to be all right, she is. Now, let's just hope Derry can measure up to her.*

CHAPTER FORTY-FIVE

The ocean looks vast and serene when we pull into the dock area. Nellie ties the horse to a post and pats her nose. "We'll be back soon, fella. Here's a snack for you." She puts a portion of oats in front of the animal who immediately ducks his head into the bucket.

"We can keep an eye on the carriage from the dock, Mam, though horse thievery doesn't seem as common here as it used to be in Boston."

"I think that's because there are so many horses in Ireland. In Boston, they were at a premium."

We check the roster and learn that the ship from London is on course and will dock at Pier Six. It's now quarter past one. "Are you hungry, Nellie? There's a sandwich shop over there," I say, pointing.

She shakes her head. "I'm much too excited. But if you want something, I'll wait for you at the pier."

"I think I'll save my hunger for that lamb Mamie's preparing."

The two of us head to Pier Six. Heads turn to stare at the lovely young woman in her blue dress, but she's oblivious to them. Eyes straight forward, she strides to the waterfront and begins to scan the water, her hand sheltering her eyes from the sun.

"I cannot believe I'll see him again. It's been so long." She jerks around to face me. "What if he's changed? What if he doesn't love me anymore?"

"He will," I answer, certain of the truth in my words.

At two-fifteen, the pier bell chimes. A dock worker picks up a megaphone and shouts, "Ship 1420 from London now in sight!"

I feel Nellie trembling beside me. She gives me an excited glance and says, "Can you see it?"

I cannot. A small crowd has gathered, and everyone is scanning the horizon trying to get the first glimpse of the ship. Finally, a young boy near the dock's ropes yells, "There it is, off to the left. I see the sails."

All of us pivot to the left and stare at the horizon. Nellie stands on tiptoes and tugs at my sleeve. "There it is, Mam." She points. "Right there."

At first, there is nothing. Then, I see it. Two tiny white sails off in the distance. Nellie grabs me around the waist and squeezes. "He's coming. Good Lord, he's actually in sight. My Derry." She waves frantically, knowing full well he can't see her in the crowd now gathered with us.

"Yes, love. Yes. But it'll be another hour till he's here."

"I don't care. He's here. My Derry is almost here."

We stand there squinting into the sun for another thirty minutes until, finally, the ship draws close enough that the harbormaster sends out the barges to pull her in. The passengers standing at the ship's rail are still a jumbled mass of images, one indistinguishable from the other. With each second that passes, Nellie's energy escalates higher. Tears fill her eyes as she stares at the accumulation of humanity at the rail that somewhere contains the only man she's ever loved.

"Oh, oh!" she exclaims, and points toward the ship's bow. "There he is. See, Mam. See him waving to us. He's standing right there with Neo. He's so much thinner, but it is Derry."

I fix my eyes to the deck near the bow of *The Poseidon*. In all truth, the only way I am able to pick out Derry is to see Neo's dark face. It looks like he's the only Negro on the ship. But, she's right. It is Derry. And yes, he is thinner, but still a strong, handsome young man with the shock of brown hair falling over his forehead. His resemblance to Kathleen takes my breath away for a moment. The instant he recognizes Nellie, his joy registers by the lift of his face and the intensity of his waving. He is overcome with elation.

Whatever miracle Neo worked to get him home to Dublin, I know that Nellie, Derry, and Kathleen will be grateful to him for the rest of their lives.

The barge clunks against the pier and the deckhands attach their lines and begin to tug the ship further in so they might tie it to the pilings. Anchors clatter down the sides of the ship and she finally jolts to a halt. When the gangplank is lowered, people scramble to disembark. Neo and Derry are near the front of the line. Finally, the two of them race down to the dock, their knapsacks bouncing from their shoulders.

Nellie runs toward them, her arms extended. "Derry!" she calls.

When he spies her, he takes off in a fast sprint toward her. When they are together, he holds her out from him, saying, "My love, my pretty girl." When he takes her into his arms, he holds on as if he never wants to let her loose again. "Nellie, I love you with all my heart."

I am elated, knowing nothing's changed.

She stands taller, and just as their lips meet, I am distracted by a glint of metal hitting the left corner of my eye. I jolt my head to the left and see Joseph O'Neill raising a revolver from under his arm. Screaming, I run toward him, my feet feeling mired in quicksand. He jerks and sees me, his eyes flaring with obscene hatred. I collide with his body, and hearing a deafening explosion, tumble back onto the dock.

As I fall, I jerk my head toward Nellie. She and Derry run toward me, their soundless mouths agape in horror. *Good, they're all right.* I try to lift myself to sitting but am too weak. Blood soaks the front of my dress. *Oh, Father, he's shot me. I cannot move.*

Screams.

Strangers.

Why are they crying?

Nellie falls to her knees beside me.

Dear Jesus, don't let him hurt Nellie.

"Mam, hold on! Mam! Mam! We'll get help."

"Kam. Take me to Kam." *Did I speak?*

Nellie and Neo look at each other. Both are crying.

Derry says, "Be very gentle in moving her."

My sweet Irish boy.

I'm in the bed of a wagon. A blanket covers me. Nellie cradles my head.

"Hold on, Mary," Neo whispers, beside me. Derry whips the horse.

Galloping.

Yelling.

Blessed darkness.

Light.

Flowered wallpaper.

Fearsome pain in my wrist.

"Kam?"

"I'm here." He lies on his back beside me on the bed as Nellie, Derry, and Neo hover nearby. Her blue dress is torn. Tears streak her cheeks.

Dearest, don't cry.

"Mary, lie back and breathe," Kam says. "Please don't move. They're transfusing blood from my radial artery into your wrist."

Shock. *Stay calm for both of our sakes.*

"How?" I whisper.

"Neo made the incision and affixed a tube to the inside of my artery. He stitched the other end to your vein. We must lie very still so as not to dislodge the tube. Do you understand?"

I close my eyes. Memory of something I read. *Recipient often dies. Yes. All right. I've had a wonderful life. Mathair Chriost. Daniel! He's waiting for me! The nuns were right. There is more.* I drift to Daniel's embrace. My feet never touch the ground. I am so happy.

Kam, Nellie, Kathleen, all of you, I love it here. I'll see you again. I will watch over you from wherever I am. Don't forget me. I love you.

EPILOGUE

DUBLIN, IRELAND, 1905

My name is Kate O'Byrne, and I'm a reporter for the *Irish Times*. Don't look surprised. I'm aware women are seldom hired as journalists in today's world. Oh, yes, quite aware. The editor at the paper, one Mr. James O'Dornan, has made that clear since the first day I applied for a job. And the second day. And nearly each application day since.

Seven years ago, fresh out of St. Mary's college, I answered an ad in the *Irish Times* to be a typesetter, thinking that would get my foot in the door. Mr. O'Dornan puffed on his soggy todóg and looked down his red-veined nose at me through the entire interview. His nostrils flared and his eyes were a squint. You'd think I smelled worse than his putrid cigar.

"Miss O'Byrne," he said, "are you aware that newspapering is a tough job, a job where men fight over stories like Nutty Curran himself." He paused. "Oh, sorry, love. You've likely never heard of Nutty Curran."

"Actually," I answered. "I have, sir. Matthew Nutty Curran was the heavyweight boxing champion of Ireland and would probably have been the same in England but the Brits decided not to recognize his matches because they weren't held on National Sporting Club premises." *Thank you, Jesus, that Da is a boxing fan.*

O'Dornan shoved his stogie between his teeth and chewed, then belched out a big puff of smoke.

I wasn't hired that day to be a typesetter. Or anything else at the newspaper. So, I took a job as a governess and began working on my book. A novel at the start, but as I wrote it, things happened that turned it into something like a biography. Magical things from dreams at night and waking.

I knew I was a good writer. Certainly, all the nuns had told me that since second grade. But it surprised even me that once I started the book, my words felt carried on angel's wings to my mind. What no one knew was I had a co-writer guiding me. Her name was Mary Boland Kelly, the angel grandmother I scarcely knew.

I was quite surprised when *Croi Làidir* won the Jonathan Swift Literary Award for best new novel three years ago. Once that happened, it was difficult for O'Dornan to ignore my application to be a reporter. He knew it would have made him seem foolish, especially in Ireland where writers are revered next to God Himself. And I made sure O'Dornan was aware of that.

I love being a reporter—everything about it; from meeting and interviewing newsmakers and politicians to the ordinary people who make Ireland the magical place it is. Of those in the villages, many are still living under thatched roofs. But living, an operative phrase if ever there was one. Thank God we haven't had a famine for quite some time, and the home rule movement gains momentum every day. My da, Derry, back when he was a young Fenian, was actually imprisoned for his part in the rebellion against the British, but in time, he realized that real gain would come from inside. Now, he's part of the British

Parliament, carrying on the diplomacy the great Dan O'Connell started so many years ago.

When people interview me about the book and its inspiration, I tell them something obscure about the creative winds that embrace Dublin, and that's partially true. But in my heart, I know my real inspiration is my Grandma Mary.

Before he died, Grandda Kam told me she was "soft as lamb's wool" but "nails tough"; that when Mary Kelly got something in her craw, she gnawed at it until it was chewed up, spit out, and done. *Laidir*, that's what Irish people called her. And for good cause.

At thirteen, she left Ireland during the Great Famine, having buried her mother and baby sister. Determined to get to Boston in America to find her da, she was tricked onto a coffin ship by a woman she trusted, only to learn that the woman had sold her as a sex slave to the crew. Grandda Kam met her on that ship and told me she said, "After they all molested me in their stinking cabin, I wanted to die—throw myself overboard to the sharks as others had—but there was something in me determined to survive. And I did."

My mam says I'm like her; that I have some of her grit in my bones, and I believe that's true. Just ask Mr. James O'Dornan.

My grandma died when I was only three years old, so my memories of her are hazy. When I close my eyes and think of her, though, the sensation is of safety. Absolute trust. A sense she's been guiding me all my life.

I first dreamed of her when I was twelve. I saw her so clearly—young, with red hair streaming behind her and riding a chestnut stallion bareback along the Irish Sea coast. She sat that horse like a professional jockey, she did. The waves breaking around her didn't faze her or slow the gallop even a little. And she was laughing.

For months, she was silent in my dreams. When she finally spoke, she was older and I could almost feel her arms around me. *Kathleen, tell my story.*

Tell her story? How could I do that? I never really knew her. But like any good reporter-to-be, I knew how to do research. Starting with my mam and da, I heard tales of bravery and derrings-do to rival any Celtic legend.

She was a midwife who saved many women in Boston. On a visit from America, Dr. Molly O'Halloran shared miraculous tales of life-saving surgeries on terrified young women. "Mary never gave up on a patient," she said, her eyes shining with affection and admiration.

But my grandma was no saint. Mam and Molly told me a story of them crafting a devious hoax on Molly's brother, Sean. That explained a lot. I have faint memories of him, none of them terribly warm. When I learned he had my mam committed to an asylum for the insane, I lost any caring feelings I might have ever had for the man. Last I heard of him, he was considering a run for America's presidency. He lost.

My grandma was an Irish-American woman with virtues and faults like anyone else, but she inspired me to follow my dreams and write a book about her. Through dreams and misty memories, through reminiscences from those who loved her, and from her notations in the medical books Molly left with me, I learned all about the woman. And loved her.

My grandma, Mary Boland Kelly. Thank you.

ABOUT THE AUTHOR

Jeanne Charters is a veteran of the broadcast television industry. She was vice president of marketing for Viacom TV and opened her own broadcast ad agency, Charters Marketing.

Charters grew up believing she'd be a stay-at-home mom and live in her hometown in Ohio for the rest of her life. However, after four children and a divorce, Charters ended up in Albany, New York, where she met and married Matt Restivo, her husband of thirty-five years and counting. Charters and Restivo moved to Asheville, North Carolina, after retirement. Beyond her novels, she has also written for magazines and newspapers.

ABOUT THE AUTHOR

DAUGHTERS OF IRELAND

FROM OPEN ROAD MEDIA

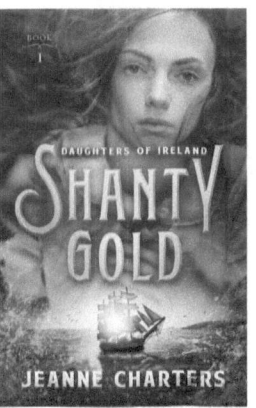

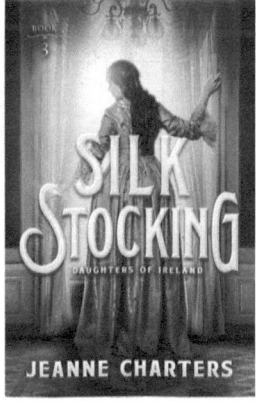

OPEN ROAD

INTEGRATED MEDIA

Find a full list of our authors and titles at www.openroadmedia.com

FOLLOW US

@OpenRoadMedia

.

www.ingramcontent.com/pod-product-compliance
Lightning Source LLC
Chambersburg PA
CBHW020430030726
47495CB00006B/1732